Kevin Doyle was born and brought up in Cork. He holds a Masters in Chemistry from NUI (Cork), and worked for a number of years in the chemical industrial sector in Ireland and the United States. He has been published in many literary journals, including the *Stinging Fly*, the *Cork Review*, *Southwords* and the *Cúirt Journal*. He has been shortlisted for a number of awards, including the Hennessy Literary Awards and the Seán Ó Faoláin Prize, and has won the Tipperary Short Story Award and the Michael McLaverty Short Story Award. He has written extensively about Irish and radical politics and, with Spark Deeley, he wrote the award-winning children's picture book, *The Worms that Saved the World*. *To Keep a Bird Singing* is his first novel.

KEVIN DOYLE

To Keep A Bird Singing

·THE·
BLACK
·STAFF·
PRESS

First published in 2018 by Blackstaff Press
an imprint of Colourpoint Creative Ltd, Colourpoint House,
Jubilee Business Park, 21 Jubilee Road,
Newtownards, BT23 4YH

With the assistance of The Arts Council of Northern Ireland

LOTTERY FUNDED

Printed and bound by CPI Group UK (Ltd), Croydon CRO 4YY

A CIP catalogue for this book is available from the British Library

ISBN 978-1-78073-171-1

www.blackstaffpress.com
Follow Kevin on Twitter @kevidoyle

For Mary Favier

Prologue

Albert Donnelly stood in his garden. The sun was shining and he could hear birdsong – blackbirds and thrushes whistled and chirped. It was June and everything was lush. At the end of the garden the river flowed. There had been rain over the weekend and the current was strong. On the opposite bank was a pair of swans. They were under a willow. Sometimes they visited, crossing to peck on his lawn and borders. Occasionally they wandered as far as the rose beds. Albert's brother, Robert, liked swans. They were the only thing that excited him any more.

Turning from the view, Albert looked for Robert. He was parked in his chair on the terrace, overlooking the garden. Their house stood fifty or so feet higher up than the river and provided a vantage point. Cork's main public space, Fitzgerald Park, was across the river; the grey, stone crenellations of University College were beyond that, and the spire of the Protestant cathedral, St Fin Barre's, was there in the distance.

Albert waved. Robert was five years older and was dressed plainly in a black polo neck and light-grey slacks. There was no response. Albert waved again and then wondered what Robert looked at all the time. What did he see now? It wasn't clear.

The house was called Llanes. Sometimes people asked why, but Albert wouldn't reveal the origin of the name. A family secret, he claimed. Originally the house was a retirement home for army officers, going back to the British times. After independence it came under the jurisdiction of the Irish army and, by and by, an officers' association had taken possession of it. It was in private hands until Albert acquired it in '70.

There were eight rooms upstairs; downstairs, a drawing room, a library and a private cinema, as well as the modernised kitchen. Below were floors that had once acted as the service area for the retirement home. There was also an outdoor swimming pool – covered over now. An ingenious construction. Fed by the nearby river and controlled by a sluice mechanism, it mimicked one of Cork's famed public works – the outdoor baths on the Straight Road. It was thirty-five feet in length and twenty wide with a plunge pool for diving at the side. Albert couldn't remember now why he had covered it over. Was it the drudgery of maintenance or the desire to have a bigger garden?

His thoughts were interrupted by the ringing of the phone. Before mobiles the landline had been the only phone for the house. Sometimes it had been difficult to hear it if he was outside or down by the river, so he'd had a ringer bell installed on the outside of the house, on the ivy-covered gable.

He walked up the garden and then climbed the steps to the terrace. There was a rest area halfway up, a stone seat opposite a fountain. He paused beside it. A robin was sitting on the fountain lip. 'The grace and beauty of God to you,' Albert said. Twenty-six steps to go. He felt fit and able for them. A little breathless but that was natural at his age. He was seventy-two and in good shape really. Ill health had not visited him like it had Robert.

When he reached the terrace he went directly to his brother. 'Did you hear the phone, Robert?' he asked. 'Well, I heard it. All the way down there I heard it. I waved, did you see me? You must have.'

There was no response. Albert bent down. For a second he scrutinised the freckles on Robert's nose. The brown dots had faded and spread out; they were no longer distinct. As a boy he had examined those freckles closely, often when Robert was asleep. Tony, their brother, had had plenty of them too. But Albert had none, not one single freckle, and he had never liked that about himself. He whispered, 'The devotion of Christ and the love of Christ is the reward. Robert, you will sit at His right hand.'

There was no response again. Albert took his brother's veiny hand and squeezed it. At one time Robert was the most senior police officer in Cork city. He had risen to the rank of chief superintendent. Now what was he? Albert didn't understand his brother's illness. He didn't like it either. He continued squeezing the hand until he saw pain in his brother's eyes. He squeezed harder then and tears formed. He whispered, 'We are chosen to sit at His right hand.'

Albert's suitcase was still in the hall. Standing beside it was a Romanian cross packaged in a protective cardboard sleeve. Albert had transported it from Bucharest and what an ordeal that was. It was purchased legally, nothing to do with that. No, it was the shape. Carrying a cross, even a small one, at his age was not easy.

He looked around. He couldn't remember why he had come inside. Was there something he had to do? He looked back in the direction that he had come from. Robert was still outside. Albert had shifted him closer to the French windows and faced him into the wall. His brother had to make an effort and right now he wasn't making any.

Albert stared. He became irritated and pinched his wrist. Why had he come inside? It wasn't the swans. What had the swans to do with inside? He saw a loaf of fresh bread on the counter and the newspaper beside it. That was it, now he remembered.

He looked at the phone display. It registered one call; the number was unavailable. Albert dialled the voicemail. There was a single short message: 'Brian Boru is back.'

Punk

1

In the charity shop people stopped to look; Noelie Sullivan too. The Ireland Hearse was passing. It had been appearing on the streets of Cork for a number of days. Instead of a coffin, it carried a floral wreath that spelled I-R-E-L-A-N-D in green, white and gold. Behind the hearse, a sole mourner followed. She was tall, dark haired and she held a shawl around her head and shoulders. People who knew about these things said she represented Cathleen Ní Houlihán, the mythical figure used to portray Ireland in literature. Behind her, a small float trundled along supporting a flock of expertly painted cardboard sheep. Salvos of 'baaaa, baaaa' interspersed with Chopin's Funeral March could be heard intermittently. In the front of the hearse, a large plump man puffed grandly on a cigar, regaling the onlookers with, 'Everything's fine. Business as usual for me. Austerity is good for you.'

The agitprop had caused a stir. There had been an argument on local radio and a city councillor had even suggested using an obscure by-law, to do with the misuse of hearses, to legally remove the procession from the city's streets. He claimed the hearse was a provocation and alleged that it demeaned the people of Cork, whom he pointed out were not sheep. Inside the charity shop, however, bargain hunters hurried for a view. In the rush, a woman lost her balance and fell awkwardly against a stack of boxes. A collection of LPs spewed across the linoleum. One record, by eighties punk band Crass, entitled *Penis Envy,* slid as far as the feet of a small boy who picked it up. The album cover depicted the oversized face of a sex doll. His horrified mother quickly took it from him and hurried to the till, where Noelie Sullivan was haggling with Mrs MacCarthaigh over the price of a copy of Beevor's *Stalingrad.*

'I'm surprised to see this filth on sale in here,' the mother said.

Mrs MacCarthaigh, in her sixties, small of stature and with white hair, took the LP and examined it. She was certain she had never seen anything like it before. 'Good God,' she declared, and put the album in the bin. Noelie Sullivan reached down and retrieved it.

Penis Envy by Crass. Released in London on 1 August 1981. Noelie reckoned that maybe three or four copies of the LP – at most – had ever made it across the Irish Sea to Cork. The punk scene in the city was small back in the early eighties, and the political punk scene was even smaller. So to see the album now after all this time, well, that was a surprise.

He studied it. In good condition, very good actually. He heard Mrs MacCarthaigh say, 'If you're interested, there's more over there on the floor.' He turned. Chopin's Funeral March was fading and the Ireland Hearse was moving on; the shop returned to normal duties. He saw the pile of LPs.

'I'll be back for the book.'

Gathering the records, he took them to where the light was better. *Never Mind The Bollocks, Here's The Sex Pistols* happened to be on top; that unmistakable yellow sleeve, the punk typeface. *The Slits* by The Slits was under it. But it was only when Noelie saw *Inflammable Material* that he paused. *Inflammable* was the first album by the Irish punk outfit Stiff Little Fingers. It was a famous LP, bursting out of Belfast in the late seventies. It was the sticker, though, that caught his attention. Slapped on the top right-hand corner of the black sleeve, the circular label was supposed to make the Fingers more commercially palatable at a time when punk wasn't. It should've read 'Includes the Hit Single "Alternative Ulster"' but now there was only: 'Inclu it Single "Alternat ster"'.

A wedge was missing. Torn out. Some people didn't like the stickers and Noelie had been one of those – back then. Too commercial. Smacked of marketing. Fuck marketing, right, we're punks ... But in this case the job had only been half done. Most of the irritating sticker remained and now it stared at Noelie. Impossible, he concluded.

Bargaining Mrs MacCarthaigh hard, he beat her down to €1 an LP and left twenty minutes later with a treasure trove of eighty-seven albums. *Stalingrad* he got for €3 – a neat €90 all in. He was robbing her he knew, but the records, he was sure, were his. They had vanished from his flat twenty-six years earlier, in April of 1984 to be precise. The theft marked the beginning of a run of bad luck for Noelie.

His LP player was nothing fancy. Designed for converting vinyl to MP3 format, it played decent nonetheless. He fixed up the plugs at the rear of his amp and checked the needle for fluff. He wondered what to play first and decided on 'Ready, Steady, Go' by Generation X. He'd always liked them. Placing the LP on the turntable he lifted the needle onto song 4, side A. The punk anthem took off.

Noelie turned the volume as high as it would go. His neighbour downstairs was at work. He went to the window, lifted the sash and looked out. Douglas Street was long and narrow. It was often choked with traffic, like now. Generation X continued at full pelt in the background.

The Rats album had sealed the matter. In 1978, Bob Geldof and Co. came to Cork to sign copies of the band's second release, *A Tonic For The Troops*. Noelie waited with his buddies one morning for Geldof to show. This was well before 'Sir Bob' and 'Feed the World'. Geldof was still a raw punk, an upstart, and liable to say anything. He was one of Noelie's heroes. Geldof insisted on signing Noelie's copy of *A Tonic* on the vinyl's label

– not on the record cover as was convention. Bob Geldof and The Boomtown Rats, Cork, 1978. In the charity shop, when Noelie saw the same scrawl on the label, any lingering doubts about the origins of the collection vanished.

He selected *Signing Off* next, the UB40 album with the reproduction of a UK benefit form on its cover. Taking the vinyl from its sleeve he noticed an edge of paper jutting out. He tried to remove it but it was attached in some way. Slipping his hand inside he worked it free. It was a page from a book, *Garrison's Survey of Notable Irish Historical Figures*. There was a biographical sketch of Brian Boru, regarded as the last High King of Ireland, and beneath that a graphic of the king in his regalia. Turning the page over, Noelie saw a typed list:

<u>Brian Boru File</u>
Document x 7
Photograph x 5
Double-8 clip x 1

He looked at the front again and then at the list once more. Putting it aside he placed the UB40 record on the turntable and selected 'Food For Thought'. The reggae number opened with a long sax introduction. He had seen UB40 live in their heyday. Lots of the big bands played Cork back then – The Damned, The Undertones, The Stranglers, Siouxsie Sioux. He was at college at the height of the punk era, an undergraduate first and then a postgraduate. For much of that time he had also worked part-time as a kitchen help, spending all his money on gigs and records. A couple of times he'd even travelled over to London to the Hammersmith Palais and the Roundhouse.

A long time ago now, he realised, and strange to be reminded of it all again, all that energy, the heady mix of music and politics. Life was not as straightforward any more.

2

There were three on the Portakabin roof and they squabbled as magpies do. What was it? One for sorrow, two for joy, three for a girl and four for a ...

Noelie flapped his hands at the birds and they hopped across the container defiantly, their talons flicking off the metal roof. A plastic sign announced 'Dineen Slate and Tile. Office'. The door was open but there was no one inside – just a desk, a chair on wheels and a halogen heater.

Next to the Portakabin there was a large doorless shed housing various types of slates arranged on pallets. Patio slabs too – Nepal Sky, Ochre Sand, Connemara Grey and Cork Red. Noelie examined one and wondered if it really was a local stone or just a marketing ploy.

A dog barked somewhere. At the rear of the yard he saw a house on the other side of a low dividing hedge – a bungalow, whitewashed a long time ago. Noelie found a gap and went through. A man in a navy boiler suit stood beside a red Hiace.

'Hey?' Noelie called.

The man started to walk towards Noelie. He was sixty and had a limp. In his left hand he held a ratchet.

'Just wondering about something is all.'

'We're closed.'

'Not slates or tiles, don't worry.'

'I said I'm closed.'

'Ajax Dineen?' asked Noelie.

'What's it to you?'

'Some stuff arrived into the charity shop on Castle Street. Mrs MacCarthaigh, the lady in there, said you were the man brought it in. Bits of furniture and things. But there were records too, punk records.'

'So?'

'So you don't look like the sort of man that'd be into punk.'

Dineen was mostly bald and what hair he had was white and plastered to his pate. He scrutinised his visitor.

'My place was broken into way back,' explained Noelie. 'I won't go into it but a couple of things were taken. Some cash, an antique clock and those punk records of mine. At the time they were my pride and joy ...'

'Don't know anything about that.'

Noelie put up a hand. 'No sweat. I'm not looking to cause trouble, I'm just curious. How did you come to have the records like?'

Ajax put the ratchet into his trouser-leg pocket. His expression softened. 'How you so sure they're yours?'

Noelie explained about Bob Geldof. He also mentioned reporting the theft to the gardaí at the time. 'I have a copy of the report still. All eighty-seven records are listed on it. It's a perfect match.'

Ajax considered this and then nodded over Noelie's shoulder. The slate-and-tile yard was on the edge of the city, off the Old Mallow Road. Further out was mostly countryside. Noelie looked.

'See the hill yonder?'

There was a rise about half a mile on. Crowning it was a Celtic Tiger mansion with huge dormer windows. Even from where they stood, Noelie could tell it was a large house.

'That place has seven bedrooms, every one of them en suite. There's a gym and a games room as well. Everything you care to mention, that fella up there has it. Wouldn't be surprised if there's a helipad as well.' Ajax was standing beside Noelie now. 'Where d'ye think the tiles and patio slabs for his mansion came from?'

Noelie worked it out. 'You haven't been paid.'

'In one. Every morning I see him driving his two daft sons into private school in town. Big Land Rover too. New vehicle, no less. But can he pay me what I'm owed? No siree. Not on your life. No money for poor old Ajax.'

Noelie examined the mansion again. Did some former punk reside there? Surely not. 'Did he have my records?' Noelie asked.

Ajax shook his head. 'No, no. He's just an example of what I'm dealing with. I inherited these three garages up Dillon's Cross way. On a back lane there. An aunt of mine passed away. The garages were hers. We weren't close but that's not the point. Them records were in one of the garages. Along with a lot of other rubbish.'

Ajax's dog came over. He was one of those lovable rogues. He lay in front of his owner looking for a tickle but got half a shoe instead. Noelie obliged. He rubbed the dog along its belly.

'My aunt rented those sheds to this man for years. For pittance. Don't know what the connection was. When the sheds came my way I said I was putting up the rent. Not by much now, I'm not greedy. I was making it more reasonable, that was all. I had unbelievable trouble even getting this man to respond to me.' Ajax frowned. 'Anyway, the rent fell due. Last month this is. But not so much as an extra cent from his nibs. I went this way and that way about it. Met him finally, the once only. He came here. He claimed he had an arrangement with my aunt. High-handed about it, he was. But no paperwork. Not a single line to prove anything. Wouldn't budge, wouldn't pay the extra either.'

'So you ...?'

'I cleared one shed. Just one – I'm not unreasonable. I moved his stuff into the other two sheds. Most everything's in there. The few things I couldn't fit in I decided to pass on to herself on Castle Street. Move him along like.' Noelie frowned but Ajax was adamant. 'Look, this fellow has money. He's not short.'

'So this man, this sheds guy, he's the one that had my records?'

'Exactly.'

'What's his name?'

Ajax shook his head. 'Not so fast, boyo.'

'Look, I already told you, I'm just curious.'

'No deal.'

Noelie got up from patting the dog. 'Okay so. But this man, he look like an old punk to you?'

Ajax guffawed. 'The opposite. This man's in security, the top end. Did the yachting regatta last year, the one that all the la-di-das were at. That's what I mean like. He has money this man.'

At an internet cafe Noelie googled the regatta and found the name he was looking for in the credits: Cronin Security Group, proprietor Don Cronin. A further search uncovered an address in Montenotte. Noelie knew the area. It was on the northside of the city, along one of the many hills that bordered the Lee Valley. At one time the area was the preserve of Cork's grandees – big-house territory with large gardens to match. But in time and with the various changes that came to the city, the majority of its spacious lots were chopped up and sold off in portions to developers. Montenotte was no longer exclusive but it was still on the right side of desirable.

Grant Lane was tucked away in a quiet corner. A cul-de-sac, it snaked its way downhill until it met one of Cork's many sheer red-stone cliff faces. Noelie didn't fancy the narrow lane so he left his Astra up on the main road. Cronin's place was the last house down the lane and unlike its neighbours, a new build. A sign warned of a snarling Alsatian guard dog.

The gate was open and he went through. A silver Mercedes was parked in the drive. Noelie pushed the doorbell and heard a sing-song chime. A medium build of a man in his late fifties answered. He was tanned, in a Marbella sort of way. Either he loved golfwear or he had just come from eighteen holes. Unlikely to be an old punk, decided Noelie.

'Yes?'

Noelie put his hand out. 'Don Cronin?'

The man looked at Noelie's hand and didn't reciprocate. 'Do I know you?'

'Noelie Sullivan. I was wondering the same. The Arcadia Ballroom, The Stranglers, The Slits, The Damned – any of that lot ring any bells?'

Cronin looked perplexed, and a touch bemused. 'What are you talking about?'

Noelie withdrew his hand. 'It's like this. You used to own some punk rock records. A decent collection. Crass, Nun Attax, The Clash and the like. A few first issues as well. Was wondering how you came by them?'

Cronin's expression remained bewildered so Noelie continued. 'Up in Dillon's Cross there. You've been renting some lock-ups, I'm told. You had stuff in them in storage, including my old record collection. So, to cut a long story short, I was wondering how you came by them, my records like?'

The confusion on Cronin's face vanished. 'How did you get my address?'

'Does it matter? See the records were robbed from my flat. I'm talking 1984 here ... A long time ago, admittedly. But a crime is a crime, right?'

The silence grew long and Noelie understood that a connection had been made. He watched Cronin scratch his head.

'Wait a moment, I need to make a call,' he said and turned to go down the hall but then changed his mind. He smiled at Noelie. 'Look, come in.'

Noelie hesitated but Cronin insisted. He stepped into the hall. 'Make your call, I'll wait here.'

Cronin had the phone to his ear. He turned to check that Noelie was still there and then walked out of view. In a nearby room, Noelie saw a large marble fireplace with tall stand-alone vases on either side of it.

Cronin returned.

'Got it now?'

'There's been a mistake. I'm very sorry about this. Noel O'Sullivan, you said?'

'No 'O'. Just Sullivan.'

'Actually, it does seem likely that you're talking about my property. I've been having some difficulty with a landlord. I do own some LPs.' He paused. 'You think some of them are yours?'

'There's no thinking about it.'

Cronin smiled. 'But we can sort this out, right? If it's a matter of money?'

'It's not.'

Cronin looked past Noelie and attempted to shepherd him down the hall. 'Tea, coffee? A beer? Look, come in.'

Sudden wild barking outside made up Noelie's mind for him. 'Another time,' he said. He was out the door and through the gate before Cronin could stop him.

'What's wrong?' called Cronin.

Noelie walked quickly up the steep lane. At the first bend, he saw a white Audi approaching at speed. He turned back. He was lucky that a lot of the houses round there were enclosed by walls or high hedges. The first gate he tried was locked but the next along opened. Inside was a large house. A mature garden sloped away on one side. Noelie heard the Audi outside. It stopped. Car doors opened. He heard men's voices and a dog barking. Noelie made his way to a large rhododendron and ducked under its canopy; he stood in deep shade.

A moment later the gate opened. Two men entered with a dog on a leash. A frail voice called out, 'I'm ringing the police.' Noelie spied an elderly lady at the door of the house. She brandished a mobile phone.

The visitors were courteous. They explained that they were with Mr Cronin. Her neighbour, they emphasised. There had been a burglary attempt at his place and they were looking for the intruder. A standoff ensued. Unfortunately the dog got excited. It had picked up Noelie's scent.

'I'm talking to them now,' called the woman shrilly.

The men opted to leave, dragging the dog behind them.

Noelie remained hidden. What was going on, he wondered, and why had Cronin's overreacted? Eventually, he went as far as the gate and looked out. There was no one around but there was no knowing what was around the next bend either. He decided not to take the risk. Heading down the garden, he stayed out of view. It was a beautiful property, one of the old, undivided domains. Two monkey puzzle trees stood at the bottom.

Reaching a low wall, he climbed it and entered another garden. This was smaller and there didn't seem to be anyone around. He waited a moment and then walked out the front gate like he had been visiting for afternoon tea. An hour later he was back home.

3

Noelie had the upstairs flat at 78b Douglas Street. It had been his home for nearly twelve years, since his return from New York in '98. There was a decent-sized bedroom, a large sitting room with a kitchenette to one side and a small bathroom. He had made it cosy, fitting a better kitchen and repainting it fully. An entire wall was dedicated to bookshelves, very overstocked.

Ani DiFranco was playing when the downstairs front-door bell sounded. Noelie was expecting a visit and figured it would be either Cronin or his goons. In the event of trouble his plan was to exit by a landing window outside his flat door. But it was only Ajax.

Noelie lifted the sash. 'What's up?'

Ajax was spitting. 'You've fucked up, that's what's up. Open the door.'

Noelie took the precaution of putting his father's old poker under a newspaper by the sofa and went to open the door. Ajax barged through, fuming. 'Even at my age I'm still surprised at how stupid some people are.'

Checking there was no one else outside Noelie followed his visitor upstairs. He guided Ajax to his best armchair and asked if he wanted tea.

'Fuck tea. What's with you? Do you have any sense?'

Noelie was bemused. 'What's up?'

'He's gone apeshit, that's what's up. You don't realise who he is, do you?'

'Cronin Security.'

'You fuckwit. A couple of hours after your visit, he's out to me. Wouldn't give me the time of day before that. Now suddenly he's sitting in my kitchen. There's cash on the table for everything he owes me, plus two more years in advance at my new rate.'

'You're laughing so.'

'Do I look like I'm laughing?' Ajax half stood. 'If I was a few years younger I'd break your fuckin' front teeth.'

Noelie wrinkled his forehead. He didn't mind Ajax letting off steam but dangerous talk could get out of hand.

'I shouldn't have got rid of those records. It was a mistake. A rash act. I need them back.'

Noelie shook his head. He filled the kettle and clicked it on.

'I'm not asking, Noel or Noelie or whatever it is you're called, I'm telling you.'

Noelie spoke slowly. 'First thing, they're not your records, they're mine. You off-loaded them to Mrs MacCarthaigh and I purchased them from her. Second, the records were mine in the first place, from way back. Like I said, there's even a garda report.'

Ajax stood. Placing a hand on his bad leg, he winced and approached Noelie. 'Cronin called me again just now. Asked if I had the records back yet. I said I was planning on calling to see you. A few minutes later, two cunts arrive out to me in a fuckin' Land Cruiser no less. Walk right in the back door and stand looking. The younger one's holding a crowbar. Didn't scare me but scared the life out of the missus. Understand now what we're dealing with. I have until midnight.'

Noelie figured that Ajax was telling the truth; he certainly looked bothered. But what was up? Why did Cronin want the records back?

'Play along please. Hand over the records.. I'll even pay you.'

'You're not curious?'

'I couldn't give a flying fuck. I just want the records back.

How much?'

Noelie wandered over to the front window and looked out. There was no one down on the road other than his neighbour from across the way. She had her digital camera out and was snapping the regs of a few parked cars. She was in a one-woman war with City Hall over disputed disability parking rights.

'Well, how much?' pressed Ajax.

'Make me an offer.'

'Two hundred.'

Noelie guffawed.

'You cunt.'

'My dear man, those records are valuable. Some are first issues. A few are even signed. There's an actual Nun Attax EP in that lot. Can't be got nowadays, not for any amount of money.'

'You tell me then.'

'Two grand. But that price is a favour to you. If I went on eBay ...'

'Deal.'

'Deal?' repeated Noelie alarmed. 'Serious, you'd pay me that much?'

'I don't have it on me but I can be back in an hour with the full amount.' He limped over to Noelie with his hand outstretched. 'Deal?'

Noelie shook his head reluctantly. 'Actually no, I was codding. I'm not interested. I told you the records are of sentimental value.'

Ajax didn't appear to hear what Noelie said. 'I need to see them, okay, if I'm to shell out so much.' He went over to Noelie's CD collection. He looked around and under the counter. 'Where are they?'

'Did you hear me? I'm not selling.'

Suddenly Ajax lunged towards the bedroom door but

Noelie got there ahead of him. 'Out of bounds, if you don't mind.'

Ajax tried to push through but Noelie easily held him off. The older man glared. He pointed at a framed poster on the wall. It was given to Noelie by an ex, a long time back. The subject was an elderly woman clouting a fascist skinhead with her handbag. The text was in Swedish but the graphic underneath was unmistakable: it showed a clenched fist shattering a swastika.

'What are you anyway? Some sort of nut?'

'You telling or asking?'

Ajax cursed again. Noelie shepherded him towards the armchair but he wouldn't sit.

'Tell you what,' said Noelie. 'I'm curious, I really am. You tell Cronin I'll speak to him. Tell him I'll meet him somewhere in public. I'll deal with him and that'll take you out of the picture. Okay?'

'That's not okay.' Ajax went over to the flat door. 'You thick fuck, you'll learn.'

4

What did Noelie mean, sentimental value? Why did he even say that? It had little enough to do with anything sentimental. It was seeing the records again, realising that the collection was intact. That was odd for sure, and after all this time too. But there was something else. The break-in hadn't been straightforward. Noelie's records disappeared along with some other items – an antique clock and some money. At the time Noelie had been involved in a campaign opposing the visit to Ireland of US president, Ronald Reagan. There had been a plan to disrupt Reagan's walkabout in Ballyporeen where his great-grandfather hailed from. Following the break-in the protest never took place.

Sleeping lightly, hovering in the middle world between flight and rest, Noelie was alert to every noise. It was still dark when he opened his eyes. An alien blue light bathed the ceiling. At the window he saw a squad car below on Douglas Street. He heard voices next, his downstairs neighbour Martin's among them. Boots plodded up the stairs. Noelie's flat door suffered some hefty blows. He opened up to two uniformed cops, both bulked out in stab vests. The younger one, hand on truncheon, looked confidently at the ready.

'Noel Sullivan?' the older garda asked.

'Speaking.'

'You're under arrest.'

Noelie didn't move; he shook his head. 'Why?'

'An assault earlier tonight near Blackpool Credit Union.'

'I've been here the entire evening.'

'Well, you're coming with us now.'

Noelie still didn't move. The younger cop advanced and poked him roughly with the truncheon. 'Now, get dressed.'

They observed him while he put on clothes. Downstairs, as they were leaving, Martin called out generously, 'I've got their badge numbers.'

Noelie was stuffed into the back of the squad car. The vehicle smelled foul. It also brought back some very unhappy memories.

He was taken to the main garda station in the city, Anglesea Street, and was put in a room with two chairs, a table and a recording contraption on the wall. He declined tea and was left there. There was a single window and below it a long slicing mark that looked like smeared shit.

A detective finally arrived. He had light red hair and red eyebrows, as well as a generally red complexion. Thirty-five maybe. He placed a photograph on the table between them; a family snap job.

'Know him?'

'Ajax Dineen.'

The detective pulled out another picture, a cheap digital printout. It showed a face caked with blood, eyes battered and woefully swollen.

'Know him?'

Noelie drew back in shock.

'Same man,' said the detective. 'First picture his wife loaned us, the second picture was taken a few hours ago up at University Hospital. He's barely able to speak.'

Noelie picked up the printout and examined it. Could be a forgery but he doubted it. Anyway, what would be the point? It certainly looked like Ajax.

'According to his wife you did this.'

Noelie shook his head. 'Not me.' He met the detective's stare. 'I mean it, not me. I wouldn't do something like that even if I had something against him, which I don't.'

'She claims you were bothering him earlier, that you took some things belonging to him and wouldn't give them back.'

Noelie saw no reason not to explain. He told him about finding the records in the charity shop, and then about Ajax and the lock-ups. He mentioned visiting Don Cronin but didn't elaborate on how that had gone.

The detective wrote everything down. When he finished he asked about the lock-ups. What did Noelie know about them?

'Nothing. Mr Dineen there, he was the one who mentioned them.'

'Know where they are?'

Noelie shrugged. 'Dillon's Cross, around there.'

'Can you be more specific?'

Noelie shook his head. The detective sized him up. He stood and picked up his notebook.

'You have a name, by the way?' asked Noelie. 'Aren't you supposed to tell me that?'

'Barry.'

'First or second name?'

Noelie didn't get an answer. The detective left and he waited another long while. The pictures remained on the table and he examined them again. The bludgeon job looked real, too real. Over records? Noelie couldn't believe that. For one, Cronin had trouble remembering them. He wasn't playing them too often either, stored in those lock-ups.

So was Cronin just teaching Ajax a lesson? Because he had acted the mick, moving Cronin's gear from the lock-ups – that was brazen. Noelie recalled something else though, that comment: *Do you know who he is?* So who was Cronin when he wasn't being top dog in Cronin Security Group?

He tried the door but it was locked. He rattled the handle and shouted a few times but no one came. Eventually he kicked the door but that had no effect either. He returned to his seat and waited. Resting his head in his arms he must've dozed because when he woke it was with a start. The interrogation room door opened.

Detective Barry spoke to someone in the corridor and then moved aside to allow a second officer to enter. This older man wore a lighter-coloured uniform reserved for senior officers; there were red epaulettes on his shoulders. It was over twenty-five years since their last encounter but Noelie recognised him straight away.

Denis Lynch still sported the same Saddam Hussein-style moustache. He was jowlier about the face and had put on weight. Clearly, he had been promoted a few times since their previous encounter. Noelie's old adversary would be in his mid-fifties now.

'Like old times,' said Lynch, affably putting his hand out.

Noelie looked away. Lynch didn't react. The smile left his face though. He nodded to the detective to leave.

Noelie had seen Lynch's name a few times in the intervening years. Mostly in relation to drug finds. More recently Lynch had been in the newspaper to do with a community initiative on the southside of Cork. The photograph accompanying the article showed Lynch in the company of a few of the city's councillors, including a prominent member of Sinn Féin. Considering Lynch's reputation for ill-treating republicans during the Troubles, it was something of a treasure shot.

Lynch sat down. He looked at Noelie. 'You've a long memory.'

'Ever wonder why?'

'That's in the past now.'

'Of course,' agreed Noelie. 'In the meantime you've been promoted. Got the stripes, I see. Whereas a mere insect like me,

I'd be better off forgetting, right? Who the fuck cares anyway?'

Lynch reached across the table and retrieved the digital print of Dineen. He looked at it. 'You've had a run-in with someone of interest to me. Don Cronin. I'd appreciate your help.'

'Really?'

'You said there were lock-ups.'

'Can't remember now.'

Lynch held Noelie's gaze. 'I don't want to get offside. I'm guessing this has nothing to do with you. I'm guessing you're stuck in the middle of something else entirely. And I don't particularly care what that is. But Cronin I'm interested in. You ever heard of the Hennigans, the drug family? On the southside? He's close to them.'

'I stay clear of those types.'

'Not for long more, I'd say.'

'Meaning?'

Lynch nodded to the photos.

'I've a set of punk rock records. Why would they be of interest to the Hennigans?'

'Tell that to Mr Dineen.' Lynch leaned into the table. 'Where are the records now?'

'Why? You're interested in punk too, is it?' Noelie paused. 'What do you want with my records?'

'There's an ongoing investigation. In other words, until I say different, everything, and I mean everything, to do with Cronin is relevant. Including your records – is that clear?'

Noelie didn't reply.

Lynch was more conciliatory. 'Look, let me have one look at them. If they are what you say they are, then you can have them back right away. It's no big deal surely?'

Noelie smiled. 'Normally I'd agree. In fact I'd be happy to help, being an upstanding citizen and all. But this isn't a normal situation. For one, you're not normal. You're a fucking

26

sadist and I remember that.'

'I'll get a warrant.'

'Get a warrant.'

'And maybe, while I'm at your place, I'll find something else – weed or something more unsavoury.'

Noelie suddenly banged the table with his fist giving Lynch a fright; the senior cop looked annoyed.

'I know,' declared Noelie. 'Get a warrant and when you're at my place, maybe you'll find explosives. You'd be the right pig of a hero then, wouldn't it? Imagine the headlines: "Red Brigade Cell Rumbled". Underneath, a picture of yourself and the byline "Our Intrepid Hero Saves the Day Again".'

Lynch said nothing. They stared at each other. Eventually Lynch pushed his chair back and stood. He wrote a number on the side of the digital print.

'In case you change your mind.'

'Don't worry, I won't.'

'Never say never, Noelie.'

'Oink, oink.'

5

Noelie took a taxi to his sister's. Ellen lived in Bellevue Park, a quiet area on another of Cork's numerous hills. Noelie liked the red-brick three-storey house. It had character, large rooms and gardens at the back and front. Ellen had done well for herself. While Noelie was in college doing a chemistry degree, Ellen had gone into retail and eventually started her own business. Her first venture was a tiny boutique selling hats and scarves. This was in the mid-eighties and there was a recession then too; the business went bust. Design college followed, part-time, and after that, following a spell in France, she tried again. This time it was ethnic clothes and she was successful.

A husband followed. Coincidentally, Arthur was also a chemistry graduate. After working for a few years, he went to business school and was later head-hunted to the pharmaceutical operation L&G Health where he had since been promoted a few times. Now Arthur travelled a good deal, mainly within the EU, and was an expert of some sort on quality and regulation law.

Noelie and Arthur didn't get on. They were different in outlook and temperament, and had argued one too many times at the Christmas dinner table and other family events. Bush's Iraq war, the Celtic Tiger when it roared, even global warming divided them. Noelie's erratic career hadn't helped. He had abandoned his PhD in '85 and moved to the States where he worked mainly on the lab bench for the next thirteen years. After a messy, difficult break-up with a woman he had spent almost eight years with, he had returned to Ireland in '98 and found work almost immediately. He wasn't prepared for what happened next. Made redundant in 2004 after the firm was downsized, he eventually got another position – on a lot less money. That job only lasted until the financial crash in 2008. Now, at forty-nine, he was signing on again and had been for nearly nineteen months.

'Sorry I asked.'

Ellen shook her head. 'Look, out of nowhere you arrive here and ask to stay the night. I mean do you realise how early in the day it is? It's only just past nine. Who turns up at this time of the morning and asks to stay the night. You're in trouble, right?'

Noelie watched his sister put her breakfast things in the dishwasher. Arthur had already left for work and normally Ellen opened her boutique for 10 a.m. Not that there was much business now – austerity Ireland had seen to that.

To change the subject he asked her what she thought of the Ireland Hearse. 'They're all on the dole, I bet,' she replied.

After Ellen left for work, Noelie wondered what he should do. The obvious option was to go home and he was tempted. At some point he would also have to face Cronin.

Shane was the only other person in the house. At sixteen he was Ellen and Arthur's only child. Noelie got on well with him. Music was their connection. Young Shane had his own band and Noelie had been to one of their gigs – there had been only one – at The Old Oak pub. That move had scored the uncle plenty of kudos.

Shane was easily capable of spending the entire morning in bed – he had finished school for the summer – so Noelie went to rouse him. The teenager had long shaggy hair and bore an unfortunate resemblance to Rory Gallagher, Cork's renowned electric guitarist. Noelie's advice was to lose the look and the hair – it was too generic for Cork – but the advice had been ignored.

Otherwise, Shane was cool. Posters of Nirvana, The Clash, Bombay Bicycle Club and The National were placed around his own Old Oak gig poster. The opposite wall was a hand-painted take-off of Lou Reed's *Berlin* album cover. Not a bad attempt either. Dark. Apparently Shane's dad wasn't wild about it.

Noelie called up the stairs to Shane and told him of his good fortune – finding his record collection in the charity shop. He reeled off some bands and record names. Punk was not Shane's thing but Noelie knew that his generation had plenty of respect for the genre. The Jam, The Clash, The Ramones and New Order were legendary and probably always would be. Also because Noelie had seen many of the bands perform live he had plenty of stories. At one time The Phoenix Bar and The Arcadia Ballroom in Cork were massive venues.

Being a teenager, Shane felt hungry as soon as he was awake. He came downstairs almost immediately and Noelie enquired about a pot of fresh coffee. Shane obliged. He also put Noelie on the house computer, which was password protected.

Noelie wasn't sure what he was looking for. He googled combinations like 'Hennigans and Cronin' and 'Hennigans and Cronin Security Group' but these searches yielded zilch. He added Lynch's name only to find out that his old nemesis was now a garda inspector – a high rank indeed.

He tried the term 'Brian Boru' and came up with tons of links to the last High King of Ireland. The majority were mundane articles from Irish history. Others referred to pipe bands and Irish clubs named after the historical figure; most of those were in the US and Australia.

Shane brought Noelie his coffee and looked at the screen. 'Wouldn't have put you down for a Celtic warrior, Uncle

Noel,' he quipped. Noelie allayed his fears and a moment later he heard The Clash's 'Spanish Bombs' blasting out on the house sound system; fine system, too. Shane put his head back round the door.

'That suit you?'

'Spot on.'

Noelie abandoned his search for the ex-High King and returned to Don Cronin. Almost immediately he found something. Tucked away on an old website was a biog. Apparently Cronin Security Group had escorted a shipment of medical equipment for free to Chechnya in 2003 during the war there – hence the plug on the site. The short biog boasted that 'Don Cronin was a serving member of An Garda Síochána from 1971 until 1997, spending the majority of his service in Garda Special Branch in Cork ...'

Noelie sat back and said, 'Well, fuck me.' An ex-garda then. Not any old ex-garda either, Special Branch. With thirty or more years of service. He thought about this. A one-time Garda Special Branch officer now in bed with the Hennigans – according to the inspector anyway. So, were Lynch's interests legit? Or was it personal? Or could it be a bit of both? After all, cops hated crooked ex-cops.

Noelie surfed for a while longer, reading an article about house repossessions and another on Gerry Adams. Apparently Adams was now being feted in Spain, where they were hoping he'd play a role in persuading ETA to go down the peace-process road. The irony of it made Noelie smile – the alleged IRA man now rehabilitated into the role of wise statesman.

Closing the browser, he went to the kitchen where he found his nephew tucking into a strange breakfast: scrambled eggs, black pudding and sausages all rolled up in a orange tortilla. The teenager could hardly get the wrap in his mouth.

'Looks mega,' said Noelie.

Shane shook his head. He regularly reprimanded his uncle

31

for using, as he put it, the lingo of 'the youth'. Knowing it would wind him up, Noelie did it even more. He said goodbye and received a muffled acknowledgement in return.

In the back garden a side gate opened on to a private lane that travelled along the side of Holy Family Church. Eventually it joined Military Hill. Noelie stood at the intersection and looked around. Setting off downhill, he was immediately overtaken by a slow-moving silver work van; it pulled in ahead. Warily he crossed the road and, at the bottom of Military Hill, kneeled to tie his laces. He saw that there were three men in the driver's cabin. They avoided making eye contact.

St Luke's Cross was his best option. It was a busy junction and there were a number of exits. He went into O'Keeffes. The corner shop now did a major line in deli foods. Jacob's was joined on the cracker shelf by Sheridan's, Carr's and Miller's. Plenty of varieties – gluten-free, wholewheat, savoury, paprika. Even GM-free. Noelie waited. Outside, the van appeared and as it did he ducked, left the shop again and ran down the narrow lane immediately outside. Crossing Summer Hill, Noelie made it on to Mahony's Avenue and kept running. He had just decided that he had lost them when he heard tyres zipping over the corrugated road surface. He looked back and saw the van bearing down on him. A Fiesta came to the rescue. Mahony's Avenue was narrow and the Fiesta's driver panicked at the sight of the speeding van. Noelie heard horns blaring and the beginnings of a shouting match – 'Pull over, pull over ...'

At the next intersection, the traffic was one way. Almost out of breath, Noelie ran counter-flow and into the railway station. Platform 1 was deserted and he walked to where a notice declared 'End of Platform'. Pedestrians were advised that they should go no further but Noelie hopped over the barrier and continued quickly on to the tracks.

He hurried into the rail tunnel. There were lights at the entrance but he was quickly surrounded by the dark and the cold. All he could hear was the hollow echo of his footsteps.

The tunnel was an engineering feat for its day. Opened in 1855, it travelled for five kilometres under a series of hills that stood on the northside of Cork's Lee Valley, linking the riverside rail station with the flat countryside inland. There were a number of smoke shafts, needed in their day for the coal-powered engines. Between the second and third shafts Noelie recalled that there was an alcove with a shed for tools and for the track workers to rest up in. As a young lad he had been into the tunnel a few times – for the dare and in search of a chase from the workers.

He found the alcove after a long walk. It was smaller than he remembered and the shed wasn't much to look at – more a lean-to. But it was dry. Using the dim light from his phone he settled in a corner, glad to rest. By night time it would be safe to move again.

Bonfire Night

6

There was dull yellow light as far as Noelie could see, right down Douglas Street to Frank O'Connor House. Cars were parked nose to tail on one side and he figured that someone could easily be in any of them waiting for him to reappear. After a long day and most of the night in the train tunnel, he didn't feel like taking any chances.

Backtracking to Sullivan's Quay he walked downriver. On Dunbar Street there was a patch of waste ground. He scaled a high wall, crossed three gardens and crouched outside the back window of his neighbour Martin's flat. It was dark inside. He tapped the window quietly and repeatedly until a crack of light appeared in the curtains. Putting a finger to his lips he warned Martin to be quiet.

They went into the sitting room. It was warm. 'Where've you been?'

'Don't turn on the lights.'

'Your place has been trashed.'

Noelie cursed. 'When?'

'Some time yesterday, I guess in the afternoon, while I was at work. The door was busted in.'

'Anyone there now?'

'Don't think so. It was quiet all evening and during the night. But this character called. Asked if I knew you or where you were. Big ears on him. Didn't hang around.'

Noelie thought about this. 'Still have the records?'

Martin went to his bedroom and returned with a cheap canvas suitcase. He unzipped the flap and removed a towel covering the records underneath. Blondie's album *Parallel Lines* lay on top.

'Quite the collection.'

Noelie whispered, 'Lovingly gathered.'

He took the records from the suitcase and placed them in stacks on the wooden floor.

'Years ago I had a run-in with this cop. His name is Lynch. He's still around, an inspector now. Over at Anglesea Street the other night, he turned up. You can imagine my surprise. But guess what? Lynch wanted to see these records too. That's when I realised, there must be something in them.'

Martin put on the kettle and Noelie checked that the curtains were drawn. Positioning a lamp on the floor, he examined each LP thoroughly: outer sleeve, inner sleeve and then the record itself. He moved quickly through a stack of twenty and found nothing.

Martin brought tea and a cheese sandwich. Noelie ate and continued to check the records, explaining how he became entangled with Lynch back in 1984.

'There was this stunt I was in on. The idea was to embarrass Ronald Reagan.'

Martin was incredulous. 'Were you out of your tree? A stunt involving a US president. You could've been shot.'

'We never got that far.' Noelie shook his head, thinking about the time and the madcap plan. 'We were clueless. We had this black coffin filled with imitation blood. The idea was we'd take it to Ballyporeen and drop it there somewhere in public. Crazy. Anyway the cops got wind of it. My place was broken into. I didn't put two and two together initially. My records were stolen, that was all that I could think of. Later I realised I had left information in my flat about the Reagan stunt. The day we were due to head to Ballyporeen, I was hauled in by Lynch and his crew. I got a bad hiding.'

Noelie went quiet. It was the one and only time in his life

that he had been physically assaulted and it had been done by the cops. It still made him angry.

He was nearly two thirds of the way through the collection and beginning to doubt his theory when he felt something bulky. In The Fall's *Live at the Witch Trials* he saw an envelope taped to the inside of the cover. He worked it free and a package fell out. Inside was a typed document.

Statement by Detective Sean Sugrue on the matter of Mr Jim Dalton.

'Cops again.'
Noelie read on.

I, Sean Sugrue, am making this statement on April 27th 1997 of my own free will and volition. I wish this statement to be made public in the event of my death and I have given instructions to this effect to my colleague, Don Cronin.

There were four pages. The last page showed a map, hand-drawn and quite faded. 'Proposed Shopping Centre' was written over a large, shaded square. Noelie couldn't work out where the map was of until Martin deciphered another handwritten note.

'Box and Hounds?'
Noelie looked more closely. 'Fox and Hounds. It's a pub on the northside, Ballyvolane area.' It was easy after that. The map referred to the area known as the Glen. 'When I was growing up it was wilderness. But a while back the Corpo agreed to make it a public park. It's kind of rough and ready.'
Martin pointed to a cross. It was prominent on the map

and had numbers beside it. 'What's that? A church?'
Noelie didn't think so. There was no church in the Glen
Park. It was too wild for that. There were the remains of a
tannery, from Cork's early industrial history, but that was all.
He shrugged. Taking a seat on the sofa, he started to read.

My statement concerns Mr Jim Dalton who is listed
with An Garda Síochána as a missing person:

In late 1978, I was transferred from Tralee to
Union Quay Garda Station in Cork city. I worked
at Union Quay from 1978 to 1997 as part of Special
Branch and was responsible for monitoring the
activities of Sinn Féin. Specifically I observed
party functions and events in order to collect
information on members and activists associated
with the organisation. Additionally my information
was collated with intelligence collected from a
stable of informers, also administered at Union
Quay.

In September 1989, *The Ottoman* yacht was
intercepted off Baltimore in West Cork. It
contained a shipment of eleven Stinger (Type D)
missiles stolen from a production facility near
Izmir (Turkey) a year earlier. The capture of the
shipment was significant and followed the equally
significant interception of *The Eksund* arms
shipment from Libya (1987). Both operations were
particularly important in light of the emerging
peace process and played a role in frustrating
military objectives while strengthening the hand
of the Adams/McGuinness wing of the organisation.
The DST (French intelligence) played a key
role in the interception of *The Ottoman* via an

informant of theirs inside the Kurdish-Turkish community in Paris. When their source became aware that the missiles stolen in Turkey were destined for the IRA they contacted Special Branch. It was anticipated that an IRA internal investigation would take place. Since Cork IRA were involved in the importation, it was inevitable that an eye would be cast over its ranks for a potential informant.

Disinformation was an important arm of our work, and we maintained an active list of IRA personnel whom we were in a position to compromise. This involved orchestrating suspicion by the use of leaks or by the planting of compromising information on selected targets. Such efforts increased distrust and disharmony within the organisation's ranks. Even when a suspect was cleared by internal IRA there was often long-term rancour, and this was deemed to be quite useful in terms of achieving our objective of degrading and defeating the IRA.

An IRA operative was chosen as a target for such an operation only after careful evaluation. A candidate was picked on the grounds of his or her importance within the IRA's army structure, and usually some preliminary evidence was put in place to assist with a framing effort.

Following *The Ottoman* seizure, I forwarded a list of candidates that could be targeted. One individual was selected and I began preparing our campaign. However, shortly after I began this work I was instructed to change targets and prepare a strategy that would compromise an individual named Jim Dalton.

From the outset I knew that there was something wrong. Mainly this had to do with Mr Dalton's position. He was a local political activist in Cork Sinn Féin. He may have played a minor military role at some point – perhaps he had been asked to hold weapons or to transport an operative – but I was absolutely certain he was not militarily trained or on active service with the IRA in the area. My knowledge was that Mr Dalton had become involved in Sinn Féin after the 1981 hunger strikes. His wife's family had strong republican values, but he was somewhat indifferent until the 1981 crisis. I represented my view to my superiors regarding Mr Dalton's suitability, but I was overruled.

As I described above, a certain amount of work is required in advance to establish credible suspicion about an individual's allegiance. With respect to Mr Dalton, matters were hurried along and a connection in Le Havre was used along with a another high-level British Intelligence double-agent operating inside the IRA in Northern Ireland. As a result, just after Christmas (1989) Jim Dalton was questioned by internal IRA regarding *The Ottoman* interception. This was what we wanted and I understood that this was viewed positively by Garda command.

It was normal at this point to stand back and let the rumour mill do its work as it is not good to be seen to be too close to any operation. However, something appeared to go wrong and the following day I was ordered to accompany Detective Denis Lynch with instructions to arrest Mr Dalton. It was not explained to me what the problem was, but it struck me that there was a certain amount of panic in our actions. I sensed the Dalton frame-up was falling apart and that his arrest was an act of last resort in our efforts to compromise him.

Unusually, we arrested Mr Dalton as he left his place of work. The date was January 3rd 1990. We did so on the instructions of Det. Lynch, who was the senior officer, so as to ensure that the arrest was not witnessed. I assumed we would return to Cork but instead we went to Mallow, and then to an isolated house outside the town.

I sat with Mr Dalton in the back of the unmarked car during this journey. He was quite agitated and demanded to know where he was being taken. At one stage he began speaking to me in Irish.

At the house we took him inside. He got quite upset suddenly. I wasn't sure myself what was going on, but Det. Lynch directed me to check the house to verify that it was secure. This was normal practice. I was upstairs when I heard a shot and then a second report. I ran down immediately. Mr Dalton was lying on the hall floor at the back of the house. He had a bullet wound to the underside of his jaw and a second in his chest. According to Det. Lynch, Mr Dalton had attempted to wrest his weapon from him and in the ensuring struggle the weapon had gone off.

Despite my experience I had never seen anything like this before. I was very upset. There were aspects that I didn't understand and that made no sense to me. However, everything moved very quickly. Det. Lynch looked upset, too, and despite some reservations I believed his account of what happened.

Det. Lynch contacted our superior officer

in regards to what to do next and it was at this stage that I became worried for the first time. I was told, via Det. Lynch, that it was vital to our ongoing operations that the Jim Dalton informer plan hold up. We were not offered any explanation with respect to this. Instead we were instructed to maintain that Dalton was a high-level informer and that he had been put into a witness-protection programme for his own safety. From an operations point of view this was ludicrous, but I was too dazed by what had happened to argue otherwise.

That night we drove back to Cork city with Mr Dalton in the boot of our car. Det. Lynch subsequently organised for the disposal of the body.

Initially I played a full part in the cover-up. For a number of years I did not dwell on what had happened other than to say that I was not happy about it. The matter jarred with me, however, and about a year later I relayed my concerns to a senior officer in the Cork command. The officer confided to me that Jim Dalton was ready to betray the identity of a high-ranking mole inside IRA command and that this was the reason for his removal. No other details were offered. However, that was the first admission to me that the killing was not an accident.

Later on I confronted Det. Lynch directly about the killing, but he denied that it was anything other than what he said had happened – an act of self-defence on his part. I did not believe him.

I did not pursue the matter any further at the time. I am not saying that the explanation I was given by the senior officer was a justification for what had happened, but for a time it allayed my doubts. At the time much was deemed permissible when it came to the protection of sources and, in particular, highly placed confidants. A perceived threat could have very serious consequences and I recognised that. Moreover I accepted that my superiors were acting in good faith and in line with the main objective, which was to neutralise the danger to the Republic presented by Sinn Féin and the IRA.

However, in time I came to understand that this was not the case. Some years later an unexpected turn of events forced me to re-examine a number of key assumptions and relationships that I had built up in the force. This has led me to reason that the murder of Mr Jim Dalton may have taken place for quite different reasons than those given to me.

In 1997, at the time of the Good Friday Agreement negotiations, I wrote to Garda HQ in Phoenix Park, Dublin, regarding the Jim Dalton case. I was aware that the Dalton family were actively seeking information about his whereabouts. I was invited for an interview. I prepared carefully for this. I offered evidence to support the case I was presenting. I was given a hearing and I was listened to, but no action was taken. I accept now that I was naive to expect anything else.

This is my written account of these events. Furthermore I wish to apologise to the Dalton family for all the hurt and pain that I've caused them. There are actions that are unjustifiable in any circumstances, and the murder of this husband and father was one of those acts.

May the love of God be with you always and may you

find it in your hearts to forgive me.
    Signed Sean Sugrue
    Witnessed by Don Cronin
    Cork, September 12th 1997

Noelie handed the statement to Martin. He walked over to the back window. Drawing the curtain open he saw that dawn was breaking. A cat, perched on the sill, stared at him.

Noelie had wondered about the record collection and what could be in it. The idea that he would find something had become fixed in his head during his long wait inside the train tunnel. It would explain Cronin's violent reaction and Inspector Lynch's equally bizarre interest in the records. He'd wondered if he would find some information about drugs or a stash of money. But a garda execution hadn't occurred to him; a garda execution he didn't like one bit.

Martin came over. 'Ever heard of Jim Dalton?'

Noelie shook his head.

'You think this could be true?'

Noelie thought about it. Martin was in his mid-twenties. He was of a different generation to Noelie, one that came of age as the Troubles were ending. He probably had no idea what it was really like back then.

'Unfortunately it is possible. There are things that went on that we just don't know about.'

Martin nodded to the LPs. 'We should finish the job.' They checked the remaining records but found nothing more.

7

Climbing the stairs slowly, Noelie waited and listened. On the landing he saw the lengthways split in the door to his flat. There was glass on the hallway floor and more at the entrance to his sitting room. Retrieving a hurley stick from where his coats hung, he entered ready to strike. Mayhem wasn't the word for it. The table was smashed, the sofa upturned and ripped along its sides and underneath, and there was cushion filling everywhere. His books were also strewn about. Every shelf had been pulled down; some of the wall fixing had come away as well.

He went into his bedroom. It was wrecked too. The dresser was overturned and his bed pulled apart. The phone charger was where he had left it, plugged in at the side of the bed. Returning to the sitting room, he checked around the kitchenette and on the counters. Cutlery, plates, pasta, rice, biscuits and raisins were everywhere. He searched for the page about Brian Boru, realising now that it was probably significant, but it was nowhere to be found.

'Fuck,' he swore.

Downstairs, Martin let him back in. The coffee was brewed.

'Destroyed. No other word for it. Not the cops either, I'd say. Doubt even they could be that vindictive.'

'Cronin then?'

Noelie didn't know. He plugged in his charger. His phone had been dead for the best part of a day – from shortly after he entered the rail tunnel. Messages beeped in rapidly, a whopping eighteen in all.

47

'You're popular.'

Noelie was surprised. 'Believe me, that isn't normal.' Apart from one from a former work buddy, the rest were all from his sister. *Is Shane with u?* The next, *Trying to contact you. Is Shane with u?* Then, *Where are u? Shane not home. Worried. Is he with u?* All the others were variations of the same.

Noelie didn't understand. It wouldn't be normal for Shane to visit Noelie, let alone for him to stay over. He checked the time of the last message: 2 a.m.

'Something up?' Martin asked.

'I don't know. I hope not.'

He rang his sister and she answered immediately. 'Where've you been? I've been trying to contact you. Is Shane with you? Please say he's with you.'

Noelie told Ellen that he hadn't seen Shane since the previous morning.

'He hasn't come home. He went to his friend in the afternoon and then he went into town. He hasn't been seen since.'

Ellen was crying. Arthur came on the line. Noelie braced himself. 'You sure you don't know where he is. Where were you all this time?'

Noelie held the phone away from his ear. He exchanged a look with Martin and replied, 'I don't know where he is. How would I know?' He explained about his phone being dead. 'Look, I'm coming right over.'

Noelie left using the same route he had arrived by. Douglas Street was a parking nightmare so he often parked a fair distance away. He approached his car carefully, checked no one was lying in wait for him and drove directly to Bellevue Park. At his sister's, the door was opened by a neighbour. Noelie found Ellen on the sofa, red-eyed and pale.

'I've been trying to contact you all night. Where were you?'

'I was out.' He explained about his phone dying but didn't

elaborate on where he had been. 'When I got back, it was late. I never thought to check for messages.'

Arthur put his hand to Noelie's shoulder and felt his sooty collar. 'Where were you looking like that? What were you doing?'

Noelie realised he wasn't manky but he wasn't entirely clean either. He should've cleaned up properly, fully. But the idea that Shane had gone missing had unnerved him.

'I was helping someone.'

'During the night?'

He faced up to his brother-in-law. 'Leave it.'

'I want a private word.'

Arthur left and Noelie followed. There was a room off to the side that was used as a home office. They went in.

'We're worried sick. This isn't like Shane. I don't care what's going on, do you understand?'

'There isn't anything going on. I haven't seen him. Of course I haven't. If I had I'd tell you immediately.'

There was a tense silence. Noelie could tell his brother-in-law didn't believe him. Arthur left. Outside, Noelie stood in the hall unsure about what to do. Ellen appeared and came towards him. She looked like she was going to cry again.

'What are the gardaí saying?'

'They're on the lookout for him. But they won't do anything official until twenty-four hours have passed.'

'They probably have a point,' agreed Noelie.

Ellen exploded. 'They have no point. He's barely sixteen. He's never not in contact. He's good that way.' She looked at her brother. 'What if he's done something stupid?'

Noelie was taken aback. 'What do you mean? He's sound, Ellen. He was all talk to me yesterday about the band. He's in great form. Whatever you mean by "stupid", he wouldn't do it.'

In the silence that followed, Noelie thought about what he

had got himself involved in with Cronin and Inspector Lynch. Could there be some link? Surely not.

'This friend, he say anything?'

'They were supposed to hang out but his friend had a family event. So Shane left earlier than he was expecting to.' Ellen dried her eyes. 'Where were you really, Noelie? You look a state. Take a look in a mirror.'

Noelie moved to avoid his sister's eyes.

'And what about yesterday? Out of nowhere, "Oh hi, sis, can I stay the night like?" Noelie, you never the stay the night. Since you came back from America, I'd say I could count the number of times on one hand.'

Arthur appeared at the door. He said they had marked out a local area to search and that he was going to go out with their neighbours.

'I want to help,' said Noelie and offered to look around a nearby area known as the Camp Field. 'It's often used as a shortcut into town. I'll check it in a bit.'

After Arthur left Ellen returned to her question. 'Why did you show up here so early yesterday?'

'There was a break-in at my place and it was wrecked. It got to me and I didn't want to stay there.'

'But you arrived just after nine in the morning, Noel. What time did your place get broken into?'

Noelie didn't want to go into his trouble with Cronin. He also didn't want to mention his hassle with the cops. In Ellen's view, if you were in trouble with the gardaí it meant you were in the wrong; there weren't two sides to it for her.

'I stayed over with someone. Got back and saw the place.'

They stared at each other.

'I don't believe you.' When he didn't say anything, she repeated, 'I don't believe you, Noel.'

8

Noelie checked the shortcuts around the Camp Field. The kids in the area knew them all and Noelie did too. He had grown up around here. Clearly these routes were no longer in much demand. One path was overrun with brambles and nettles, another had become a graveyard for empty beer bottles and cans.

It was dispiriting work. He passed along them all once and then went back to his car. He sat there, worried. The Sugrue statement was not just trouble, it was dangerous. Putting that alongside Shane's disappearance he knew it was reasonable to be concerned: there was no way the young lad would just leave and not be in contact. He checked his watch and worked out that it was the best part of nineteen hours since anyone had heard from him. He decided to call to Don Cronin's.

At Grant Lane, he drove down the narrow hill and parked at the end of the cul-de-sac. A well-dressed, slim woman was standing on Cronin's front porch. She was on the phone. Noelie got out and called loudly, 'Is Don home? Could you tell him Noelie Sullivan's here?'

The woman hesitated, scrutinised him and went inside. Noelie tried the side gate and entered. He went as far as the silver Merc. He noticed that the car boot was open and that there were suitcases just inside the front door.

Cronin appeared. He was wearing light chinos and another of those argyle golf jumpers.

'Well, well,' he said.

'I need to ask you something.'

'Become more talkative, have we?'

'I found what was in the record collection – I found the Sugrue statement.'

Cronin didn't move, his expression didn't change either. 'So now you're in as deep as everyone else. Congratulations.'

'My nephew's missing. Since yesterday afternoon. Is it connected to this?'

Cronin smirked. 'See what I mean.'

'No, I don't. Do you know where he is?'

The security boss shook his head. 'I have no idea.'

Noelie went nearer, to the foot of the steps. 'He's just a kid. Take the records, take the statement if it's so important to you. I couldn't care less.'

'Too late. I've had visitors. Because of you and your big mouth. My lock-ups, the three I had at Dillon's Cross, were cleaned out yesterday morning. Special Branch. They took everything. So it's over for me now.' Cronin continued looking at Noelie. There was a pitying expression on his face. 'You haven't a clue, have you?'

Noelie didn't understand. 'Explain then.'

'Why? I don't give a fuck about you. You shouldn't have meddled. Look where it's got you, coming down here acting the smartarse.'

'I never asked to get involved in this. I just wanted to know how you got my records.'

Cronin put his hands in his pockets and turned to go.

'Were you blackmailing Lynch, is that it?'

Cronin faced Noelie again. 'It's a lot bigger than that and a lot nastier.'

Noelie stared. He didn't like what he was hearing. The woman suddenly reappeared in the doorway. Noelie figured she must be Cronin's wife. She had a dog on a leash, a pit bull. It snarled viciously.

'Where's my nephew?' he asked again.

'I don't know.'

'Who does then?' Noelie hesitated. 'Is Shane going missing connected to this, to whatever this is about?'

'You better hope not.'

Noelie pursed his lips. 'Give me a name, give me something.'

Cronin shook his head.

'Who is Brian Boru?'

Cronin's expression darkened. He looked surprised. 'I'll give you one piece of advice. Forget that name.'

'Who is he?'

'Push this and you'll end up lying in a ditch.'

The pit bull snarled. It wanted to attack but Noelie didn't move. 'I can't do that. Not when my nephew's missing. Who is Brian Boru?'

Cronin shook his head despairingly. 'Ajax Dineen said you were a fool. He was right.'

Noelie nodded to the suitcases. 'Where are you going?'

'On a holiday. Security isn't what it used to be.'

'Give me a name. Please.'

'You're already way out of your depth. If I was you I'd go to the nearest church and pray that none of that crowd has taken your nephew. That's what I'd do. You've fucked up, Noel.'

'Who are you talking about? What crowd?'

Cronin's wife stooped to release the dog. Noelie retreated. He just managed to get out and close the gate behind him. The dog lunged anyway and the metal gate shook from the impact.

Noelie watched Cronin turn and say something to his wife. She was on her phone again. They went inside and closed the front door.

9

Hannah Hegarty's desk was tucked away in a corner at the offices of the *Cork Voice*. She was Noelie's best friend and an old college buddy.

'The bad penny is back.'

She hardly looked up. 'Find yourself a seat. There is one somewhere. I just need to finish this.'

The only chair was covered with brochures. Noelie picked up a glossy promo for the Marquee, the city's pop-up summertime music venue. He glanced at the line-up and put it away again. Music and entertainment were the last things on his mind.

Hannah eventually paused and swivelled her chair in his direction. She wore a black muslin scarf around her neck and through her reddish hair.

'You don't look so good.'

'I'm not.'

She put out her hands and he rose to hug her. 'I'm sorry for being a prick,' he said.

'Forget it, I–'

'I've a big mouth.'

'That's true.'

They both laughed.

'I shouldn't have said what I said.'

A week earlier they had had a minor falling-out – Noelie's fault. He had dissected an article Hannah had written for the *Voice* – a pen portrait of a local politician. The *Voice* was a freebie and a fair amount of its journalism was less than rigorous. He hadn't held back. Hannah had been pissed off and hurt.

She stood. 'Let's get coffee. As you know, we have the highest quality beans here.'

She led him along a wide, brightly lit corridor. They were good friends, old friends too. At college, aeons back, they had gone out together. Two dates in total and it hadn't worked. Amazingly they had stayed on good terms. In a way, getting the romantic stuff out of the way was the making of them. Over the years they had gone their own ways but they had always stayed in contact. Now the two of them, unmarried and a lot older, felt like survivors from another era.

They reached the coffee area. It was makeshift but cosy. Hannah dropped coins into a paper cup and took the two instant coffees she'd made to a table beside a large window. The view was of a busy crossroads. On the other side were more flat-roofed buildings, all of them once part of Cork's Dunlop Tyre factory.

They watched the traffic coming and going. Eventually Hannah prompted Noelie. 'So?'

'I'm in trouble. Not me precisely, not yet anyway.'

He described what had happened since finding his record collection. He got to the Sugrue statement and gave her a brief summary. He finished with the news about Shane. 'I can't help thinking that Shane's disappearance might be connected to all of this. But that seems crazy. I'm worried about that statement though. I don't know what to think.'

Hannah knew Noelie's sister well enough and got on with her. She'd met Shane once or twice as well and agreed that the lack of contact from him was worrying.

He told Hannah about the break-in and about the damage that had been done at his place. 'Someone's very annoyed, that's clear.'

Hannah asked to see the Sugrue statement. 'Jesus,' she said when she finished reading it.

'I've checked up on Jim Dalton. It's all legit.' He explained that he had gone to an internet cafe. Jim Dalton was listed on a number of missing persons sites. One entry included a mugshot of Dalton and a contact number for his wife, Ethel Dalton. He continued, 'January gone marked the twentieth anniversary of his disappearance. The family held a press conference. There's a YouTube video of the entire thing. The Daltons are adamant that he's not in any witness protection scheme and that he isn't – and never was – an informer. Basically, they're still looking for him.'

Hannah said she had some contacts that she could talk to about Jim Dalton. She asked Noelie how much he knew about Sugrue and why he had written the statement. He admitted he knew very little about the man or his motives.

'This statement claims that Dalton was murdered, correct? By the gardaí too?'

Noelie nodded.

'So you must be thinking what I'm thinking. Like, oh fuck.'

'That's exactly what I'm thinking.'

Hannah read the statement again. 'He's remorseful, Sugrue I mean, isn't he?'

'I guess.'

A woman appeared and helped herself to a coffee. She looked youngish, pretty. Hannah said hello to her.

'The boss.'

Noelie looked again. 'She's just a kid.'

'That's how it is.'

Hannah had worked for a long time for one of the big papers in Cork. She was close to making staff when the internet happened. It was a bad blow. For the present it was the *Cork Voice* and any other freelance gigs she could get. She lowered her voice. 'She's actually okay. Got politics, a feminist. Always banging on about pro-choice stuff.'

'How bad.'

Hannah was thinking. 'Look, if there was some connection,

I mean between Shane's disappearance and you finding this document, surely they'd make contact?'

'I think so.'

'But no one has?'

Noelie shook his head. 'There's been nothing at all.' He told Hannah about his exchange with Cronin.

'You better hope "that crowd" doesn't have him, he said.'

Hannah frowned. 'Crowd, meaning ... ?' Noelie shook his head. 'The IRA? Is that what he meant?'

Noelie conceded it was possible. A crowd could be an organisation. It was certainly something organised. He put his head in his hands. 'What have I got Shane mixed up in?'

Hannah looked concerned. Noelie watched her read the Sugrue statement again.

'Should I tell Ellen?'

Hannah thought about this. She knew Noelie's relationship with his sister wasn't great.

'If you had something to go on, something that would back up the possibility, I'd say yes, but you don't. Right now there's nothing.'

There was silence again.

'The Dalton case is real, Hannah.'

'You said that already.'

'Sorry. What I mean is, what should I do? About the statement, about what it's saying?'

'Go to the guards?'

They both saw the joke and laughed. Noelie realised how much better he felt having talked things through with Hannah. He reached over and took her hand. 'Thanks,' he said. 'Really.'

Hannah glanced at her boss. 'You're giving her ideas.'

'So what.' Noelie squeezed her hand again. After a pause, he asked, 'Should I go to the Daltons, give them this information?'

They were interrupted by someone looking for Hannah.

She signalled that she'd be right there. They put their cups in the bin and walked slowly. As they did, Noelie told her the Daltons' address; it was off Cathedral Road, not far away as the crow flies.

'You're still not sure I should go?'

'Once you tell the Daltons, they'll go public. I mean they probably need to. But it will also mean a shit storm. Alleging the gardaí murdered an innocent man. You know how the cops are viewed in this city? Like gods.'

'Except it's one of their own that's saying it.'

He reminded her about what Cronin had said about Branch cleaning out the Dillon's Cross lock-ups. 'I'm thinking there are people after this information right now. If I don't do something soon, what's to stop them coming after me again?'

Hannah nodded this time. 'I see your point. Call the family so, see what they say.'

Outside, Noelie called Ellen first. In the few seconds that he was waiting for her to pick up, he hoped like he had never hoped before. But the tone of Ellen's voice alone was his answer. He could hardly hear her speak. 'Nothing,' she said, adding after a pause that she was doing a 'Missing' poster on the computer. They were going to make a hundred copies and put them up around the area immediately. She put down the phone without another word.

10

Cathedral Road was the main artery through Cork's working-class heartland of Gurranabraher. The Catholic cathedral was at the bottom of the hill. Noelie pulled in at the corner with Casement Avenue. The Dalton house was one in from the intersection: modest and well maintained.

After talking to his sister, he had called the Daltons. Mrs Dalton answered. He explained who he was and that he had information about her husband. Prolonged silence followed. Then a different voice came on the line, younger and female. Who was he? Where was he from? Was this genuine? Noelie answered each question calmly. After another long silence he was told to come over.

A young man – one of the Dalton sons or so Noelie guessed, there were no introductions – answered the front door.

'You the man who called my mother?'

Noelie said he was. He was warned that his visit had better not be any kind of a hoax. If it was, Noelie would pay.

After that he was shown into the front room. Ethel Dalton was waiting for him. She stood immediately and came towards him. She was older than Noelie, in her late fifties. She looked pale.

A polished black piano dominated the space. On the lid sat a large framed half-portrait of a man in a dress suit. From the internet mugshot Noelie figured it was Jim Dalton – dark hair and big eyes; a slight build of a man. Arranged around the main picture was a collection of smaller framed photographs.

Some were of family gatherings; one showed Jim Dalton as part of a jazz ensemble.

Ethel Dalton spoke. 'My Jim's been seen in San Francisco, in Oklahoma too. He was working in Brisbane for a while. Then in Aberdeen, in Scotland that is, on the rigs. We've heard everything, just so you know.'

The son chipped in, 'Understand?'

'Took a new life, left us, is what they say. Or he was gay. We've heard also that he was having an affair and that he just ran off with his lover. Another story is that if he had stayed in Cork, the IRA's nut squad was going to have him. So, the story goes, he was one of the lucky ones – he got out before it was too late. Served the Free State lackeys and took his winnings. So, just to repeat, just so as you know, we've heard it all before.'

Noelie hadn't mentioned the statement on the phone; he had just said that he had information. Seeing Ethel Dalton made up his mind for him. She looked and sounded exhausted. He believed she was genuine.

Unzipping his canvas jacket he took out the statement. 'I'll show you what I found. It's up to you then.'

Ethel Dalton looked Noelie in the eye.

'My Jim was an orphan. The one thing he craved in life was family. We were it, we were his family. There's four of us left. Me, my son and my two daughters. We all know he'd never leave us, not willingly anyway. So I've never cared about what they were saying, about any nut squad or any Free State winnings. I know my Jim.'

Noelie unfolded the document. As he did the door opened and a young woman came in. Her hair was cut short, shaved on one side.

'Hello Mam,' she said to her mother as she scrutinised Noelie. Unexpectedly she put her hand out to shake Noelie's.

'If you want to know how I came by this,' he said, 'I'm happy to tell you. But suffice to say that I didn't know anything

60

about who your husband was until I read it. So I have no idea if it's the truth or if it even makes sense to you. It's not pleasant reading.'

Mrs Dalton took the document and sat. There was silence in the room. Noelie asked if he could wait in the hall. They could call him when they were done.

The Dalton house reminded him of his old family home. It was well looked after. There was a little table with a phone just inside the front door. There were lots of photos and pictures on the walls. A quartet of silver framed photographs drew his attention. Noelie recognised Pádraig Pearse, James Connolly, Joseph Plunkett and Austin Clarke – four of the 1916 Easter Rising leaders executed by the British. Beside them was a wooden carving of a traumatised male face. An inscription read 'Long Kesh Concentration Camp, 1980'.

The door opened.

'Mam wants a word again.'

Ethel Dalton was standing. When she saw Noelie she stretched out her arms and took his hands.

'Thank you,' she said. Her eyes were filled with tears.

The daughter took her mother's arm. They walked to the piano. Ethel Dalton lifted the portrait of her husband and held it close before giving it a kiss. She placed it face down on the piano.

'It's over,' she said.

11

Noelie rooted in his inside pocket for the photo of Ajax Dineen. He called the number scrawled on the side. Inspector Lynch answered immediately.

'Recognise who this is?'

'No.'

'Noel Sullivan.'

There was a pause. 'I was wondering where you had got to.'

'Wonder no more. How's it all going?'

'As you're asking, I'll be calling later. Your warrant's ready.'

'Thought I'd spare you the expense and the trouble.'

'You'll bring in the records?'

Noelie guffawed. 'No, I found what was in them.' He enjoyed the silence that followed. 'The name Jim Dalton ring a bell?'

'Should it?'

'Considering that you killed him, accidentally on purpose of course, I'm thinking you might just remember. On the other hand, I am of the view that you're a callous fucker, so maybe not.'

They agreed to meet at the Imperial Hotel. There was a cafe at the front. Noelie knew it would be busy. He felt sure Lynch wouldn't try anything in a public place. Noelie went home first. On Douglas Street, he examined the window display in Solidarity Books. When he didn't see anyone or anything suspicious around he crossed the street to his front door and entered.

There was no reply at Martin's; he was probably still at

work. Upstairs, he checked all the rooms in his flat again. There weren't any surprises but it looked worse. He cursed whoever it was who had trashed his place.

The front door no longer functioned so he barricaded it shut from the inside using a chair. Emerging from a long, much-needed shower, he caught sight of himself in the bathroom mirror. He was of thin build, with a long face that he had never been wild about; his mother's side of the family. At least he had all his hair, although it was quite grey now. Hannah had suggested he get it dyed. 'Just don't do it yourself,' she advised, 'get a professional.' But he didn't like the idea.

He noticed his hill-walking gear. Since being made unemployed he had taken it up as a regular activity. It kept him sane and he tried to get away at least once a fortnight. Sometimes he went on his own, other times he went with a group from his last job. He would have liked to have gone right there and then but he needed to stay put.

He shaved and sorted his clothes – they had been thrown about everywhere. Putting on a dark round-necked jumper and jeans, he suddenly remembered the stash of cash that he kept in the flat for emergencies. He found one trainer under his bed, empty. The second was in a corner and that was empty too. €400, gone.

'Fuck,' he shouted, and kicked his ruined mattress.

He called Hannah. She was still at work. She commiserated over the money. He told her how the Dalton meeting had gone. She agreed that it had been right to tell them.

Hannah had made enquiries of her own. A detective she knew had confirmed that a notice about Shane had just gone live on the garda system; Mayfield Station was coordinating search operations. There was another thing. An ex-journalist friend of hers had been in contact, to do with an article she had done years back on the IRA and the Northern Bank robbery. She thought he could be worth talking to.

'Like I said, he's retired. But apparently he's been writing this book on the IRA, mainly on their operations in the Cork–Kerry–Limerick–Waterford area. The "geographical" south as he once described it to me. He might know something about Dalton or Sugrue even?'

It sounded promising. As it was they had very little to go on. They agreed to meet later and make a plan.

At the cafe, there was a table free beside the window. It had a view along Cork's leafy South Mall. Noelie sat down and while he waited he called Ellen. She had just returned from the garda station and was feeling a lot more optimistic. The gardaí had been very helpful and reassuring; they fully expected to find Shane.

Just as he was finishing his call, Lynch appeared. Dressed in a navy canvas jacket and dark trousers, he still had the look of a cop about him. He sat down and reached for the manila envelope on the table. Noelie moved it out of range.

'Not so quick. What about Shane?'

Even out of uniform, Lynch looked menacing. Noelie recalled the beating he had received. Although it had happened a long time ago, it still affected him.

'A missing person's report has been filed so his case is official now. Mayfield Garda Station told me that your brother-in-law had been in touch. All they have to go on so far is the location of his last text message. Oddly it's from over your way. The beacon on Capwell Road picked it up around 2.30 p.m. yesterday. His phone was switched off a while later.'

Noelie felt a bit sick – Capwell Road was quite near his flat. Shane must have a friend in the area.

'Isn't there a way of telling a phone's location even if it's switched off?'

'Yes, but it takes time. The phone company needs to agree access. It'll be done now.'

The waiter came and they ordered. When he'd gone, Lynch put out his hand and Noelie gave him the packet. He hadn't included the Glen map, only the typed confession. Lynch examined the document.

'Says in there that you executed a man called Jim Dalton.'

Lynch cocked an eye at Noelie. 'Really? Jim Dalton's in a witness protection programme. His family simply won't accept that. Cork gardaí have been over and around it with them two hundred times.'

'The Daltons don't have a very high opinion of the Cork gardaí.'

Lynch looked up. 'You know them?'

'We've talked. Actually they were quite taken with what your ex-colleague Sugrue has to say in that statement.'

For the first time Lynch looked uneasy. 'Sugrue isn't reliable.'

'The Daltons seem to think he is.'

'Towards the end of his career he went strange. Saw all sorts of things, including Padre Pio. You know Pio, the stigmata priest. He told me once that Pio occasionally sat in his car with him.' Lynch squinted. 'Is that sane?'

The inspector turned over a page and then another. Noelie waited.

'Would it complicate matters if a body were to show up?'

'What does that mean?'

'Just wondering. Like, what would it mean if a body were to turn up?'

At that moment the waiter returned. He served the cappuccinos. When he left, Lynch said, 'What body?'

Noelie smiled. He had wondered about the Glen map. When the Daltons saw it they had jumped to the same conclusion. Did the cross and coordinates on the map refer to a grave?

'Dalton's.'

Lynch held the document in front of Noelie. 'Is there more?'

'Maybe there is.'

Lynch's expression turned very sour. 'I've explained already that this an active investigation.'

'An active cover-up's more like it. Think I'm stupid? There's no investigation. You're just protecting yourself.' Noelie nodded to the statement. 'Religious nut or not I believe Sugrue. Know why? Because I know what you were like. I was on the receiving end. A leopard and his spots, and all of that.'

'I've been good about all this, Noel, but I've my limits.'

Noelie smiled. 'I'm shaking in my boots.'

They held each other's stare. Lynch glanced at the statement again, flicking back and forth through the pages. When he finished, he repeated his question: 'Is there more?'

Noelie leaned closer. 'I'll make this simple. Help me find Shane and I'll help you.'

'I'll help you with your nephew. That goes without saying.'

'I mean really help me. Tell me what's going on. What's this all about? Don Cronin implied that Shane's disappearance could be connected to this Sugrue statement.'

Lynch looked surprised again. 'You talked to Cronin?'

'Actually he was on his way to the airport. With the missus in tow. Catching a plane to God knows where. He said that I should hope that "that crowd doesn't have him" or words to that effect. Who is "that crowd"?'

Lynch shrugged. 'I don't know.'

'You expect me to believe that?'

'It's true.'

Noelie nodded at the statement. 'That's going public in a while.'

'You think anyone will believe this crap? Sugrue went gaga and there's more people than me know that too.'

'Which explains perfectly why you're sitting here with me right now. So who is "that crowd"?'

'I said I don't know.'

Noelie stood. 'You being such a hotshot cop, I'm guessing you've heard of Wikileaks? That's where this statement is going. And the other material with it.'

Lynch nodded to the chair. 'Sit down.'

'Please?'

'Please.'

Noelie did. Lynch looked at Noelie for a long moment.

'I don't see how any of this could be connected to your nephew going missing, I really don't. No one likes to admit it but boys do go missing. He could've run off. More than likely he's with someone ...'

Noelie listened. He felt Lynch was being straight with him.

'Shane's a decent kid,' said Noelie. 'He's sixteen but he's level-headed. The problem is he wouldn't disappear for a whole night and not make any contact.'

Lynch nodded. 'Missing children, teenagers, are a priority. I'll make it my business to find out where things are at. Is that good enough?'

Noelie waited. 'And?'

Lynch sighed. 'I can tell you a bit about Dalton. At least then you'll be more in the picture.' He paused. 'It's a legacy issue. There are obligations to people who helped the authorities in the past.'

'People who helped the authorities,' repeated Noelie slowly. 'Informers, you mean?'

Lynch hesitated. 'That's not a term I use. The point is the gardaí still have a duty of care to people who cooperated with us during the Troubles. The Dalton matter is about that. Dalton was put in a witness protection scheme to safeguard an identity. That's the bald truth.'

'An identity?'

'I don't know any more than that. Believe me, I'm not as high ranking as you think. The type of detail you are asking for is handled by a special unit that's only partly linked to Branch. I doubt if there's more than two people in the entire state who know who this person is. That's how it's done, that's how it has to be done.'

Noelie couldn't decide if he believed Lynch or not.

'Has anyone made contact with you or your sister about Shane?'

'No.'

'Well, it's early days.'

Noelie smiled. 'You're good, I'll say that much. Any thoughts of Broadway?'

Lynch frowned. 'What are you on about?'

'The past. Legacy issues. Acting responsibly. Duty of care to those who ratted on their comrades and so on. It's easy to see where this is leading: best to be quiet for now and let the responsible authorities handle the matter. Nice.'

'It's the truth.'

'You want to buy yourself time. Find some way to get out from under this. It's the old tactic: delay, delay, delay.'

'Can't you get it into your thick skull that I'm not out to get you. I'm trying to give you advice, Noelie.'

'Who is Brian Boru?'

Lynch shrugged. 'The last High King of Ireland.'

'Snap. Except Don Cronin knew. When I asked him who Brian Boru was it caused quite a reaction. Not a good one either. He told to me to forget I had ever heard of Brian Boru. Is that the identity then, the one you are all being so careful to protect?'

'I don't know. What I do know is that you're making a mistake going public with any of this and I mean that. Wait a day even. In case someone makes contact?'

It was Noelie's turn to feel unsure of himself.

'It's worth thinking about who you're dealing with here, Noel. Say there is someone highly placed inside the Provos with a hidden past – what do you think that person might be thinking about right now? If there was the remotest chance of some information getting out that would reveal that person's true role, what do you think she or he would do? Someone told me once you're of above average intelligence. Work it out.'

'Find Shane. You have a few hours.'

Lynch folded the Sugrue statement and slipped it inside his jacket. He stood up. 'I'm giving you good advice. Don't be rash.'

Noelie was left to settle the bill – a minor matter but annoying all the same. When he was done he went out to the hotel foyer. A group of American tourists with overloaded luggage trolleys were making their way to reception. At the hotel entrance Noelie looked up and down South Mall. Lynch was nowhere to be seen. The meeting hadn't gone well for either of them.

12

Every nook, cranny, small box and crevice had been searched. So they hadn't just been looking for the records. Noelie figured whoever had been through his place knew about the statement and the map. Clearly Branch were suspects but it just didn't feel like them. The mess was too chaotic and there was something personal about the damage that Noelie couldn't understand. The framed picture of his parents had been smashed and the photo had been taken out and torn in two. Also, his posters had been pulled down and ripped up. Even his precious framed Tom Campbell, a strange depiction of a woman's elongated face, had been jabbed through in the centre.

Standing there, he knew he needed to clean up but he was sickened by the wanton damage. Martin's sudden arrival startled him.

'You're nervous.'

'And shattered.'

Noelie realised he was exhausted. Maybe that was why he felt so low, so hopeless. Martin suggested he come downstairs. He could make tea or Noelie could get some sleep.

As the tea was being poured, Hannah arrived. She went up to look at Noelie's place and returned shaking her head. 'Pure destruction. It's like someone wanted to rip the place apart.'

They agreed that having someone break into your flat was one of the worst things that could happen. Noelie wondered again who it could've been. Martin reminded him of the man who had called, the one with the large ears.

'What time was that, d'you think?'

'I was only in from work. Six or so.'

'He could've been waiting of course. Watching for who came and went. He say what he wanted?'

'You. Were you around? I said no but that I was. I was on guard, given what I'd seen upstairs, so I camped it up a little for him. He didn't hang around.'

'Was he threatening?'

'Not really. He looked unsure.'

'A cop?' enquired Hannah.

'Didn't look like one.' Martin said, then added, 'Actually definitely not a cop. He was on the shabby side. There was something strange about him, like he hadn't been out in sunlight for a long time.'

Hannah laughed at this but Martin was adamant. 'I mean it, he was on the strange side and I don't say that about many people. Okay, it was partly his ears. They were like shovels. But there was something else too.'

Hannah reminded Noelie about her ex-journalist friend, Tommy Keogh. 'I called him and asked generally. He said he had met Sugrue once.'

'Where does he live?' asked Noelie.

'Crosshaven.'

'Could we go there now?'

'Let's do it.'

The drive took them south out of Cork in the direction of Carrigaline. Keogh lived at Church Bay, a rocky cove not far from the mouth of Cork harbour. It was about two miles on from Crosshaven itself.

'Church Bay was one of our seaside destinations when we were young,' said Noelie. 'We'd take the bus from town. Ma, Da, Ellen and me. Church Bay or Youghal, those were our two options.'

They drove in silence for a while. Noelie realised his phone was almost out of credit so he asked if he could borrow Hannah's.

He called Ellen. Her optimism from earlier had vanished. She pointed out that they were heading into a second evening without having heard from Shane. She was really worried.

After the call Noelie felt panicked too. Hannah tried to reassure him. 'It's only a day and a bit. He'll turn up, Noelie – you have to believe that.'

She changed the subject, and told Noelie a bit more about Keogh. She had visited him before.

'Not long after he retired, he had a few of us down to dinner. He was missing the company. Hacks' night out. I always got on with him. I heard he had some good sources so I've kept in with him.'

They reached Crosshaven and joined the winding road up to the coast. Noelie spoke again. 'Lynch didn't think this was connected with Shane's disappearance though. That's something.'

'Did you believe him?'

Noelie thought about his answer. 'I think so. Lynch was out of sorts in fact. I can't put my finger on it but it's like he didn't know what was going on either.'

Keogh was expecting them. There was something familiar about him. Noelie wondered if had he seen him on TV. He was in his mid-sixties, had dyed black hair and a bushy beard. It looked as though he had broken his nose at some point.

He greeted Hannah warmly and led them into a glass-fronted sunroom. Ahead, at the bottom of a precipitous cliff, there was a rocky cove; beyond that the flat expanse of the Celtic sea. The vista was spectacular.

Seafaring knick-knacks abounded. A trawler net suspended

from the ceiling held conch shells, life buoys and a boathouse steering wheel. Keogh produced lemonade. As he poured them a glass each he told them that he had heard something: a tip-off from an ex-colleague about a press conference for the next morning.

'Sugrue's name was mentioned.' He looked at Noelie. 'Is that your work?'

Noelie reluctantly nodded. 'It's possible.' The news was alarming though. If there was a press conference, then everything would be out in the open. Everything would move very quickly.

Noelie told Keogh the entire story, from the serendipitous discovery of his records to the realisation that there was something hidden in them, and on from there. In turn Keogh explained about the book he was writing.

He had heard about Jim Dalton and knew of the various rumours surrounding him. He pointed out that the Cork gardaí had previous, and reminded them of the case of Sean Corcoran. The Corkman was found shot dead on a back road outside the city and branded an informer. However, when the IRA commander Sean O'Callaghan turned himself over to the British police in 1988 he said he'd made repeated efforts to warn Branch about the threat to Corcoran's life. Branch didn't act and one theory was that Corcoran had been sacrificed to protect a more highly valued informer inside the IRA in the Cork area.

Noelie didn't like what he was hearing. He also realised now that he was running out of time.

'The main reason we wanted to talk to you is in regard to my nephew. I discovered this information about Jim Dalton, and then the boy vanished. Didn't come home and his mobile went dead too.'

Hannah added, 'It's over twenty-four hours since anyone's heard from him. He's only sixteen and never not been in contact with home. Noelie's worried; everyone is.'

Keogh nodded understandingly. Hannah continued, 'Noelie spoke to Inspector Lynch about it. He was, let's say, circumspect but he admitted that it was possible that Shane's disappearance could be connected to the Dalton matter.'

Keogh was surprised. 'He said that?'

'Not in as many words. Look, he denied Jim Dalton was dead but he did admit that his disappearance had to do with protecting what he called "an identity" inside the IRA.'

Noelie put his head in his hands. 'In truth I don't know what's going on. But Shane disappearing right now feels too much like a coincidence.'

Keogh looked at Hannah and then at Noelie again. 'I guess there's some sense in his reasoning.'

'But no one's been in contact,' continued Noelie. 'Surely if someone had taken Shane to put pressure on me or whatever, they would have made contact?'

Keogh nodded. 'So maybe there isn't any connection. Maybe there's no need to panic.'

There was silence.

'Except that I went to see Don Cronin. He's ex-Branch, Cronin Security Group. '

'I've heard of him.'

'He was cagey. He as good as admitted to me that there's something nasty at the back of all of this.'

'Nasty?'

Noelie shrugged. 'I don't know what he meant. He wouldn't say much more but the name Brain Boru popped up. Cronin said stay away from anything to do with that name or things could get bad.'

Keogh didn't say anything.

Hannah spoke. 'Have you ever heard any mention of this Brian Boru figure?'

Keogh hesitated. 'Look, anything do with informers is unsavoury. You have to ask yourself what sort of person informs. It'll be messy is what I'm saying.'

Hannah nodded. Noelie spoke. 'Could you give me a name, just something? We won't say it was you, but someone, anyone we could talk to.'

Keogh excused himself. He fetched binoculars and returned to near where they were sitting. He studied the view.

'I'm an anorak about ships,' he said. 'It's why I live here.'

A massive cargo ship was approaching Cork harbour at Roche's Point. It was stacked high with containers. Noelie shook his head in dismay while looking at Hannah.

'Calm down,' she whispered.

Eventually Keogh retook his seat and looked at them both. Noelie wondered if he had forgotten why they were there.

'What do you know about Sugrue?' Keogh asked.

'Not much. Lynch implied he was tapped, a bit mad like, but then he would, I guess.'

'It's not entirely untrue. I came across him a few times. Followed his story a little. He was a maverick in the gardaí and that interested me. But this is separate entirely to your query.'

'Go on anyway,' said Hannah.

'In the early eighties, Soviet ships used to come into Cork's upper port area. Bringing coal mainly. Other items too, mind.' He laughed. 'Including the best of vodka for the local Communist Party men. Anyway Sugrue was in a group that boarded one of these Soviet merchant ships one afternoon. This must've been about 1980 or that. Him and a few acolytes occupied the deck and proceeded to celebrate Mass, the Tridentine version if memory serves me right. I think he was a follower of Lefebvre but don't quote me on that. Hardcore anyway. It nearly caused an international incident when it emerged that Sugrue was a serving garda. He was banging on about this stuff to do with the Third Secret of Fatima and all of that. Totally cracked. Didn't go down well with the Soviets at all. That was how I first came across him. I was certain he was off to Tory Island to count sheep after that, but all he got was a rap on the knuckles. Clearly he was connected.'

Noelie couldn't see how this was relevant. Pointedly he repeated his request, 'Is there someone I could go to, in Sinn Féin or in the Provos? Hannah said you know your way around them. I need to talk to someone and I need to do it right away. Could you put in a word for me?'

Keogh chewed his lower lip.

'It would be a big help,' added Hannah.

'Anyone connected to Sinn Féin will clam up the moment you start asking about the past, especially if it's to do with informers. Like I said, no one wants to go there. It's messy and, to be absolutely mercenary about it, there are no votes in it either. The opposite in fact. These days with Sinn Féin, votes are the only thing that matters. Next general election there's even a possibility that they'll make it into government in the South. That would be a massive step for them. Remember ten years ago they were outlaws.' He paused. 'Even if I was to ask on your behalf, I'd get the same reply.'

'Someone disenchanted then? There must plenty of them, given the sell-out.'

Keogh looked taken aback. 'You think Sinn Féin sold out?'

'Last time I checked, there were still British troops up in the North.'

Keogh smiled. 'Old school.'

'I guess, but that's for another day now.'

'Look, anyone not toeing the party line is going to be well outside the fold. When you're on the outside with Sinn Féin, you may as well exist in another universe.'

Noelie looked away. The laden cargo ship was just entering the narrow mouth of the harbour. He managed to catch Hannah's eye. He felt that they weren't going to get much further with Keogh. In any case their host was panning the horizon with his binoculars again. He put them down.

'I know it's not what you want to hear, Noelie, but you'll get nowhere going to Sinn Féin. I'm only saying it so that you don't waste your time. I've been cultivating my sources for years. They're like a family with dark secrets. They close ranks totally when challenged. If you go around shooting off your mouth about an informer, you'll hit a brick wall before you've even finished your question. If I was to give you any advice it would be to go about your enquiry discreetly.'

'Except I don't have time for that.'

Keogh shrugged. He said he was sorry that he couldn't be of more help. They got up in unison and Noelie listened as Hannah and the retired journalist bantered about the old days. He could see they got on well.

At the door they shook hands. 'Come and see me any time, Noelie, if you think I can be of any further help. I mean that and I'm sorry I couldn't tell you more this time.'

Outside, Noelie and Hannah stood for a moment. Sunset was approaching. It was a beautiful setting and the sea air was refreshing.

'There's a path down to the cove over a bit. Do you mind if I take a look?' he asked.

Noelie remembered Church Bay as a rocky cove. It was still the same. There wasn't a grain of sand anywhere. He crossed the stony foreshore and went to the water's edge. Rocky ledges ran out on each side. Hannah stood nearby. They listened to the sound of the waves breaking. 'Got the slightest impression he knew more than he was saying,' she finally said.

Noelie looked at her and nodded. 'When you mentioned Brian Boru.'

'Exactly. He knew the name but he wasn't saying how or why.'

13

Hannah dropped Noelie back to Martin's; the plan was that Noelie would crash there for the night. She advised him to get some sleep. In the morning, she'd go with him to his sister's and they'd help with the search. Martin said he'd like to come as well. He was on flexi hours and could go into work later.

As soon as Hannah left, Noelie called Ellen. She had a bit of news.

'They've been through Shane's mobile phone records. It seems as if his phone was switched off near Turner's Cross around 3 p.m. In the morning, at first light, the search will focus on that area.' Noelie said he'd be there.

He had one last idea. He drove back across town and up Cathedral Road. Passing the Dalton house he considered calling in but decided against it. At the junction with Knocknaheeny, he drove into a black pall of smoke drifting across the road from a nearby bonfire. Noelie slowed to a halt; he could barely see ahead. Somewhere in the distance a lively singsong was in progress. It was a city tradition to host community fires on St John's Eve. Hundreds of bonfires, big and small, were being held around the county. When the smoke finally lifted, Noelie drove on.

Ardcullen estate was a triangle of houses off Augustine's Drive, almost at the very top of Cork's northside. It looked bleak and deserted. If there had been a local bonfire in the area it was long over with. Number 27 was on the back row. Years before when Noelie had last visited, he had found the house easily because of all the Celtic FC paraphernalia in the windows. That had since been dispensed with. There were no lights on but Noelie rang the bell anyway. On the second attempt he heard a door opening inside. A hall light came on and then a porch light. It took Goggin a few seconds to recognise his visitor.

'Fuck,' he said. 'Noelie Sullivan.'

'Can I come in?'

Goggin hesitated and looked at his watch; it was nearly 11 p.m. 'What is it?'

'Need to ask you something.'

'Now?'

'Now.'

Goggin moved aside to let Noelie pass. The two of them went back as far as 1981 when they spent an evening together in a cell in Bridewell Garda Station in Cork after a particularly spirited anti-H-Block protest in the city. They were about the same age but while in the cell they also discovered that they had gone to the same school. It was a tenuous link but for some reason it mattered to them both. A while later Noelie helped Goggin find a good lawyer after Goggin was beaten up in the back of a garda squad car; different occasion, same cause. Goggin won a few grand in compensation for the assault and Noelie wasn't forgotten.

That was a long time ago. Eventually Noelie left for New York and spent the best part of thirteen years in the States. On his return in the late nineties, he made an effort to get involved in politics again. A campaign against the privatisation of bin collections was underway. Through that he met Goggin again. He tried to renew their friendship but too much had changed.

By the turn of the millennium the electoral wing of the IRA, Sinn Féin, was busy cultivating a moderate, peaceful image. Goggin was now a party member and he seemed to be at the forefront of these efforts. He no longer wanted to debate any issue. The Good Friday Agreement, in particular, was off the agenda. Noelie found his old associate to be very defensive, as if he was now in charge of some holy canon that proclaimed that Sinn Féin and the IRA had only ever wanted peace on earth. Noelie knew that that wasn't quite the truth.

They went into a small sitting room with an enormous flat-screen TV against one wall. Goggin didn't sit but Noelie did anyway. He didn't know how to begin.

'So?'

'I need to talk to someone high up in the Provos. Here in Cork. Tonight.'

Goggin's face broke into a smile. 'Are you on something?' he asked.

'I'm serious.'

'Serious back, Noelie. Like, what the fuck? The Provos? What Provos? Haven't you heard? They disbanded. The Provos don't exist any more.'

As if to prove the point, Noelie noticed a stack of leaflets in the corner of the room. They showed the iconic Sinn Féin logo – an F plaitted through an S – printed on a background of the Irish national colours of green, white and gold. It was like the material was there to prove that Goggin was telling the truth and of course, in a way, he was. But Noelie was desperate.

'My nephew's gone missing. Happened yesterday.' He hesitated. 'I found this material about a supposed grass inside Sinn Féin. Have you ever heard of Jim Dalton?'

Goggin's face lost its bemused appearance. Noelie continued anyway. 'It seems like the cops may have set Dalton up, way back.'

Noelie's host waved his hands wildly. 'Not interested.'

'Just listen.'

'I know the Daltons, they're trouble. I don't want to know any more.'

'Just give me a name then, someone I could go to.'

Goggin went to the sitting room door and held it wide open. He looked pissed off. 'Bye.'

Noelie knew that this had always been a possible outcome but he remained sitting. Goggin rattled the door handle.

'I said get out.'

Noelie left without another word. Outside on the path, he heard the door slam shut behind him. Immediately he smelled burning rubber in the night air. Walking to his car he also heard something unusual. It was loud and it came from high up in the sky. Eventually he saw a projection of light, as straight as a laser beam, being directed downwards over the centre of the city. It was a helicopter and he guessed it was positioned over the Lee. Could it be search and rescue checking along the river's course, looking for Shane?

He sat in his car and put his head on the steering wheel.

The Lonely Woods of Upton

14

There were wreaths along the mound of earth and on each side: from Shane's mother and father, from his aunts on his father's side, from his cousins, from Noelie, from his school class, from the school itself, from his father's work colleagues. And many more besides. Shane's band had sent one in the shape of an electric guitar – it was Noelie's favourite. Carnations and lilies entwined on a body and a fender expertly shaped from green reeds. A CD of their release, *By The Cage*, was glued to the makeshift guitar's fingerboard. Alongside it was a grainy picture of Shane playing at The Old Oak. Lots of signatures were scribbled on the photo, which had been laminated and would outlive the wreaths and flowers that were already withering in the warm July weather.

Shane was found at low tide in the Lee's north channel. Some years earlier a riverside walk had been put in place on the grounds of the old Irish Distillers' site. The land was now the university's but the public had access to the route and it had become popular. A tree branch bowed like a fishing rod under a heavy catch caught a walker's eye. She took a closer look and realised that something large was snared on the branch – half in, half out of the dark water. This was in the late afternoon, on the day after Bonfire Night, and of course Shane's disappearance had been in the news by then. The walker recognised the hoodie showing a bicyclist doing a mid-air turn – an image associated with the band Bombay Bicycle Club. A female detective, Byrne, broke the news to the family.

The subsequent investigation focused on Shane's last known movements. He was at a friend's house until around 1 p.m. on the day he disappeared. He sent and received a series of text messages as he walked into Cork city centre. Analysis of this phone traffic indicated that Shane had stayed around the city centre area for about an hour. His final message at 2.32 p.m. – a text of no consequence about a YouTube video – was relayed by a phone mast on Capwell Road, a kilometre and a half from the city centre and about half a kilometre from Noelie's flat. Following this Shane appeared to move further away from the city centre. The final communication from his phone, as it signed off the network, was picked up by a beacon adjacent to Cork City FC's football pitch at Turner's Cross – a location almost in the heart of Cork's southside suburbs.

Noelie knew he was under suspicion courtesy of his brother-in-law, and Detective Byrne confirmed as much. Within an hour of the identification of the body, she took Noelie aside and informed him that Shane's disappearance and death would be fully investigated. She would need to see his flat as a priority; he could cooperate or she could get a warrant. Noelie decided to cooperate. He told Detective Byrne in detail about his involvement in the Jim Dalton affair, about his arrest in relation to the assault on Ajax Dineen and everything else that had happened in between. He also told her where he had been hiding during the critical time that Shane vanished. Later, analysis of CCTV footage from the rail station and the tunnel confirmed Noelie's account.

Those couple of days, a fortnight ago now, were still a haze for Noelie. Eventually he told Ellen more about the trouble he had got into: why he had gone to her house early on the morning of the day of Shane's disappearance, about the records and about Don Cronin's goons. As a result his sister had hardly spoken to him afterwards. Hannah had come to the rescue, accompanying Noelie to the funeral Mass and the burial.

In time, other developments had helped shift the focus away from Noelie. The post-mortem revealed that Shane's cause of death was drowning. No drugs or alcohol were found in his blood. Nor were there any signs on the body of violence or physical trauma. The report noted the presence of abrasions on Shane's fingertips. These were consistent with attempting to maintain a grip on concrete or on quayside walls.

Another factor that helped to clear Noelie was where Shane was found. The majority of river suicides in the city took place downstream of where Shane was discovered, at the bridges and quaysides around the centre of the town or in the docklands. What was Shane doing so far upriver? It was possible that he had fallen in downstream and had been carried upriver with an incoming tide but this was thought to be unlikely. A possible explanation was that he had entered the river upstream of where he was found. This led Detective Byrne to 'Bumhole', an area of waste ground beside the city's skateboard park. Bumhole was a gathering place for youngsters of Shane's age and it was rumoured to be a location for drugs and teenage sex. One scenario was that Shane had gone there before he vanished. Byrne hadn't confirmed this but it was plausible. Had something happened to Shane when he was at Bumhole?

A significant factor too – in particular for Noelie – was the time of Shane's death. A time bracket was the best that could be done – it was eventually calculated that Shane had been in water for at least forty-eight hours. Given that the time lapse between the final communication from Shane's phone and the discovery of his body was seventy-three hours, this meant that Shane had died when Noelie was hiding in the train tunnel.

Prior to Shane's disappearance, there were only two groups of people who knew about Noelie's recovery of the record collection: Inspector Lynch and his associates in

Branch, and Don Cronin and his crew. In the immediate aftermath of Shane's disappearance Noelie had spoken directly to both men: he felt sure neither was involved. Cronin was the most likely of the two to have had both motive and means, yet in Noelie's last encounter with him he had come across as someone who was parting company with the entire matter of the lock-ups. The only thing Noelie was unsure about was Cronin's reference to 'that crowd'. He took some small comfort in the fact that Shane's drowning had probably happened before he went to the Daltons – he had been nervous that his revelations had somehow resulted in Shane's death.

Ellen had latched on to other theories, including the idea that there was a girl or girlfriend involved. As it turned out there was a young woman close to the band. Noelie tracked her down to the Camden Palace, an indie arts venue in the centre of Cork. Anaïs had a beanstalk physique, a sunflower tattooed on the side of her neck and was totally out of Shane's league. She was in her twenties whereas Shane's lot were all teenagers. Fancied themselves, of course, but she had seen through that. She confirmed that the idea of her fronting Shane's band had come up once. She emphasised 'once' and implied to Noelie that one of them – Shane possibly? – was into her a bit too much for his own good and that this might have been behind the band's offer. But in any case, on her say so, the plan went nowhere. She also informed him that the boys did more drugs than was good for them, given their ages. That had come as a surprise to Noelie.

Now, two weeks on, he stood at his nephew's graveside for the first time since the funeral. He was at the cemetery for another reason but he couldn't not visit Shane's grave. Stooping eventually, he placed his hand on the damp mound. He clenched some soil, put it down and clenched more.

He only occasionally went to his parents' graves – he never got that much out of visiting. But this somehow felt different.

He didn't know if it was Shane's age or the rapport he had felt he had with him – or perhaps it was residual guilt? – but he felt the need to talk. He told Shane that he was very low and that Ellen was trying her best to cope without him. He also told him that the band had been up to visit her a couple of times. There were tears in his eyes.

'Sorry,' he said, adding, 'I don't understand ...'

Opinion remained divided on what had happened to Shane. The unspoken consensus was that it was either an accident or suicide – although no one seemed able to explain the latter. Shane, it seemed, had plenty to live for. The rock band he was in was popular; his mood before his disappearance had been upbeat. No one had been able to dredge up any particularly unsavoury interaction, apart from an allegation – unproven – that one of their songs had been ripped off by another local band. In sum, nothing made sense.

A small wooden cross stood at the head of Shane's plot; it would remain until a headstone was cut and inscribed. Noelie straightened it and said, 'I'm not forgetting you.'

He looked around. In the distance, on the far side of a border hedge, he saw movement: what looked like the top of a milk float moving along. He walked between the lines of graves and emerged onto a gravel path. Eventually he caught up with the vehicle. It was pulling a trailer, from which the driver-caretaker had unloaded hedge trimmers and a small petrol mower. The man was of retirement age, grey-haired and small. He looked up when Noelie approached.

'Wondering if you can help? I'm looking for the paupers' area. In the newspaper they said that the human remains found in Glen Park have been laid to rest there.'

The caretaker nodded. 'See the maples yonder? There a low marble wall on the other side of those. Number 72–5.

Coffin half the size of normal. Like a child's. Not much of him. But that's not the paupers' area. The opposite actually.'

Noelie didn't understand.

'That's the most expensive part of the cemetery,' said the caretaker. 'Take a look and you'll see what I mean.'

Noelie walked to the line of trees. The section was up against the outer cemetery wall. A low marble division snaked around a good half acre, marking it out as separate from the main graveyard. There were flowerbeds, seats too; many had dedications inscribed on them.

Plot 72–5 was just a mound of earth. Freshly dug as well. Unlike Shane's plot there were no wreaths at all. The grave looked very bare and lonely. As with Shane's grave the official marking of identity was just a simple wooden cross. A name was written on it: Michael Egan.

The Dalton family had held a press conference on the day after Bonfire Night at one of the main hotels in Cork; it was well organised and received considerable media attention. At the event the Daltons made public the Sugrue statement and called for an inquiry into what it alleged. The family also petitioned for an immediate search of the area in the Glen that was marked on the map.

Garda HQ in Phoenix Park in Dublin refuted all the allegations. A personal statement was also issued on behalf of Inspector Lynch. It also refuted the Dalton family's claims.

However the gardaí did agree to initiate a search of the area marked by a cross on the map. Human remains were found almost immediately. Then came the surprise. To the Dalton family's dismay, they were not those of Jim Dalton – this was established using dental records. It further emerged that the remains had been *in situ* for over thirty years, which took matters back to the seventies, whereas Jim Dalton went missing in 1990. What happened next was by no means as clear-cut. Noelie and Hannah had gleaned as much information as they could from the newspapers; Hannah also had her own contacts.

Shortly after the discovery in the Glen, an appeal was made for information about the remains. Almost immediately a local station, Red FM, received a significant anonymous tip. This led directly to a man reported missing from west London in 1970 – an Irishman in his early twenties who had been working on the buildings. He never arrived for work one week. When his rent fell due, the family he was in digs with made enquiries. Apparently they were fond of this man and had gone to some lengths to find out what had happened to him. They eventually filed a missing person's report. His name was Michael Egan.

Noelie wandered over to the grave next to the Egan plot. A headstone was already in place there: a shiny black marble commission with an inset colour picture of a dark-haired child alongside a gold cross and an offertory prayer. A solar lantern was alight. Fresh flowers had recently been placed on the child's grave and Noelie read the attached note. *Thinking of you always, Sweetie. Love, Mammy and Daddy.*

He remembered something. Looking at the Egan grave once more and then at the child's plot, he returned to find the cemetery caretaker tackling a hedge. He had ear muffs on and Noelie had to tap him on the shoulder. The caretaker shut off the trimmer and lifted his goggles and muffs.

'Well?'

'I see what you mean. It's nice there. Manicured, better cared for.'

'Premium zone. Some whizz-kid in the council had the idea. You know the way they are these days. You pay for the privilege of course.'

'How much?'

'Twice the usual. But that's not all. Did you notice anything else about the plot?'

Noelie shook his head. 'Can't say I did.'

'It's much bigger.'

'Is it? By how much?'

'That's a treble, he's in. It can take two more as a minimum. It's five grand's worth easily.'

Noelie looked back in the direction he had come from. 'No pauper so.'

'Doesn't look like it. We're wondering ourselves. Now someone did say it could be those people over in London are paying for it, the ones who helped to identify him, but in that case why a grave for three?'

Noelie eyed the caretaker. He wondered if this might be some kind of wind up, but the tired expression on his face remained.

'There'll be a headstone?' Noelie asked.

'Takes time to order and do up. A few weeks to six months is normal.'

'Any idea who'll be doing it?'

'Brennans, off Shandon Street. Them usually.'

15

At the Dalton house, Noelie examined a photo on the mantelpiece. It was of Ethel and Jim Dalton on their wedding day. A North Cathedral wedding: Ethel and Jim standing under the arched portico, well-wishers fanning away on each side. Ethel in white, the veil drawn aside; a bright smile on her face. Jim, beside her, in a dark suit with a carnation in his lapel. Ethel had inches on him in height.

Mrs Dalton came back into the room and sat on the sofa. She pulled a blanket over her knees.

'My Jim wasn't an orphan as such but he ended up as one. He was found wandering on Coburg Street. Do you know it?'

Noelie nodded.

'He should've been at school, 1960 this would be around. His mother was never that good. In those days that's what happened to you. He was taken from her and sent to the industrial school at Upton. There was just him and her. By the time he got out, she had died. So he kind of became an orphan. He never knew his father.'

Noelie put back the wedding photo. 'Did you ever hear him mention the name Michael Egan?'

Mrs Dalton recognised who Noelie was talking about. She shook her head and propped herself more upright on the sofa. 'Sharon,' she called loudly.

The daughter appeared at the sitting room door. She had a coat on. 'I'm going out, Mam.'

'Can you bring the photo, the one of your dad and the bishop?'

While they waited Noelie asked if there was any further

news regarding the allegations in the Sugrue statement. She responded with a series of colourful expletives; in short, no, there were no new developments. The Garda press office had now entered the fray and were disputing the claim that there had ever been any meeting involving Sugrue and the Garda Commissioner. The Daltons were taking legal advice but the allegations, for the moment at least, were last month's news.

Sharon returned and handed the picture to her mother. She didn't acknowledge Noelie. Ethel passed it to him. It had a light sepia colouration. A handwritten inscription on the edge read *Danesfort Industrial School, May 1963*. The subject was the presentation of a scroll. A line of boys in white shirts and dark short pants, ten or eleven years of age, were waiting their turn. Jim Dalton was third from the end. It would be difficult to identify him as the line of boys were not the focal point of the shot but Noelie decided to take Mrs Dalton's word for it. Behind the presentation there was a monument with a Celtic cross at its apex.

'That's Con Lucey there,' said Mrs Dalton, pointing at the deceased former bishop of Cork. Lucey had a reputation around Cork. Conservative didn't quite do him justice.

Mrs Dalton pointed to the next figure along, a priest in a soutane. He was tall, wore glasses and had his hair in a comb-over style.

'The Rosminian Order ran Danesfort. He was the head man.'

'The occasion?' enquired Noelie.

'This group were altar boys trained to administer Mass in Irish. My Jim was a good speaker, to do with that I suppose.'

Beside the head Rosminian there was one other priest. He was young and wore a white soutane. He was smiling. Noelie wondered about the significance of the pale garb. A novitiate?

There were other adults present too, in civvies. However their faces weren't easy to make out due to the angle the photo was taken from. Mrs Dalton didn't know who they were. Noelie wondered why she wanted him to look at the photo.

'From the *Examiner*?' he enquired, referring to Cork's main newspaper.

Mrs Dalton didn't know. After a while she continued, 'Jim was careful about this picture. He kept it to himself. I joked with him once that he must have been doing very well to have his photo taken with the bishop but he said that he could still smell the pee in his pants when he looked at the picture. Every boy there was scared half to death, he used to say. Jim was very bitter about Danesfort.'

This wasn't any surprise to Noelie. 'An unpleasant place from what I've read.'

'A prison for the poor.'

'Why did he have the photo?'

'I don't really know.'

He handed back the picture. Mrs Dalton laid it on the blanket on her lap. 'Will you get me a glass of water?' she asked.

Noelie was glad to. He had visited on a hunch. He recalled that Mrs Dalton had said her husband was an orphan. At the cemetery when he saw Egan's bare grave, he had wondered if Egan was an orphan too. There hadn't been any mention of his family in the news reports. Was that the connection with Dalton? He figured there had to be one. After all, why would a map of where Egan was buried be attached to the statement on Dalton's execution?

The kitchen was spotless. The entire house was that way, well-kept and cosy. A very ordinary Irish house apart from the republican memorabilia in the hall. Not many Irish people remembered the 1916 martyrs with such devotion.

He watched Mrs Dalton sip her water. She declared that she was poorly since the let-down at Glen Park, that she had been certain that the body that was found would be Jim's. She had seen the end of the road and was ready for it. She had decided long ago that her Jim was dead. Finding his body was all that remained.

She put her hand out for Noelie's and squeezed it.

'An informer is lowlife, the lowest. We're republicans here, as you know.' Noelie nodded. 'It was the worst thing they could ever say about him and about us. Jim's good name was taken. They said he was a tout, a collaborator. We've had to live with that.'

Picking up the photo again, Ethel Dalton added, 'He wanted this photo but I wouldn't give it to him.'

Noelie didn't follow. 'Who?' he asked.

'Sugrue.'

'Sean Sugrue? He was here?'

'A few times.'

'Branch business you mean? Harassing Jim?'

Mrs Dalton frowned. 'No. This was long after Jim disappeared.' She thought for a moment. 'Three times at least.'

'What did he want?'

'You see that was why I had no doubts about the statement you brought to us. The minute I saw Sugrue's name on that document I knew it was probably what we were looking for.'

Noelie remembered. Mrs Dalton had certainly not hesitated. At the time, with all that was happening, it didn't fully register with Noelie but now that she said it he understood.

'So what did he want when he was here?'

'He was interested in Jim's involvement in Sinn Féin. He knew quite a bit about him, I'll tell you that. I wouldn't tell him anything though. He got the message too.'

Noelie nodded. 'So it was police business?'

'No. He was adamant it was a private errand. He was clear there. I got the impression he was sorry about something. I didn't know what of course. This was around the time of the first IRA ceasefire, '94, I think, right? Or '95, maybe it was. I thought it was to do with that actually. Mending bridges and all that stuff.' A look of repulsion came over Mrs Dalton. 'He was quite religious, you know?'

'So I've heard.'

'Wanted to say the rosary with me, with all of us. That's what convinced me he was involved in Jim's disappearance. You could tell he was guilt-ridden.'

Mrs Dalton closed her eyes. Noelie suppressed his impatience.

'What else did he ask about?'

'It was all to do with Jim. What was he like before he disappeared? Had he spoken about anything that seemed suspicious, looking back. Was he worried? That kind of thing.'

'And?'

Mrs Dalton suddenly heaved herself up from the sofa. She went to a sideboard and opened a set of doors. Noelie saw a shelf of books all neatly lined up with years printed on their spines. 1990 was the first. She retrieved 1994 but returned it and took out 1995.

'I've kept a diary for every year. In the beginning it was for notes, to keep track of who said what. But in later years it became a way of dealing with Jim's absence. The last few years I haven't put much in them at all. There's been nothing to report.'

She skimmed through 1995 until she came to February. 'Here it is.' She read the entry.

16 February
Sean Sugrue called. He was in Special Branch in Cork and knew Jim. He wanted to pray with me. He asked if Jim spoke about the Provos and what he said. He was interested in anyone Jim didn't like or didn't trust. He

asked about a person called Brian Boru. I told him Jim wasn't in the Provos, that he was in Sinn Féin.

'This Brian Boru,' Noelie asked, 'what was that about?'
She shook her head. 'I can't remember.'
'Why did you write it down so?'
'Don't remember that either. It was fifteen years ago. See I put things in the diary because they seemed important to me at the time. But why exactly I thought that, I don't recall now. Why?'

Noelie told Mrs Dalton that he didn't know who Brian Boru was but he seemed to be someone or something important inside the IRA. He asked if her husband had ever mentioned the name. She shook her head.

'So Sugrue was here a few times and he wanted to pray with you all. Anything else?'

Mrs Dalton returned to the diary. The next few pages were empty. She returned to the very first entry in that year, on 1 January, and offered it to Noelie to read.

One day you will walk in. You will be at the door and you will stand there and you will smile at me. I won't believe it is you. That moment when I know it is you and that you really are present and have come back will be the happiest moment of my life. I won't actually believe it is you until I hold you. Then I will hold you so tight that I am sure I will squeeze the life out of you. I will never let you out of my sight again.

It was sad, and when Noelie looked up he expected to see something like sadness in Mrs Dalton's eyes but instead she beamed.

'What is it?'

'I remember. Sugrue was interested in the photo because he knew someone in it.'

Noelie retrieved the Danesfort picture and examined it again. 'You mean other than your husband?'

'Of course. Well, he didn't know Jim was in it. He was waiting out in the front room, where the piano is. We had got the photo framed and put up on the wall by that time. He was looking about, as you do.' Mrs Dalton looked very pleased. 'He asked me about it and why we had the photo. When he realised my Jim was in it too he became quite excited.' She looked at the diary again and flipped through all the August entries but there was nothing. 'I should've written something about all that, shouldn't I?'

Noelie felt like screaming yes but he only nodded.

'Well, it's not always easy.' Mrs Dalton suddenly looked sad. 'It gets me down. I used to think I'd never give up on Jim but there's been setback after setback. I don't know any more. I despair of ever finding him.'

Noelie understood. He waited a while and then probed again.

'Sugrue wanted to take the photo away to make a copy of it but I wouldn't give it to him. No way.'

Noelie went through every page in the diary for 1995. He found one other reference to Sugrue in November. All it said was 'Sean Sugrue called again.'

He looked at the Danesfort photo once more and then showed it to Mrs Dalton again. 'Any idea who it was he recognised?'

Ethel Dalton looked. 'I don't,' she said. 'I'm sorry.'

16

There was an obituary for Sean Sugrue in the January 1999 edition of the *Garda Gazette*. Born in County Clare, he joined the police force in 1966 at the age of eighteen. Ten years later, while serving in Tralee in Kerry, he foiled a bank robbery at the main post office and was wounded. Subsequently, he received the Scott Medal for Bravery and two years later, in 1978, he acquired his detective's badge and moved to Special Branch in Cork. From then on he worked in counter-terrorism. Notable successes included his involvement in two foiled IRA gunrunning attempts – the interception of the *Jenny May* off Dunmore East in 1980 and *The Ottoman* near Baltimore in 1989. In late 1997, he took early retirement from the gardaí in order to pursue an ambition to be a lay missionary. The following year, before taking up a post in Romania, he died in a car crash. He was survived by wife, Annette, and children, Tomás and Meabh.

Noelie looked up Annette Sugrue in the phonebook. It was not a common surname so he phoned around explaining that he was doing research on Scott Medal winners. Bingo on the seventh call – Mrs Sugrue lived in Mitchelstown, about thirty miles from Cork.

Noelie decided to visit immediately. On Hannah's advice he dressed up and put on a shirt and jacket for the meeting. At the front door he smiled and explained about the research he was doing. Mrs Sugrue was in her late fifties, grey-haired and thin. She wore a blue cardigan, a white blouse and a black skirt. Noelie was reminded of a nun.

She didn't want to talk and she was sceptical. Noelie

expanded on the Scott Medal thesis, explaining the importance of a book on courage given Ireland's present woes. 'If more people spoke out a few years back this country might not be in the state it's now in.' He got nowhere with this angle however and changed tack, asking instead about her late husband's religious convictions and how they had influenced his life. Mrs Sugrue relented.

'Come in,' she said, adding as a qualification, 'my son's here.'

Noelie wasn't sure what that meant. 'This really won't take long,' he assured her.

He was shown into a front room with sofas arranged around a big empty fireplace. There were a series of professional pictures of Sugrue on the wide mantelpiece. In the main portrait, Sugrue was in uniform wearing his Scott Medal. He looked exceedingly proper and po-faced.

'Fine-looking man,' Noelie said.

'He was.'

At that moment Noelie saw the son. He appeared at the doorway looking blankly at Noelie, a large man but younger than Noelie.

'Mammy,' he said.

Mrs Sugrue promptly led him away. She returned a few minutes later. 'What do you want to know?'

Noelie told her that he knew a good deal about her husband already. He was particularly interested in his willingness to speak out. He produced the statement about Dalton. 'This was very brave.'

Mrs Sugrue moved away. 'Are you a journalist?'

'I'm not.'

'What do you want then?'

'I'm the person who found this document. I know the Dalton family. They're desperate for information. They still haven't found their father's body.' Noelie moved nearer. 'This is an extraordinary statement, no? Basically your husband is saying that the gardaí executed ...'

'It was a long time ago.'

Noelie waited. He expected Mrs Sugrue to say more but she remained silent. She wouldn't look at Noelie.

'Garda HQ have rejected your husband's claims. They're saying this meeting with the commissioner never took place.'

'It took place, I was there. Not at the meeting, of course, but I accompanied Sean to the gates of Garda Headquarters in Phoenix Park. The meeting happened.'

'You're certain?'

'Of course I am,' snapped Mrs Sugrue.

'Is there any documentation, something that would support what you're saying – an appointment card or a letter even?' Noelie nearly said email but he realised that they hardly existed back in 1997.

'Sean never discussed work with me. But that meeting did take place. It's not a time or an appointment that I'm ever likely to forget. His retirement came immediately afterwards.'

'Because of how that meeting went?'

'That and other reasons.'

Noelie waited for clarification but none came. 'Your husband implied in his statement that there may have been something sinister going on. Did you know anything about that or what he was thinking of?' He read from the statement, '"... the murder of Mr Jim Dalton may have taken place for quite different reasons than those given to me." What did he mean by that?'

Mrs Sugrue stared.

'Mrs Sugrue?'

'I have no idea what he meant.'

'Any information might help.'

She shook her head again.

'Yet a few months later he was dead.'

'What are you saying?'

'Just that he appears to have made a very serious claim, and then within a short period of time he died.'

'God called him home.'

Noelie frowned. He hadn't heard that sort of phraseology in quite a long time. 'A collision with another car, I understand?'

'It was a single-vehicle crash. The car went out of control and they hit a wall.'

'They?'

Mrs Sugrue didn't answer. Instead she said, 'Sean was going to go abroad. He had signed up for a two-year contract. He was attending a meeting to arrange the details.'

'To Romania. It seems like an odd place to go, as a missionary I mean.'

Noelie's observation was met by a cold silence. Mrs Sugrue shook her head with the sort of finality that made Noelie think he was about to be shown the door.

'Don Cronin was a friend of your husband's?'

'He was.'

Noelie explained that the statement about Jim Dalton's death had been in Cronin's possession for quite some time. Did she know anything about that?

'He's not someone I either like or trust. We never got on.'

A sudden sharp noise like glass breaking startled them both. Mrs Sugrue left immediately and went down the hall. Noelie followed. The hallway had a musty smell that brought back unhappy memories of aunts in Clonakilty reciting endless decades of the rosary. He went quietly as far as the kitchen door. Mrs Sugrue was outside in the spacious back garden attempting to corral her son, who was dodging her like a rugby player avoiding tackles.

The kitchen had an ancient feel about it too. Noelie saw glass on the floor near the stove. His eyes were drawn to a neat arrangement of bowls on the table. One contained silver medals, miraculous medals he realised; he had had one as a child. Another held cotton squares and a third, folded prayer cards. On a tray nearby there were hundreds of glossy white boxes neatly stacked. Noelie examined one. It contained a medal and chain carefully arranged on a cotton pad. There was a card with a picture and information printed on it. He put a box in his pocket and returned to the front room.

Mrs Sugrue came back. 'I'm afraid I can't give you any more time.'

Noelie smiled graciously. 'You've been very generous – I appreciate it.' He put away the statement.

'One more thing.' Before Mrs Sugrue could say anything, Noelie had produced the Danesfort photo and put it in front of her. 'This picture belonged to Jim Dalton. He's in it.' Noelie identified him in the line of boys, adding, 'Your husband was very interested in this photo. According to Mrs Dalton he recognised someone in it. I was just wondering if you have any idea who that person might be?'

Mrs Sugrue reluctantly took the photo. There was a long silence.

'Mrs Sugrue?'

When she looked up Noelie saw that her eyes were glistening.

'Where did this come from?' she asked.

'It was Jim Dalton's.' He explained the background to the photo.

Mrs Sugrue sat down. Noelie said, 'I can come back another time.'

'You must leave.'

'Okay.' Noelie put out his hand for the photo. 'What is it?'

'Are you doing this deliberately?'

Noelie didn't understand. 'Doing what?'

'Please go.'

Noelie was shown to the front door. At the gate he looked

back at the house. He wondered what to do. Clearly Mrs Sugrue knew something but he didn't want to pester her. Back in his car he called Hannah and got her answering service. She texted a while later to say she'd be home in the late afternoon. She suggested they meet at her place.

17

Occasionally Noelie volunteered at Solidarity Books. The shop was run on a shoestring budget and needed all the help it could get. As he had committed most of the next morning to manning the till, he decided to press on and do some more digging around Sugrue's death. He called into Central Library.

Noelie found the press reports of Sugrue's death quickly. The *Irish Times* piece was brief, stating that the car, a Ford Granada, had gone out of control near Clonmel, a town about sixty miles from Cork. A single-vehicle crash, the occupants were unlucky to hit the only stretch of wall that there was for a few miles in either direction. Sugrue, aged fifty, was declared dead at the scene. The driver of the car, a Father Tony Donnelly, aged sixty-seven, died en route to Cork's University Hospital.

The report in the *Examiner* was more detailed. Road conditions were described as good at the time of the crash; it wasn't raining. Sugrue's career in Special Branch in Cork and his Scott Medal for bravery were noted. There was additional information about Father Donnelly. Born in Cork, he attended Farranferris Seminary College, later opting to become a priest in the Fathers of Charity order. After a spell at their school in Omeath he transferred to a teaching post at Danesfort Industrial School, eventually rising to become principal. Father Donnelly was also the elder sibling of retired Cork garda boss, Robert Donnelly.

Noelie reread the section. When Ethel Dalton showed him the Danesfort photo, she had said that one of the prominent figures in the picture was the principal at the industrial school. He was a Rosminian, she said. So who were the Fathers of

Charity? He made a quick trip downstairs to Reference and found a listing for Catholic Orders: the Fathers of Charity were also known as the Rosminians.

Returning to his seat in Local History he mulled over the coincidence. So was the man killed in the car crash with Sean Sugrue the same Rosminian as the one in the Danesfort photo with young Jim Dalton? Surely not. That would be quite bizarre.

He realised that he needed to confirm the identity of the priest in the Danesfort photo. One option would be to confront Annette Sugrue again but he wasn't enthusiastic about doing that.

Obtaining information about Danesfort Industrial School was easy. The previous year a comprehensive report, the Ryan Report, had been published about the industrial school system in Ireland. It was available online in Reference. Noelie returned downstairs and waited a few minutes for a computer to come free.

Danesfort had its own chapter. It had been proposed as a reformatory school for the Cork area in the middle of the nineteenth century. A judge came up with the idea. It was situated fourteen miles south-west of Cork, initially on a substantial two-hundred-acre farm. In 1873 it was formally incorporated into Ireland's mushrooming network of industrial schools and was placed under the control of the Rosminians. The order, named after an Italian priest, Rosmini, ran one other reformatory school in Ireland – at Clonmel in Tipperary. They also ran a number of other educational establishments for boys, dedicated to training novices for service with the order in their missionary work overseas. They were represented in England, Scotland and Wales; also in Tanzania, Kenya, India and the Antipodes.

Children sent to Danesfort were to receive an education but they also had to work on the farm, which paid for the running of the school. Corporal punishment was systemic and accounts of life at the reformatory school were awash with allegations of brutality and physical abuse. As one survivor put it, 'You never forgot that you went to Danesfort.'

Noelie read through a number of personal accounts of life at the school and farm. They made for difficult reading and after he finished the second one he felt he knew quite enough about the punishing regime at the institution. He gathered his notebook and pen and went outside on to Grand Parade.

It was sunny. He sat on one of the square granite blocks that peppered the wide pavement. Cork's Grand Parade had been revamped in the noughties. It was pedestrian friendly and there were spaces for hanging out. It was the unemployed who were now making most use of the reconfigured public space. Along from Noelie, a group of men his age were diving into cans of Dutch Gold. A strung-out junkie had propped himself up against a coffee kiosk that had been set up but had never opened.

Noelie wondered about his own situation. Somehow this recession felt much worse. Back in the eighties when he left for the States it had been with a certain amount of bravado. He wanted to get away from Cork and Ireland and the bleak economic situation back then had given him the impetus to get going and get out.

Now it was a lot different. People were leaving in droves again but he had no inclination to join them. Been there, done that. He didn't have it in him to do it all again.

He texted Hannah to see if she was home from work yet. She replied enthusiastically: *Have v interesting news for u. Come over asap.*

18

Hannah's apartment was in a block of flats overlooking a section of the Lee's south channel where the river changed course and fell over a weir. It was an impressive view and atmospheric, especially at night when the quaysides and cathedral were illuminated.

Noelie sat with a beer taking in the vista. Hannah was on a call to her mother and when she finished she joined him. He told her about his visit to Mrs Sugrue and how she had got upset. He also went over the discovery he had made in the library.

'So Jim Dalton and the head of the industrial school are present in the Danesfort photo, dated 1963. Thirty-five years later, it appears that the same man, Father Tony Donnelly, is in the car when it crashes, killing both him and Sugrue. In the intervening period, in 1990 to be precise, we know that Sugrue played a part, unwittingly it seems, in Dalton's execution.'

Hannah took the Danesfort photo from Noelie and looked at it. 'I agree that is strange.'

'To put it mildly.'

'So has this some connection to Danesfort, to the industrial school?'

Noelie smiled. 'Possibly. Except what is "this"?'

Hannah shook her head. 'I think we should go to Danesfort. We need to find out who was principal there in 1963. There should be some record that we can check.'

She noticed the glossy white box that Noelie had taken from Mrs Sugrue's place lying on the table. She picked it up and took out the miraculous medal, holding it to Noelie's neck.

'A lovely Catholic boy you are too.'

He confessed to his act of theft. Hannah examined the card inside. 'You do know who this is, don't you?'

'No idea.'

'Leslie Walsh. He is, was, a prominent developer here. Killed himself a few weeks back, around Bonfire Night actually. I remember because there was quite a bit of talk about it at work. He threw himself off the Elysian Tower.'

'Charming.'

'Which led a posse of people to conclude he must've been in financial trouble.'

The Elysian was also known as the largest glasshouse in Ireland. A luxury, glass-fronted skyscraper, it was completed at the end of the Celtic Tiger era and had remained largely empty following the crash. It was located beside the City Hall.

'And was he?'

'Seems not. There's been no real explanation about what happened with him. Anyway this card is to do with his month's mind. It's next week, at the Mass Rock in Glenville.'

Noelie knew vaguely that Glenville was in north Cork. He had never heard of any Mass Rock there though.

Hannah read the prayer on the memorial card.

Would that I could utter so strong a cry that it would strike all men with terror, and say to them: O wretched beings! why are you so blinded by this world that you make, as you will find at the hour of death, no provision for the great necessity that will then come upon you?

Noelie frowned. 'A rap on the knuckles.'

'Sounds like it, doesn't it?'

On the page facing it was a picture of Walsh with his hands clasped in prayer. Just behind him was an image of Jesus wearing a bloody crown of thorns.

'He's twenty, if that, in this photo. He was seventy or more when he died.'

Hannah turned to the back cover. There was an emblem and the initials LTBL. The emblem showed a white-robed Jesus standing with a hand raised near a mature tree; some branches had leaves, other none. In the background there was a Celtic triquetra.

'Seems like Walsh was serious about religion. Is that his connection to Mrs Sugrue?'

Hannah stood suddenly. 'I think it could well be. That reminds me.' She left and returned with a photocopy of a newspaper article. 'Keogh came by. He thought we'd be interested in this. He said to tell you that he was sorry about Shane, to give you his condolences.'

The article was from 1980: 'Church Group Arrested on Soviet Freighter'. There was a photo with it. Hannah pointed out Sean Sugrue and Noelie recognised him from the pictures in Mrs Sugrue's house. In the newspaper article, Sugrue was in civvies with three others. They held a banner showing the Virgin Mary and the words, 'Fatima. I come to call for the consecration of Russia to my Immaculate Heart.'

'Cripes,' said Noelie.

As far as Noelie knew, the Virgin Mary had appeared to a few sisters at Fatima in Portugal. It was claimed that she had imparted secrets to the girls and one had to do with Russia spreading evil around the world, which was widely interpreted at the time to be a warning about the rise of the Soviet Union.

'So Sugrue was from the weird end of the spectrum.'

Hannah nodded. 'I think that's Keogh's point too.'

Noelie put the miraculous medal and the memorial card back in the box. 'That your news?' he asked

Hannah shook her head and smiled. 'That's only a taster. My news is serious news. The remains found in Glen Park.'

'Go on.'

'Curiouser and curiouser, so to speak. I spoke to Brennans, the stonemasons. They've been paid in full and in advance, so they're very happy.'

'But?'

'They haven't actually spoken to anyone.'

'Maybe the undertakers are handling it?'

'No, they're adamant they're dealing directly with whoever is paying. They've had communications. The payment came through via bank transfer. At the same time they got an email detailing the sum of money and what it was for. As you'd expect.' Noelie nodded. 'So Mrs Brennan wrote a quick reply saying thanks for the business and send us the inscription and the stone type as soon as you know what you want. Her email bounced. She sent a second email, thinking there might have been some error in the first but that bounced as well. She couldn't work it out. So eventually she took the matter to her granddaughter, her "internet expert" as she described her. Ever heard of a "disposable" email address? It's for one-off use. An email can be sent from the address but then the address voids itself and cannot receive any replies.'

'Someone doesn't want to be contacted.'

'Exactly.'

Noelie thought about this. 'Why?'

'That's the six-million-euro question.'

Noelie went to the window. Down below on the riverside there was a wooden wharf that was also part of the flat complex. A yellow rowboat was tethered to the wharf and was swaying majestically in the current.

'Someone wants Michael Egan to have a proper grave. The same person must also know his story.' He remembered something. 'Weren't you going to ask that detective friend of yours about the Egan investigation?'

Hannah's tone turned to one of pained sufferance. 'I did, Noelie dearest. And I had to have a drink with him too which is not my idea of fun. So in other words you owe me.'

Noelie pretended he hadn't heard Hannah. 'So what did he say?

'The investigation is low key.'

'What does that mean?'

'Another way of saying it's not high priority.'

19

They took the South Ring out of town. At Bishopstown
Shopping Centre they swung onto the Bandon Road. While
Hannah drove she told Noelie about her Facebook idea. There
were a number of industrial-school survivor groups on social
media. She had looked them over and made enquiries. One of
the admins on one survivor group's page had replied.

'Basically he knows of someone who has done quite a bit
of work on Danesfort. He'll get back to me as soon as he can
with a number or an address. Not bad, right?'

Noelie didn't do Facebook. He had taken against
Zuckerberg and Gates and their ilk. His one-man boycott of
Facebook was a source of derision for Hannah. She smiled at
Noelie. 'What was that? I didn't catch that?'

'I guess,' he mumbled.

Danesfort was located in the village of Upton. The turn-
off was only seven miles out from Cork. They took it and the
road immediately narrowed. Hannah drove slowly. A tractor
appeared and they were nearly forced off the road to make
way for it. At the next junction the signpost directed them up
an even narrower road. Noelie was doubtful.

'In case you're expecting anything grand, there isn't even
an Upton proper. It's a pub, if I recall, and an old train terminal,
long closed.' After a pause Hannah added. 'Historically
interesting though. During the War of Independence, Upton
railway station was the site of an infamous Old IRA ambush.
Except the boys didn't cover themselves in glory on this
occasion. A lot of civilians were killed, a few of their own and
one British soldier, I think.'

Noelie was impressed. 'You just happen to know all this?'

Hannah smiled her warm bright smile. 'You forget my family are republicans from Kerry. It's in the blood. Though, actually, that's not how I know about Upton. I did a project on it at school. About Irish ballads and the history behind the songs.'

Noelie slapped the dash. 'This is why I hired you.'

'Very funny.'

They passed over a low hill with a picturesque valley further on. A few specimen Celtic Tiger houses had collared the views. They were large offerings that sported elaborate rock-faced frontages, dormer windows and double garages like they were going out of fashion. Noelie recalled Ajax Dineen and his neighbour who wouldn't pay for his tiles and patio slabs.

Noelie had gone back to see Ajax a short while after Shane's funeral. Maybe it was a case of misery loves company but he wanted to apologise for all the trouble he had caused. He didn't get further than the front door. Ajax's wife cursed him. Noelie was still numb from Shane's death so Mrs Dineen's anger hardly registered. She could've hit him with a two-by-four and he doubted if he would have felt a thing.

They had been driving around in circles. Eventually Hannah pulled in at a farm gate and they examined the map. It wasn't detailed enough. When the next car came along they hailed it. The driver pointed over the ditch at the tree line.

'You're looking at it. It's behind the trees.'

Noelie eventually saw what she was pointing at. There were a few sizable buildings but they had all been painted lime green. If the intention was to camouflage the industrial school complex, they had been successful.

'The entrance is back along. Doesn't look like much.'

They retraced their route and found the gate. The property was now home to a local community care unit. A narrow road went through a small wood before arriving at a large open quadrangle. Noelie was reminded of a barracks square. There were vehicles parked in a line – cars and disabled-access minibuses. Noelie saw a man in an electric wheelchair being escorted through a doorway.

A one-way traffic system was in operation so they continued, eventually arriving at the front of the main building – an imposing two-storey stone structure. Noelie had seen pictures of the industrial school from the forties. They were black-and-whites; if anything the monochrome shots had accentuated the school's austere appearance. However, in all the old photos there was an open vista in front of the main school building. This was now gone due to the line of tall birches.

Noelie recalled that a number of the boys who were sent to Danesfort mentioned how large the main house seemed to them on arrival. This was down, in part, to them being children but also because they all came from small homes and hovels. One said the countryside around looked beautiful but the main building reminded him of a mental home.

Noelie and Hannah got out of the car. Noelie had brought the Danesfort photo. He walked off to see if he could figure out where it was taken from. He wandered towards the tree line and settled on a spot. The church bell in the photo and the current one looked similar. He tried to match these up.

A man appeared at the church doorway. He stood looking at them for a while and then approached. He was dressed in a plain dark suit and it was only when he came close that Hannah saw his priest's collar. He was in his late thirties, a moon-faced look about him. He smiled, revealing one entirely black molar. It was disconcerting.

'Welcome.'

Hannah explained that they were interested in the old industrial school and the Rosminian records of those who had attended. The priest was a Rosminian but told them that there had been a big fire at the Danesfort complex in the late sixties that had badly damaged the original school building. The facility was rebuilt in the seventies and at that point it was offered to the state for use as a community health facility. The Rosminians still retained rooms at Danesfort as a retreat centre but the bulk of the site was now in community care with the local health board in charge.

Noelie came over. The priest suggested that they give their names in at the office if they were going to wander about – it was a health and safety requirement. Noelie enquired if the records to do with Danesfort were available.

The Rosminian shook his head. 'All moved to Clonmel. A number of years ago now.'

Hannah showed the Danesfort photo to the priest, and told him that they were trying to identify the two Rosminians in the shot. The priest laughed diplomatically and said that it was well before his time. He excused himself, saying he had duties to attend to. He reminded them again about registering at the office.

'There might be photos inside,' suggested Noelie. 'They love to put up portraits of former principals in these places. Let's have a look.'

Inside the main entrance, they found themselves in a long musty hall. A sign directed them to the office at the far end. As he walked towards it Noelie checked the photos on the walls. They showed scenes from the seventies and eighties, after the complex became a care centre.

They exited on the other side into the square. 'There's a "you're in the army" feel to this place even now,' observed Hannah.

Noelie agreed. 'A lot of the boys that were in Danesfort

went away as soon as they were released. Left Ireland, I mean. Emigrated and just never came back. Fits with Egan a bit too, doesn't it, him ending up in London as a navvy. Except something brought him back to Cork.'

'And got him killed.'

'Exactly.' Noelie looked around. 'So was Egan here?'

'That we have to find out.'

'I bet he was.'

'You'd bet your punk collection, would you?'

Noelie laughed. 'Maybe not that.'

They left disappointed. Before pulling back on to the road, Hannah nodded in the downhill direction.

'The site of the Old IRA ambush is that way. Fancy a look?'

'Why not.'

It was only a short distance. There was a pub and, across from this, a monument in the form of another Celtic cross. Beside it was the entrance to Upton rail station. The rail line was long out of use but the red-brick station building, including the raised platform and rail siding, had been restored.

They walked in and around. The woods protecting the former industrial school were only a short distance away. Noelie guessed that state inspectors might well have alighted at this station. Invariably Danesfort got good reviews when it was inspected. The stories of cruelty and abuse took decades to surface, emerging slowly as the Danesfort boys became men and found the courage to speak.

Hannah began singing. She had a lovely voice and Noelie was glad of the intrusion. She sang lines from a well-known ballad about the Upton ambush.

Let the moon shine out tonight along the valley
Where those men who fought for freedom now are laid
May they rest in peace those men who died for Ireland
In the lonely woods of Upton for Sinn Féin.

'Another string to your bow,' he said.

Hannah smiled. 'I don't sing enough any more.'

They were silent. It was pleasant around the station: undulating farmland on three sides and the woods close by. There was a warm breeze.

'Strange to think that a battle happened here.'

'Weird. People dying for freedom in one place and up the road they were beating it out of those young boys.'

'That's Ireland for you.'

They returned to the car. Hannah didn't start the engine immediately. She had let down the side window and was staring at the view.

'Something up?'

'Just thinking.' She looked at Noelie. 'We get on well together, don't we?'

'We do.'

'It's been great spending so much time together this last while.'

Noelie looked at her. 'I know. Like old times.'

Sometimes he wondered if there was a chance for something more between him and Hannah. What held him back was their friendship. He was afraid of upsetting it, of losing her.

'So all those years ago, did we just meet at completely the wrong time? Was that it?' she asked.

Noelie smiled. 'You gave me the bullet as I recall.'

'Well, you couldn't stand still for a minute.'

'And you were a poseur. Red-haired Siouxsie Sioux.'

They laughed. What had saved them then was that they

hadn't hurt each other. There was probably an element of luck to that – both of them were too preoccupied with music and politcs and other things. Still, it was why they had been able to resume their friendship when they met up again after Noelie's return from the States.

Hannah started the engine. Noelie knew he was circling around his feelings for Hannah, trying to work them out. Something was shifting, that was for sure, and he had a sense that the same might be true for her. If these weeks had taught him anything, it was that life is precious. If there was a chance for happiness, he didn't want to let it slip away.

'Lennox's for chips then?' she said, bringing him back to the present.

'You bet.'

20

The ferry to Sherkin Island was a fifteen-minute hop from the fishing village of Baltimore in west Cork. It was pleasant and windy on board, just on the right side of comfortable. Noelie had been to Sherkin a few times before, once on a weekend-long camping trip, another time just for the walk. He recalled that the island had some great beaches.

'Black Gary – that his real name?'

'That's the name I was given.'

'Didn't your mother ever warn you about meeting people through the internet?'

Hannah put a hand on Noelie's wrist. 'I'll mind you. But just to reassure you, he's not actually from the internet. We got his name from someone on the internet but apparently he's not online himself. He doesn't even own a mobile phone, if that's any consolation. He's an amateur historian who knows quite a bit about Cork's industrial schools. The bonus for us is that he attended Danesfort.'

Noelie remained sceptical. 'If we're murdered and chopped into pieces, I'm blaming you.'

They reached the island and disembarked on to an empty pier. 'He knows we're coming, does he?'

'I left a message at the Jolly Roger pub. Apparently that's the way to make contact.'

'Got an address then?'

'Black Gary, Sherkin Island, County Cork.'

'For fuck's sake.'

'City boy.'

They waited a while but no one showed. Noelie approached

a man coming in on a small punt. He knew Black Gary.

'A mile along, white bungalow. You can't miss it.'

The fisherman was right. Black Gary's place stood out on a low hill. The small cottage looked south-east towards the harbour mouth and the sea. The front door was open and, despite it being summertime, a turf fire smouldered.

'You found me. Thought you would.'

Noelie figured that Black Gary was in his sixties. He wore a flannel shirt, jeans and a fisherman's cap, which he removed as he greeted them. He still had all his hair though his face was deeply lined. They sat around the table over tea. Gary was in Danesfort during its final two years, from 1964 to 1966. After that he was in Clonmel for another four years. He was separated from his brother and sister when he went to Danesfort. In 2001, he finally managed to reconnect with his brother who had moved to the United States in the mid-seventies after a short stint in Dublin. He showed them a picture of the two of them on Golden Gate Bridge; they were both beaming. They had also traced their missing sister using the Salvation Army but that didn't end well. She was in London but turned down the opportunity to meet them. They couldn't understand why but she wasn't for turning.

Hannah produced the Danesfort photo. 'We're trying to identify everyone in this. It's dated 1963, so shortly before your time.'

Putting on his glasses Black Gary immediately pointed at the man standing beside the bishop, the head Rosminian. 'Father Tony Donnelly.'

Hannah winked at Noelie.

'Strict man, proper like.' Black Gary laughed. 'Very holy. He'd stop you in the hall or out on the yard and say, "Recite the Our Father with me." He was that sort of way. Eccentric.'

'Anything more?' asked Hannah.

'He had favourites, they all did. You could fool him but

122

if he worked out what you were up to he'd half murder you. He wasn't disliked. He was okay really. His brother was a different matter.'

Noelie recalled the newspaper report of the car crash that killed Sugrue. 'The one in the gardaí?'

Black Gary shook his head, 'No, this brother wasn't a cop. I'm talking about Albert Donnelly, the youngest brother. Didn't look much like Tony in fact. People often said it. I kept well away from him. Sometimes he looked after the farm at Danesfort. The Donnellys themselves were farmers so I suppose they knew what they were doing.'

Black Gary nodded. 'Not far off slavery. Hard work, often used as punishment too. Anyway this Albert Donnelly was sometimes at the Danesfort farm.' He paused, remembering. 'There would be these crows out in the fields, lots of them, pecking and scavenging. Albert used to say that the crows worked for God as well. He was a harsh taskmaster.'

Hannah drew Black Gary's attention back to the photo. 'Any of the boys in the line look familiar?'

Black Gary peered. 'It's not a good photo, is it?'

'Not the original, that's for sure. A copy of a newspaper cut-out, we're reckoning.'

He shook his head. Noelie pointed to the novitiate. Black Gary looked dejected.

'Actually I thought it was more the history of Danesfort that you were interested in. I didn't mean to drag you all the ways down here for little result.'

Hannah reassured Black Gary. Confirming Father Donnelly's identity was worth it alone. Noelie asked if the name Jim Dalton meant anything to Black Gary. It didn't.

'Michael Egan?'

Black Gary shook his head again. Pointing at the bishop of Cork, he added, 'I wrote to Lucey, you know. He was often out at Danesfort, walking around blessing people. You'd think there was a blight on the place, the amount of holy water he flung about. Never even replied to me.'

Hannah smiled but Noelie looked disappointed. Black Gary noticed. 'Tell you what, I'll ask around. I'm in contact with a lot of people. Not on the internet – I just go and meet people. Let me write down the names you're interested in and I'll make some enquiries.'

Black Gary made some notes. He asked if he could get a copy of the photo. Hannah said she'd send him on one.

They were done then but Black Gary suggested a walk. Noelie felt unsure but Hannah seemed keen. Out on the boreen it was pleasant. He had never married, Black Gary volunteered. Just didn't happen for him. Broke a heart or two though. He asked Hannah and Noelie if they were an item.

'She's spoken for,' Noelie parried. 'Has a fellow that works in Qatar. Perfect set up. Earns loads and only about occasionally.'

Hannah stuck her tongue out at Noelie.

The island itself was compact. The main beaches were ahead and as it was July there were more people about than usual. Black Gary pointed to places as they walked. 'Cape Clear Island, out there on the horizon. Roaringwater Bay is over there.'

Noelie decided to risk a flyer. He told Black Gary Jim Dalton's story, about him disappearing and being accused of being a garda informer. Did he know anything about that or have any republican contacts?

Black Gary didn't. He had no time for the IRA himself on account of them bombing a pub in Birmingham in 1974 that he himself had occasion to be in once in a while. 'Too many head-bangers, if you ask me.'

Noelie carried on to the matter of the human remains found in the Ballyvolane–Glen Park area, on the edge of Cork city. 'They've been identified as Michael Egan, an Irish navvy from London.'

Hannah explained they were trying to find out if he was in Danesfort or not.

'Not easy at all to get that type of information,' he pronounced. 'You'll have to write to the Rosminians in Clonmel. All the Danesfort records are there now. But they'll make it very difficult for you if you're not family. And you'll have to pay as well.' Black Gary's tone turned sarcastic. 'Don't you know the Rosminians are fierce short of money these days.'

They reached the main beach on the island. It was wide and sandy. Noelie spotted the headland where he had camped once before and recalled why the location was so good: it had a great view out to sea and was beside the best beach. Black Gary suddenly stopped.

'Did you say Ballyvolane?'

Noelie nodded. 'The Egan remains were found in Glen Park. That's in Ballyvolane.'

'They had their farm there.'

'Who?'

'The Donnellys had their own farm – the Donnelly farm we called it. I was there one time. It was big. Now that was a place where you had to work hard. Harvest time and thinning work. All day long too.'

'Paid work?' asked Hannah.

'My arse.'

Noelie wanted to make sure he understood correctly. 'So the Donnellys had their own farm at Ballyvolane and boys from Danesfort went there to work?'

'It wasn't unusual,' clarified Black Gary. 'A lot of industrial schools had arrangements with local farms. The Donnellys were just availing of a handy situation. Anyway, who was going to object? Not us. Weren't they giving us good-for-nothings an opportunity in life?'

Noelie thought about this. 'Except Ballyvolane's quite a

distance from Danesfort, isn't it? A good fifteen miles I'd say. Not a small distance in the fifties and sixties.'

'Sure that was an issue. Sometimes if you were sent to Ballyvolane, you went for quite a while. A week would be the shortest time. But there were boys that went there for longer periods as well, months at a time I mean.'

Noelie nodded.

'It was cosy. Boss man at Danesfort was a Donnelly and Albert sort of consulted at Danesfort too. What could you do? If you were picked you had to go.'

Black Gary walked down as far as the water's edge and skimmed some stones. Noelie hung back and Hannah noticed.

'That's interesting, isn't it?' she said.

'Can't beat Facebook. Always said it.'

Noelie ran off before Hannah could thump him.

They ended up back at the pub. They ordered pints and took a seat by a long window looking out over Baltimore Harbour. Black Gary was too well known for his own good though. Almost everyone had a few words with him as they came and went. When Noelie got the opportunity, he asked about the farm again.

'Where exactly was it then?'

'Don't know the area at all and I've not been there since.'

Noelie thought about this. There had been a lot of development in the Ballyvolane area of Cork. When he was young, it was the countryside but it was far from that now.

'Albert Donnelly, can you tell me anything about him?'

'I've done my best to forget Albert.'

Black Gary was a jolly man, for all his past troubles, but he looked unhappy now. A ferry was coming across and they all watched it for a while.

'He disliked me. Don't know what it was but he took agin me big time. So I kept out of his way. I knew of a boy who ran away while at that farm and was badly beaten by Albert.' He stopped as if he was thinking about this. 'He was always saying that we were what we were because of how we were born. Do you get me?'

Noelie nodded. 'Out of wedlock, you mean?'

'He'd say it to your face that you were a bastard. He was very mean. I was afraid of him.'

Noelie exchanged glances with Hannah. Black Gary continued. 'He hated how I looked too. But like I say his brother Tony wasn't that way. He was harmless enough. Strict but harmless.' Black Gary shook his head. 'Albert puts me in a bad mood even now.'

On the ferry back, they huddled close to ward off the breeze on deck. Noelie was quiet.

'We need to find out more about the farm.'

'Yes. Albert too.'

'Is he alive, I wonder?'

'Every chance. He'd be in his seventies now, mind.'

21

Noelie found an entry in the phonebook for a Donnelly in the Glen area. As soon as he saw the house, though, he realised that it was unlikely to belong to the Donnellys he was interested in. It was a small suburban house in an estate. He enquired anyway; he was correct. The occupants weren't from the area and had bought their house just before the Celtic Tiger boom. The owner directed Noelie to a different house on the far side of the green, beside a tall electricity pylon.

'Timmy's an original. Mystery he's still alive with that thing standing on top of him.'

Noelie crossed the green. While he waited at the door for an answer he could hear an unpleasant buzz from the high-voltage lines overhead.

'Ted Toner's your man,' said Timmy. 'Lives in Blackpool. Ask for him down there, everyone knows him and he knows everything about these parts.'

Noelie found Toner's house easily; his daughter answered the door. He explained what he was looking for and was shown inside. Toner was one of those prim gents who looked a little too gaunt and frail for his own good. He could easily have been in his nineties. He spoke in a quiet voice and scrutinised Noelie for a long time before deciding that he was interested in talking to him.

'The Donnellys were pig farmers but a good bit of their land was in tillage too. The middle boy was head of the gardaí in town.'

Noelie knew he had struck gold. 'Still alive, do you know?'

The old fellow thought about this. 'Haven't seen his death

notice yet and I watch for those things. He'd be in his seventies, I guess.'

'Any of the Donnellys in this area now?'

'None hereabout at all. The farm was sold on, '71 or '72 I'd say. They made good money from it too. Sold it over the father's head. We called him Old Donnelly. He would never have given it up. There's been a Donnelly connection to this area since way back and Old Donnelly was very proud of that. Apparently one of the Donnellys had a run-in with Cromwell too. He stayed around here, can you credit that?'

Toner suddenly laughed. 'Old Donnelly lost a leg in the war we were told. Maybe that was what made him so bitter. But we would see him sometimes and we would be terrified by it, his one leg. In those times an artificial leg didn't look anything like it does now. It was just a metal peg in fact. He drank a good bit and sometimes to frighten people he would take off his leg and wave it about.'

'What about the original Donnelly house?' asked Noelie. 'Is that still there?'

Toner looked unsure. 'It was knocked down but there's something about that too. I have a picture of the original house somewhere. It was a big house.' He went looking among a stack of books but gave up. 'She moves things all the time on me,' he complained.

The daughter overheard the comment. 'It that me he's bad-mouthing?'

Toner smiled and put a finger to his mouth. 'The tables are turned. I have to watch what I say.'

Noelie asked about the Donnelly brothers.

'There was Robert, the garda. Tony was a priest.'

'A Rosminian, right?'

Toner nodded and recalled that Tony had died in a car crash a number of years back. 'None of them married.' He winked. 'They were all too holy for that.'

'What about Albert?'

'Yes, he was the youngest, I remember that. An interesting thing, though – there was no missus in the house that I ever knew of. So Old Donnelly must've had some liaison, mustn't he? Maybe there's scandal there?'

Noelie asked about the Donnellys' connection to Danesfort Industrial School. Toner only knew about Tony Donnelly being one of the priests out there. Noelie enquired about boys from Danesfort working on the farm and if Toner had ever heard anything about all that. He hadn't.

'Quite possible though. They had a big farm and around here people didn't stick their noses into the Donnellys' affairs.' He added, 'Did I tell you Old Donnelly was a Blueshirt? He was a big shot in them too.'

The Blueshirts were Ireland's home-grown fascists. The movement emerged in the thirties and was particularly strong around Cork. Following its decline, a brigade of volunteers, largely made up of ex-members, travelled to Spain to fight for Franco.

Toner explained, 'See, Old Donnelly was in the gardaí first. My father remembered that. Going right back now, I am. He was in the Old IRA, joining the gardaí with the formation of the Irish Free State. He'd have been pro-Treaty. But he was drummed out in the thirties in the purges.' Toner wrinkled his forehead. 'You could try the library for more on that. It'll be there somewhere.'

He went over to a set of boxes and began rooting in them. Now that he had worked out that Noelie had a serious interest in the past, he was determined to find the information that he knew he had somewhere. His daughter reminded him that he had a doctor's appointment. Eventually they agreed that Noelie would have to call back another time. He had one last question.

'Do you remember where the Donnelly farm was located?'

Toner got his specs. Noelie showed him a map. He examined it for a long while. 'This is a terrible map,' he said. 'Where's Conway's Cross?'

Noelie pointed it out.

'So a hundred acres from Conway's Cross going back as far as the Glenville Road.'

Noelie found the Glenville Road and they agreed on a rough area that had once been the Donnelly farm. Noelie shaded in the zone on his map.

He drove to Conway's Cross. It was all built up now, with rows of houses on the undulating hills. He was generally familiar with the area from when he was young and he realised immediately that Glen Park was close by.

After looking around, he crossed the busy North Ring road and scaled an embankment. On the far side, below him, stood Glen Park. It was wilderness surrounded by development on all sides. A narrow river ran through it. This joined the Bride which eventually met up with the north channel of the Lee.

The embankments came in close at one point forming a canyon with steep sides. Noelie knew the Egan remains had been found close to that area. He walked along the embankment ridge until he could just see the dig site. There was fencing around the zone and signs warned that the location was unsafe for walking. Looking in the opposite direction he could also easily see where the Donnelly farm had once been. He called Hannah on his mobile.

'What's up?'

'The Donnellys are no longer in the area. The farm was re-zoned and built on back in the seventies. But I've been able to work out the rough location of where their farm was and it's near where the Egan remains were discovered. As the crow flies, I mean.'

Noelie noticed walkers entering the park, a group of women. He continued, 'Just saying now, but if you were looking for some place to hide a body, you could do a lot worse than choose the place where I'm standing right at this moment. Everything around is built on, but this spot was never going to be disturbed. Too inhospitable. And a local person would know that.'

'Perfect then.'

'Looks that way.'

22

On his way home Noelie called to see his sister. The previous day he had received a message from Byrne, informing him that the investigation into Shane's drowning had formally concluded. With nothing new or suspicious to report, the file on the teenager had been turned over to the coroner who would, in due course, set a date for an inquest.

Ellen looked even worse than when Noelie had last seen her, a week earlier. She had lost more weight, her face was drawn and her eyes looked sore and red. He had also heard that she had closed the boutique, albeit temporarily. Given how much Ellen loved her store and how much effort she had put into it over the years, he knew this was bad news.

They sat in the kitchen. He asked about Byrne and she told him about the conclusion of the police investigation, confiding that she had hoped until the very end that something significant would be discovered. Anything at all would have helped.

'I don't understand and that's the worst thing. Maybe I could live with the finality of it if I could work it out.' She added that things were at rock bottom between herself and Arthur. 'I don't know any more how this will all end.'

Noelie offered to make tea but Ellen didn't want any. They sat there. When their father died in '83, following a long illness, it had been a severe blow. Ellen had taken it worse than Noelie, maybe because she was the special daughter. But their father's death didn't compare to this.

Ellen continued eventually, 'Byrne said that Shane could have been in the water as early as teatime on the afternoon he went missing. So there are a few hours where he's not visible. No one sees him and he doesn't show up on any CCTV footage anywhere. So where was he? He must've been indoors.'

Noelie asked if anything had emerged from talking to the teenagers that hung around the skateboard park but Ellen shook her head.

'Byrne claims that they put pressure on a dealer down there but that didn't yield anything. There's CCTV footage from the skateboard park but nothing at this Bumhole place. It's behind trees, out of the way.'

Shane's movements on the day he went missing had been examined in great detail, but it was still unclear why he was over near Turner's Cross, close to Cork City football grounds. Had he met someone there and who? The tip-off that Noelie had got about drugs, from the artist at the Camden Palace, had remained with him. But Noelie didn't believe it could be anything like that. Or was he being naive?

'Byrne went over everything with us again yesterday. She has your back Noelie, I must say that. Although one thing did come up.'

Noelie was alert immediately.

'At first I didn't understand it, so I double-checked. The night that Shane never came home, remember, you arrived here the following morning after getting all my text messages? I remember asking you about the day before, why had you come here so early in the morning. You arrived by taxi and asked about staying the night.'

Noelie nodded. 'I do remember.'

'See the thing is, you told me that the reason you came here was because your place had been broken into. Except that yesterday Byrne said that your place was broken into on the afternoon Shane went missing. So when was your place broken into, Noel? Or are you telling me you were broken into twice?'

Noelie was caught. He had never fully explained to Ellen the sequence of what had happened in those days before Bonfire Night. He hadn't really thought there was any point in getting into it during the search for Shane, especially since the police hadn't thought there was any connection to his disapperance when he'd told them. Afterwards, the family situation deteriorated even more. Ellen and Arthur hardly spoke to Noelie before or during the funeral.

'I'm sorry I came here.'

Ellen didn't understand. 'What? What do you mean?'

'I mean that morning – I'm sorry I came here that morning.'

His sister moved nearer. 'Did someone follow you? Did they see you here? Maybe they saw Shane here too.' Ellen's voice rose. 'Noelie?'

'There isn't a connection.'

'Jesus Christ,' his sister screamed. 'You bastard.'

Noelie didn't like where this was going, in part because he was unsure of his own ground. If this was all about a mole inside the IRA, that was bad enough but it was starting to look like it was about more than that.

He stood as well. 'I need to go.'

'Do that. Walk away like you always do.'

That comment got to him – she knew it would. It was very unfair, especially given what was going on with him just now. He turned and faced her.

'Don't lecture me about walking away or about being a coward. That's not who I am and you know it.'

'Get out.'

Noelie walked out without another word.

At home, he sat on his wobbly sofa. His confrontation with his sister had shaken him but he was also wracked by self-doubt. He should never have gone to his sister's house that morning after leaving Anglesea Street Station. He hadn't been thinking straight. The bizarre thing was – and this was even stranger given the argument he'd just had with his sister – he had gone to Ellen's house precisely because she was family. He was in trouble, but it wasn't only to do with the records and what he had got himself embroiled in. He hadn't been feeling great anyway. He had had that stupid argument with Hannah – entirely of his own making – and he was starting to feel the pinch from being so long unemployed. It had been on his mind to emigrate again – a lot of people were doing it – but at forty-nine? He didn't want to, except what was he to do around Cork? The recession was getting worse. The truth was he had gone to Ellen's because it was a sanctuary of sorts. She was family, but it had been a mistake.

He put his head in his hands. 'I need to stay busy,' he said aloud. He wondered about going over to Solidarity Books. They were a good crew and they always needed help. Sometimes being around people who just saw things differently – more like how he saw them – was the right medicine. There was also talk about a new anti-water tax campaign getting underway. Maybe that was what he needed; maybe he could put his energies into that.

He looked around. His place needed fixing up too. He had used the break-in as an opportunity to declutter the sitting room but he realised now that he had gone too far: the flat looked bare. The big job, still pending, was to replace the wall shelves that would hold his collection of books. For now they were stacked in front of his window like a makeshift barricade. He could get started on that, it would keep him occupied, but he lacked the will.

The Danesfort photo caught his eye. He fetched it from the table and looked at it once more. Was the industrial school the key? Dalton and Danesfort were linked. There was also a connection between Danesfort and the Donnellys. Crucially too there was the car crash involving Father Donnelly and Sugrue. These events were separated by years, decades actually, and yet he felt they could be linked. Why exactly was Jim Dalton killed?

He thought of Ballyvolane and the Egan remains. Until a few hours ago that bizarre business had made no sense at all to him. It wasn't that it made perfect sense now, but the proximity of the missing navvy's burial place to the Donnelly farm could be significant. Especially if it was established that Egan had attended Danesfort.

He put on coffee. Turning on the radio he chanced on Lyric FM and heard Latin jazz. He turned the volume up higher. When he lived in the States he had made a few trips down to the Mexico border, to Cormac McCarthy country. A different time, a different life. He thought of his long-standing girlfriend from that time, Spade. He had really liked her. Where was she now? They had spent years together and had nearly got married.

Nearly. That word – Noelie wondered sometimes did it sum him up. Nearly embarrassed Ronald Reagan, nearly completed a PhD, nearly stayed in the States, nearly got married. Now he had just about nearly fucked up everything for himself in Cork too.

He focused on staying calm. Music always made him happy. He was starting to feel calmer when the window shattered. A sound followed that was so loud and sharp he couldn't hear for a while. A light flashed too and he was thrown backwards. Landing on the ground, he didn't know if he lost consciousness or if he simply lost his bearings. When he eventually opened his eyes again all he could see was thick dust and what looked like ticker-tape drifting about in the air around him. There was a horrible acrid smell and something fell, from nowhere it seemed – a piece of hot metal.

He lay there. An alarm was going off somewhere and he heard a muffled voice calling out, 'Noelie, Noelie? Are you in there? Noelie?'

Month's Mind

23

Douglas Street had been Noelie's home since his return from New York. During the Celtic Tiger years he was nearly in a position to buy his own place – a combination of having steady work and access to easy credit. But in the end he opted not to. He could have afforded a place in the suburbs but he didn't fancy living there. As a result he had put quite a bit of work into the Douglas Street flat and he had come to see it as his own. Now, he realised, he wouldn't be coming back.

The problem was the landlord. Noelie had avoided him over the years but that was impossible after the explosion. He had wandered through the smashed-up living area with his workmen in tow, muttering about the extent of the ceiling collapse and the huge expense he faced. Noelie got an 'At least you're okay' but it was only token. Eventually his landlord informed him that he wasn't intending to repair the upstairs of the property immediately. Noelie needed to understand that it was a difficult time for landlords. There was a surfeit of properties about and the student market had collapsed. Just in case Noelie was wondering, the landlord didn't have anything else in his portfolio either.

Hannah came through for him again. Noelie was kept in hospital for observation on the night of the blast. The next day he went to Hannah's. Martin was there too but he moved in with his boyfriend in Kinsale until his place was fixed up; the landlord had promised to do that. Hannah told Noelie he could stay as long as he wanted.

★

During the tidy-up, in preparation for his departure from the flat, Noelie got plenty of opportunity to think about what had happened and to appreciate how lucky he had been to escape more or less uninjured. The pipe bomb had been filled with nails and screws. These were now embedded in an arc on the walls and ceiling of the flat. Some of the projectiles were no more than a centimetre in length, others were large and long. He found oily nuts, ball bearings and even a four-inch nail. One screw, a stubby flat head, perforated his framed photo of Brooklyn Bridge, embedding itself halfway through the studded partition behind. Another made it half a centimetre into William Trevor's *Collected Short Stories*. The shreds of Chomsky's *Deterring Democracy* were dispersed throughout his place like confetti. That book and a history of Contra war in Nicaragua had borne the brunt of the blast and were, in effect, no more. In a type of Chinese-fortune-cookie-meets-radical-insight, Noelie recovered one shred that read 'American imperialism applause'.

What had happened didn't really bear thinking about. He had been saved by his books. Stacked in tight formation near the window, they had taken the force of the blast. Without them he would either be dead or maimed.

He tried to shrug it off, quipping to Hannah that very few people could claim to have been physically saved by their book collection. Hannah, however, wasn't in a joking mood. She warned Noelie a couple of times to cop himself on. They both agreed about one thing though: if they'd needed proof that they were on the right track, they had it.

Noelie was carrying crates from upstairs down to the hallway when he heard his name being called. A young woman stood outside his front door. She wore a black cropped jacket and colourful leggings. Her black hair had purple strands woven through it; it was plaited into a single long braid.

142

'Noel Sullivan?'

'Yes.'

She nodded to the damage. All the windows were still boarded up. 'What happened?'

He went to the door to get a better view of his visitor. Her hands were dug into her jacket pockets. 'Someone tried to kill me,' he said.

'You've been upsetting people.'

'You think?'

'My mother does.'

'Your mother?'

She put a hand out. 'I'm Meabh, spelled the Irish way. Sean Sugrue's daughter.'

Meabh was in her late twenties. She wore lots of eyeshadow and was taller than Noelie.

'My mother said you were asking about my father.'

'You could say that.'

'I'd like to know more, about your interest I mean. Is there some place we could talk?'

He decided on Charlie's, a pub down on the quayside. It was a short walk away and offered more ambiance than the bomb site that was now his flat. As they walked Meabh explained that she lived in Amsterdam but that her mother had phoned her a few days earlier.

'So you've come from there?'

'I have.'

Noelie was impressed.

'My mother and I don't speak too often. I've been in Amsterdam for a long time. I was surprised. Something you said unsettled her.'

'I showed her a photograph.'

'She didn't mention any photograph.'

It was nearly two weeks ago and, although plenty had happened in the interim, Noelie easily recalled the meeting and the sequence of exchanges between him and Mrs Sugrue. He felt sure it was the photograph.

'She say exactly what bothered her?'

'Not in so many words.'

They were soon on the quayside. The nearby footbridge was the only crossing for some distance either upriver or downriver. It was thronged with students coming and going from the nearby colleges. Meabh nodded downriver to the hills in the distance.

'What area is that?'

'St Luke's Cross. Montenotte. Why?'

She explained that the last time she was in Cork she had looked for a place her father used to take her. 'A limestone church with a steeple. It was on a hill. I found a place that I thought was it but it turned out to be a Protestant church, so that wasn't the right place.' She looked thoughtful.

'When was this?'

'1999, I think. A bit after his death.'

Noelie pointed out that there were plenty of hills in Cork with churches on them. Did Meabh know the name of the area? She didn't. Noelie was surprised by her lack of knowledge of the city.

'Didn't you grow up around Cork?'

'We avoided Cork even though it was close. We lived in Mitchelstown. I even went to college in Dublin.'

Noelie figured it was probably to do with her father's occupation. Special Branch officers were often careful about where they lived and socialised. With Sugrue's interest in the local IRA it was probably a sensible precaution. Mitchelstown was around thirty miles north of the city.

They arrived at Charlie's. It was empty apart from two barflies. Noelie suggested a window table and got drinks.

A pint of Beamish eventually arrived; Meabh had a glass of water.

'So what exactly brings you to Cork?'

'You.'

Noelie frowned. 'I'm a minor celebrity but for all the wrong reasons. What do want with me?'

'My mother told me about the statement that you turned up with. She mentioned Jim Dalton as well. Afterwards I looked online and there were some reports about the Daltons and their allegations. I'd like to see the statement. Do you have a copy?'

Noelie did but not with him. He told her what it said and explained about the mystery surrounding Jim Dalton's whereabouts.

'What's your interest in this?' she asked. 'Why did you visit my mother?'

Noelie took a drink of his pint. There was a directness about his visitor. It was not a trait Noelie disliked but he realised he needed to be careful too.

'I'm happy to explain but maybe first off you should tell me why you're really here.'

Meabh looked towards the window. It was lunchtime and staff from nearby City Hall were spilling out on to the sunny quayside.

'A long time ago something happened to me. When my mother called it was because of that. She spoke mostly about you and the fact that you had visited, and she mentioned Dad's statement. She called it a confession. Then she asked me how I was.'

Noelie waited. He looked quizzically at Meabh and eventually she continued.

'It was how my mother said it, how she asked. She's never really asked before and I just knew something important must've happened. Someone or something had got to her and that was

145

why she was calling. I guessed it had to be to do with you.'

Noelie nodded.

'We're estranged,' said Meabh. She laughed at her words. 'Actually it's more than that, we don't get on. We haven't for as long as I can remember.'

Noelie thought back to his meeting with Mrs Sugrue. 'She wasn't my cup of tea either. A bit on the holy side really.'

'She's devout.'

'That's one way of putting it. When I visited, your brother was running amok. Don't think he liked working with all those miraculous medals.'

'He doesn't have a choice. He was in rehab for quite a long time but she took him out of it and now he's mostly at home with her. Personally I don't think it's good for him.'

There was a further silence.

'I had trouble before. It was pretty bad. My mother didn't take my side.'

'Trouble?'

'A man did things to me. When I was young.'

Noelie was taken aback. He hesitated, 'You mean ...?'

'It happened at one of my father's events ... I didn't tell anyone right away.'

'Your father's "events"? What were they?'

'My father was very religious. We often went to these gatherings. A priest might visit from France or Germany. A Mass would be celebrated with him. It was quite a big part of my growing up, my early years anyway. When I finally said it to my mother, she accused me of making it up.'

'Was it someone she knew?'

Meabh shrugged. 'I was never able to identify who it was. I never saw his face.'

Noelie thought about this. 'What did your father say?'

'It was kept from him although I didn't know that. My mother said she'd told him but she hadn't. But I was growing up, I knew it had happened. I went through a bad time. I started cutting myself and one day my dad confronted me about it. So I told him. He burst into tears.'

Meabh stopped; she was upset. 'The thing is he believed me right away,' she continued eventually. 'Afterwards, I often thought he must have known something all along.'

Meabh excused herself and went to the bathroom. Noelie ordered another round of drinks. When she returned he saw that she had redone her mascara. She looked wan.

He pushed a glass in front of her. 'I got you something stronger, with bubbles this time.'

She smiled.

'For what it's worth, I'm really sorry,' he said.

She sipped her drink. 'The bubbles are good.'

They sat for another while. It was almost too quiet in the bar. Eventually Meabh spoke again.

'Don't get me wrong, I've survived. I've come through it and that's what matters.'

Noelie nodded. He proposed a toast to surviving.

'Tell me about this bomb,' Meabh asked.

'I'm lucky to be alive. It was a pipe bomb, one you throw. It's designed a certain way, using an elbow joint. It came in my window. But my flat was trashed a while back and all my bookshelves pulled down. I have a big collection of books and these were arranged on the floor. The piece of pipe caught on the curtains and landed in front of books. That saved me.'

'Someone tried to kill you.'

'Or maim me at the very least. It was reported in the newspapers that "I'm known to the police". Some hack or other put that around. The subtext is I'm mixed up in drugs and with druggies. So that's the official story. However the real reason that that bomb was put in my window has to do with your father, or more to the point with what your father witnessed all those years ago. I've been following up on the

147

statement he made and I've looked into the main matter your father was concerned with: Jim Dalton's death. There's something strange going on.'

Meabh told Noelie what she knew from reading the news online. They talked about Jim Dalton and he told her about the theory that there was a mole operating high up inside the IRA or Sinn Féin.

'Dalton could've been killed to protect this mole's identity. If that theory is true then there are motives aplenty for the bomb that came through my window. The stakes here are very high, particularly if this person is still in the organisation and above suspicion.'

Meabh was quiet. Noelie continued.

'Your father admitted to being involved in the death of Jim Dalton but the gardaí are denying that Dalton is dead. They claim he's in some witness protection scheme. They won't say anything more. But the Dalton family believe their father is dead.'

'What do you think?'

'With no body it's very hard to say for sure. But your father's statement reads as authentic to me.'

'Could I see it? Is that possible?'

Noelie nodded. He suggested that Meabh call over to Hannah's later. She could have dinner with them if she wanted.

A while after, outside Charlie's, Meabh told him that she was booked into a hotel nearby. To pass some time she was going to have a look around Cork in the afternoon.

'Looking for that church?'

'I guess.'

'Any reason in particular?'

'Pigheadedness. And that church is the only direct link that I have to what happened to me.'

Noelie nodded. They exchanged mobile numbers and parted.

24

There were shades of Southfork about the property. Although the dimensions were Irish and not Texan, the large modern house with paddocks on two sides had a *Dallas* feel about it. Noelie had gone to the same national school as its owner. Jerry Casey's father had been some type of civil servant, whereas Noelie's had been a factory worker. Casey was good at school but not exceptional. In due course he moved to a private college and for a long time afterwards Noelie never saw him around.

However Noelie's sister and the Casey girls stayed friends. So Noelie kept up with his friend's progress that way. To his surprise Casey became an army cadet. Stints in the Lebanon, Cyprus and Bosnia followed.

Noelie dithered about whether to make the approach. He needed information badly and Casey might know something or someone who could get it for him. But it was risky and they hadn't been in touch in years.

He drove up the manicured driveway. The doorbell was answered by a young woman. Foreign-looking, Spanish or Italian perhaps. He enquired if Jerry was home. The man who came along the hallway had aged a lot. Casey was rounder too, particularly about the face. A smile appeared when he recognised who was calling; Casey's dimples were so prominent they had earned him the corresponding nickname at school.

'Jesus,' he said, holding out his hand. Noelie received a hearty handshake. 'Au pair,' Casey explained, indicating the young woman who had answered the door; his wife was still at work. 'She's in the army too. We're all army here,' he added happily.

They looked at each other. 'It's been a long time.' Casey said then, adding immediately, 'Everything all right?'

'Not really. I want to ask you something. I hope you don't mind.'

They went down the hall. Casey offered his condolences over Shane. He asked after Ellen. They arrived in a huge open-plan kitchen.

'Tea, coffee? A beer?'

'Glass of water,' said Noelie.

'Let's have a beer.'

Noelie was adamant.

'Okay, you've the look of a man who's here on business.'

'It's kind of like that all right.'

Casey returned with a tall glass of water and suggested they go into a different room, a quiet sitting room.

'You have a nice place,' observed Noelie.

Casey nodded but remained standing. 'Okay then, if this is not a social call.'

Noelie stood again. 'I'm sorry if I've come across like that.'

'Not a problem ... Shoot.'

'As you probably know, I was in the papers.'

Casey nodded. 'Bombs are an army thing and I paid attention. I was quite taken aback to see your name. It seems you were lucky.'

'To put it mildly.'

Casey nodded. 'So you were the target? That wasn't any mistake?'

'No mistake. Someone tried to kill me.'

Noelie wasn't sure what kind of an explanation to give but Casey helped him out. 'You used to do some community action stuff or so I heard anyway. Way back. Is it something to do with that? Or drugs or something? Have you crossed paths

150

with the wrong people?'

Noelie nodded. 'The gardaí are saying that. Drugs or druggies. A source of my own has mentioned the Provos or possibly some dissident IRA types. But I don't think so myself. My politics are far left not green nationalist, if you get my meaning. I don't have any real associations with republicans. I know a few from this or that campaign, but that's as far as it goes.'

'Sure.'

'The cops are being good but I don't know if they're telling me the whole story. I'd prefer to have the heads up, just for the future, you know.'

'I see where this is going.'

'The forensic guys let slip that the army take a look at all home-made bombs. You keep a sort of database on them. Apparently a lot of the bomb types and techniques are linked or can be linked to each other. So I was wondering maybe ...'

Casey shook his head.

' ... if it was the Provos or one of their people whether you might be able to find out for me? Get me a lead, any lead?'

'I can't. Listen, it's not that I wouldn't like to help but it's not my area. I don't have any business with ordnance. And if it's an ongoing investigation, as I'm guessing it is, I'd be risking trouble just putting my nose in.'

Noelie held his old friend's stare and then looked away. He could see the edge of the paddock. A beautiful brown colt was standing there looking into the distance.

'No harm in asking, right?'

'Of course not. I'm glad you did. I'm glad you thought of me but I'm sorry I can't help. I really am.'

Noelie felt embarrassed now. Casey looked awkward too but he wasn't for budging. 'Look, have a beer,' he suggested.

'No, really.'

'A pint then? Some evening?'

'I'd like that.'

As teenagers they had both been on a Gaelic football team that was featured in a recent photographic portrait of Cork. Noelie enquired if Casey had seen the picture? He had. But did Noelie know that their old team captain had died of throat cancer only last year? Noelie didn't. They spent a while talking about that and the various others characters that they both still knew or knew of. It transpired that another member of that team had died too.

Casey accompanied Noelie outside. He was contrite. 'What about the cops, Noelie? You're well within your rights to press them for more information. Particularly if you're worried about your personal security. You're the aggrieved party. I could give you a name.'

Noelie declined the offer. He explained about Byrne and how he had got to know her through Shane's case.

'She suggested waiting to see what forensics come back with. She's straight though. If I need to go back to the gardaí I can go to her.'

Noelie left and drove a short distance before pulling over. It had been a long shot but he was disappointed. He wondered what he could do next. They were getting close to something, but what? They needed more information.

The meeting with Casey had reminded Noelie about Ellen. She had phoned a few times since the blast but he hadn't answered the calls. Her place was on his way back into town – maybe he should call in?

He decided against it. He didn't want more trouble and he had no idea how Ellen had taken the news of the bomb. The last thing he wanted was another confrontation.

25

Hannah cut carrot cake, putting the slices on to three plates. As she poured coffee, Noelie went to fetch the Danesfort photo. He had taken up residence in Hannah's spare room. There was a single mattress on the floor and his boxed belongings took up most of the remaining space.

Meabh had changed into black leggings and a baggy black V-neck jumper. When he returned, Noelie sat beside her and showed her the picture. He explained about the presentation of the scroll and identified Jim Dalton for her.

'Do you recognise anyone?'

Meabh looked at the picture carefully and then shook her head. Noelie pointed out the head Rosminian.

'Here's the strange thing about this photo. The man who was in the car with your father when it crashed, killing them both, is this Rosminian priest.'

'Okay,' nodded Meabh.

'Given that Jim Dalton's also in the photo, that seems odd to us.'

'For sure.'

'The priest's name is Tony Donnelly. He's one of three brothers. There are Robert and Albert too.'

'Well, I do know the Donnellys.'

Noelie and Hannah exchanged looks. 'How?'

'I've met Robert Donnelly a few times. He and my father were good friends. He was my dad's boss in the gardaí, but he was often in our house too, he's distantly related to my mother.'

'Really? Did you ever meet Tony Donnelly?'

Meabh peered at the photo again. 'I don't think so but I may have.'

Noelie told Meabh what they knew about the Donnellys and their association with Danesfort, and how Jim Dalton had ended up there. 'Your father visited the Daltons a number of times. He saw this photo at their house and, according to Mrs Dalton, he was very interested in it. But we don't really know why.'

There was silence.

'How did you find out that your father had been killed, Meabh?' asked Hannah

'I was at boarding school at the time. I was very shocked. I knew my father was going away for a few months. Then out of nowhere, he was dead. It was terrible. I was left with my mother and I hated her by then.'

'How was your father when you last saw him?'

'The same as always, I think. I was much better by then. We talked about me, about my plans. I was bothered about him going away but he assured me it was only for a short while.'

'Did he say why he had resigned from the gardaí?'

'No, but he wouldn't have. He was private about work and my mother never allowed me to ask him anything about it.'

'Your dad died within months of approaching Garda Headquarters with the information that he had. It looks as if he claimed that there was some sort of criminal cover-up inside the gardaí and that didn't go down too well.'

Meabh nodded. 'I wish I remembered something but I don't.'

Hannah pointed to the photo. 'An idea we have is to identify the other boys in the picture. Most of them should still be alive. Someone might recall something that could help us work this out.'

Noelie got up. He was frustrated too. At the window he looked out on Washington Street. 'What about Facebook?' he asked.

Hannah's laptop was nearby. She checked but there were

no new messages. 'I'll put out another request.'

Noelie sat down again. 'This photo bothered your mother. She wouldn't say why. Afterward I wondered if it had to do with seeing Tony Donnelly. That would've reminded her of the car crash and that would've been upsetting. But now I'm not so sure. Could it be something else?'

Meabh shifted on the sofa, tucking her legs under her. 'I've decided to visit her. I'll go in the morning. I wasn't going to but now I feel I should. I'll ask her.'

Hannah knew from Noelie how difficult Meabh's relationship with her mother was and offered to go with her.

'It's okay,' said Meabh. 'I'm better dealing with her on my own. You said you'd show me the statement.'

Noelie fetched his copy. Meabh read it and they waited. Hannah offered Noelie more coffee but he decided against it.

'I'll never sleep.'

'That's the idea – we have work to do.'

Hannah was annoyed with Noelie. When he told her about his unsuccessful trip to see Casey she had reacted badly. He wasn't keeping her informed, she complained. What if something had happened to him. From now on she needed to know where he was. In a bid to reduce the tension, Noelie had joked that things weren't as serious as all that. Hannah really lost it then. He hadn't ever seen her so angry. His life was in danger, he needed to realise that.

Meabh indicated the paragraph near the end of the statement. 'This could refer to me.'

Some years later an unexpected turn of events forced me to re-examine a number of key assumptions and relationships that I had built up in the force. This has led me to reason that the murder of Mr Jim Dalton may have taken place for quite different reasons to those given to me.

Meabh told Hannah about her self-harming and her eventual confrontation with her father.

'My mother still blames me for telling my dad. She had kept it from him. She never wanted him to know, I guess.'

Noelie spoke. 'Say you're right, Meabh, how does that connect to the murder of Jim Dalton?'

'That's the big question,' agreed Hannah.

'Let's assume some things for a moment. Meabh's dad is involved in Jim Dalton's death. He's suspicious about what's going on and gets an explanation that's not adequate. Time passes. Then out of the blue he finds out that Meabh was assaulted. However, something connects too. This line "I was forced to re-examine a number of key assumptions and relationships that I had built up in the force" is key. So what's the connection?'

Hannah took the statement and leafed through it again. Noelie got up and went across to the window. On Washington Street a group of women were wandering towards the town centre; they were in high spirits.

They were being watched, that was the other thing he and Hannah had agreed on. Whoever threw the bomb into his flat clearly knew they had been asking questions. Who was watching and were they watching right now?

He turned back to Hannah and Meabh. No one had answers. Noelie tried again. 'The Danesfort photo – your mother reacted badly to the picture but what did your father see in it?'

Meabh looked at Noelie. 'I don't follow.'

'Mrs Dalton said your dad became animated about this photo one time he visited. He wanted to take it away and make a copy. Apparently he recognised someone in the photo. Who?'

'Tony Donnelly perhaps? The other unidentified figure, the novitiate? Hardly the bishop?'

'What's the timeline? Do you remember when you told your father about what happened to you?'

'I remember exactly. I told him on my birthday. I was fourteen. 5 November 1994.'

'And your dad visited Mrs Dalton for the first time in early 1995,' said Noelie. 'I have the date somewhere. Mrs Dalton kept a diary.' Noelie went to his room. He returned with his notebook. '16 February 1995.'

Hannah looked satisfied. 'They're roughly in sequence. Meabh's right. Her admission in some way led to her father re-examining the Dalton murder.' She smiled at Noelie. 'Finally two pieces of this bloody jigsaw fit together.'

Noelie agreed. 'But what was it about what Meabh told him that made him go back to the Dalton killing?'

There was silence.

'So after discovering what had happened to his daughter, Sugrue approaches Mrs Dalton. He sees the photo. Something more is confirmed, something else has fallen into place for him. Is it seeing Jim Dalton, albeit as a boy, in the picture? Or is it Tony Donnelly? Or is it someone else?'

'It could be Danesfort,' offered Hannah.

Noelie thought about this. 'It could be Danesfort,' he repeated slowly. 'Yes, maybe that's it. Maybe it wasn't a person at all, it was the place.'

Hannah had the picture. 'It's a creepy photo, isn't it? Something about all those boys in a line like that. The podium with the head and the bishop presiding over the order of things. Makes me sick.'

Meabh looked upset.

'You okay?' asked Noelie

'You were asking about the past. I do remember one time I came home from boarding school. My dad was off sick from work. He usually made time for me, but not on that occasion.' She looked at them both. 'It's what my mother blames me for, that I brought all this trouble down on him. She said to me once that I had killed him.'

'Are you really up to that meeting tomorrow?' asked Noelie. 'I mean someone could go with you. I could go.'

Meabh shook her head again. 'It wouldn't work. I have to deal with her myself. It's important. And I'll have the element of surprise on my side. She's not expecting me.'

Hannah drove Meabh to her hotel. When she returned Noelie was sitting near the riverside window, looking at the view. She joined him.

'Something I meant to say to you. Remember the miraculous medal and the white box you lifted from Meabh's mother's house?'

'For Leslie Walsh, sure.'

'There's a rumour about him. He was in trouble a good few years back. To do with boys. Seems he was in a seminary college too at one time. Anyway the word is he paid a substantial sum of money to keep the story out of the papers. Admitted no liability though. The settlement also involved a confidentiality clause. My boss at the *Voice* mentioned it and she's no idle gossip.'

Noelie looked at Hannah. 'So you're thinking ... what?'

'What happened to Meabh – I'm just saying, maybe this is all a lot more sordid than we realise.'

'Fuck,' he said.

'I know,' she replied, taking his hand. 'But we owe it to Meabh to keep at this. Come on, we made good progress tonight. We'll crack this eventually.' She got up. 'I'm beat. You must be too. Things will look better in the morning.'

He heard Hannah in the bathroom and then go into her room. Her door closed and the apartment went silent.

26

Noelie arrived at Henderson's Photography as it opened and was directed upstairs. The technician had just arrived too and was taking off her jacket. She made a quick examination of the Danesfort photo. Noelie enquired if she could make separate prints of every face in the picture.

'The copy is poor,' she said, describing it as a copy of a copy. She noted the inscription date at the side. 'Himself might be worth asking – he might know where you can find the original.' The owner, Henderson, had a big interest in old photos and was in various clubs that specialised in city and county pictures. 'He'll be in later so I could ask him.'

Noelie agreed it was worth a try. He'd call back in the afternoon. In the meantime he ordered an enlargement and copies. The scanner was nearly as loud as an electric generator. As he watched the technician working a hand touched his wrist, giving him a fright.

It was Casey. He smiled reassuringly and dropped something into Noelie's pocket. He addressed the technician, 'I want to order some prints but I forgot to put up a parking disk. I'll be right back.'

Noelie retrieved the item from his pocket, a note. *I'll be in the cafe around the corner from Liam Ruiséal's bookshop.*

The technician came to the counter with Noelie's order. The faces of the Danesfort boys were very snowy. Noelie couldn't even see a likeness for Dalton. The quality was hopeless.

Noelie found the cafe. He saw Casey at a table in the back and ordered a coffee.

'This is a surprise.'

'Turn off your phone and take out the battery.'

'Why?'

'Trust me.'

Noelie did as he was told.

'I'm not hanging about so listen. I asked about your matter. Just casually. Truth is I do know a few in ordnance from different assignments over the years. I was careful. Had other business there and just mentioned your matter in passing.'

'I appreciate it.'

'An hour later army intelligence paid me a visit. Two of them. Asking me why I was asking about the bomb at your place.'

Noelie didn't follow. 'Army intelligence?'

'They're known as G2,' answered Casey. 'A small unit, a stay-out-of-the-limelight operation. Serious people.'

'You're joking me.'

Casey shook his head. 'I'm not. The thing is they also knew that you were out at my place.'

'What?'

'Exactly.'

Noelie told him that he had got more careful since the bomb. He felt he was looking over his shoulder all the time now. 'I'm certain no one followed me to your place.'

'They don't have cars up your backside any more, Noelie. If they want to know where you are they track your phone. They'll have your number so it's not difficult. The question is why do they have your number.'

Noelie was startled. He had figured with the blast that he was being watched. He and Hannah had talked about it. He wondered now if everything he had done and everyone he had spoken to was known about. 'Fuck.'

Casey watched Noelie. 'You're surprised, I see. That's comforting. I was wondering – G2 have a very tight remit. They're national security, end of story. Get my gist?'

'Christ.'

Noelie knew he owed Casey an explanation but what should he tell him and where to begin?

'I've been asking some questions, that's all.'

Casey put his hand up. 'It's better I don't know. Consider this a favour, for old times' sake.' His tone turned cautious. 'I didn't say anything about why you were over. I said we just talked about our mutual football friends, and that you were in my head afterwards, not having seen you in so long. I only asked about the blast because I knew you – that was how I passed it off.'

'Did they believe you?'

'Don't know but it got me off the hook. But I better not be seen with you again.'

Casey's coffee was untouched, Noelie's as well.

'My advice to you is look at your phone communications. They'll have your number tagged but they'll also have everyone in your circle identified too. Pick up a second phone. Keep it anonymous but bear in mind it won't stay that way for long. Meantime keep your real phone active. If you don't, they'll put two and two together and look afresh. The other thing is don't have your main phone with you if you don't want them to know where you're going. Got me?'

Noelie nodded.

'Last thing: the new smartphones can be used as listening devices as well. They have the means. They can be activated even when they're switched off. That's why it's essential to take out the battery.'

Casey stood. Noelie stayed seated and in shock. It was hard to believe what he had heard and yet it explained a lot.

'You're sure they were army intelligence, not Branch or anyone like that?'

'I'm certain. Sorry.'

Noelie stayed on after Casey left. He drank his coffee

in a daze. To distract himself he looked at the Danesfort enlargements. They were disappointing. His thoughts returned to army intelligence and why they might be involved. They were clearly all over anyone who was interested in the pipe bomb too. The question was, did they know who had thrown it? Or worse, had they done the job themselves?

Noelie couldn't remember the last time he had used a coin-operated phone. He found one, though, outside the main post office and called Hannah.

She twigged straight off that something wasn't right. 'You okay?'

He said that he had a new draft of his CV. Could she spare him a few minutes to take a look at it? He'd be right down.

Hannah took the hint. 'I'll be waiting.'

In the post office he purchased two pay-as-you-go mobiles and then went directly to the *Voice's* office. They talked out in the corridor. It was quiet compared to the last time Noelie was there. He asked Hannah to leave her phone on the windowsill and they talked quietly a short distance away. He told her what he had learned from Casey.

'Oh fuck,' she said. 'We're naive. I was reading about all this new surveillance technology only recently. It's a game changer.'

They agreed that Casey's news did seem to confirm that recent events were connected to a mole inside the IRA.

'Danesfort, the Donnellys, they must be tied to this informer in some way.'

Noelie was quiet. He found the idea that someone or some part of state security may have had a hand in attempting to kill him quite distressing to say the least. Who were these people? Rogue operators? Or had they political clearance? If so, how high up did that go?

Although they had never said a whole lot on the phone to

162

each other the problem was that Hannah had a smartphone, an Android.

'They can be activated remotely and used as mics. I bought this for you,' he said, handing her one of the pay-as-you-go mobiles.

Hannah swore a number of times. 'Welcome to 1984.'

The full implications dawned on them. 'From now on extreme care,' she told Noelie.

She told him her news to cheer him up. 'First Facebook. A man named Caffrey was in touch. Lives in Thurles. Retired. He has an OAP card so he can get the train. He suggested meeting at 2.30.'

'Today?'

'I guess he has time on his hands. What do you think?'

'Let's do it.'

'I provisionally agreed to meet at the train station as he's arriving that way. We could get a coffee there.'

Hannah's other news concerned the stonemasons. 'They apologised for not getting back. The inscription arrived by the same method as before, a self-destructing email. It's confirmation of sorts.' Hannah had written it down. She read it out to Noelie.

Michael Egan
1950–1970
Duagh, County Kerry
'But in the dark he learned to creep
When all the guards were fast asleep
And in his house of spinning pearls
He hopped about in loops and whirls.'
PG

Noelie didn't really understand. 'What does that confirm?'

'Philistine.'

'Don't call me that, not that,' he mock protested.

'PG is Patrick Galvin. It's from a poem in the preface to his trilogy, *The Raggy Boy*. The point is Galvin spent time in an industrial school. *The Raggy Boy* is in part about that.'

Noelie shook his head in disbelief. 'How do you know all these things?' He hugged her.

'Confirmation then. Egan was in an industrial school. Which part of the Gulag we don't know for sure yet but it could easily have been Danesfort.'

They were both silent.

'This person paying for the grave, why is he or she opting to remain anonymous?'

'Embarrassment, fear, likely the latter.'

Noelie nodded. A colleague came looking for Hannah to ask if she could help him with a computer problem. She said she'd be right there.

'So we'll meet at the train station.'

Hannah nodded. 'Just one thing though. Meabh's story last night set me thinking. She was saying how she heard nothing about her dad's statement over in Amsterdam. Figures, right? Cork's just a dot on the planet and what happens here is never going to be earth-shattering. But if that's true how did this person paying for the headstone hear about it? It seems they could be living in Australia, going by where the payment came from.'

'The Irish press out there. There are a few papers for the emigrants. In New York there were plenty.'

'They cover big items, sports and cultural news. Why would they report the remains found in lowly Glen Park?'

'I see your point.'

'Leave it with me. I'm way behind with work but if I get the time I'll do a quick article. Mention Danesfort, Egan, Jim Dalton and all that stuff. I could post it on Indymedia and the like, here and in Australia. I'll put a contact email with it too. You never know, it could generate something. I think we have to reach out. There's no time to lose.'

27

Noelie decided to head back to Hannah's. To his surprise, he found Meabh waiting outside the main block entrance.

'Not answering your phone?' she asked.

'Long story. You okay?'

'Sort of, not really. I was wondering if I could ask a favour. Do you know Glenville? There's a Mass Rock just outside it. My mother's on her way there now.'

Meabh's visit home had ended before it had even got under way. Her mother was dressed up and on her way out the door as Meabh arrived. She didn't want to speak to Meabh or talk about Noelie's visit.

Noelie and Meabh went upstairs. He asked her if she wanted to come in for a coffee but she said she didn't have time.

'I got to thinking about what we talked about last night, about what happened to me and how it could be linked to my father's death. There's this other man who was close to my dad and to Robert Donnelly. I've only just found out that he's dead. It's strange because this man helped our family, me in particular. He paid for my college fees.' Meabh sighed. 'That's where my mother was going, to this man's month's mind. It's a Mass said for someone–'

'Hang on.' Noelie went into the spare room and retrieved the box with the miraculous medal. He showed it to Meabh. 'Is this him?'

'Where did you get that?'

'Actually I took it from your mother's. I was intrigued but I had no idea who he was. Hannah recognised him though. He was a big player in the property market in this city. Apparently loaded.'

Meabh looked at the card with the picture of young Leslie Walsh.

'How did your father know this man?'

'Let There Be Light.' Meabh pointed to the initials on the back. 'It's an organisation my father was in. Mr Walsh was in it too.'

'Who or what are they?'

'They're religious. They do good works, that type of thing.' Meabh showed Noelie the emblem. 'I heard the story of this many times. Jesus is present. The tree represents nature, life and growth. Jesus is protecting us all.'

Noelie thought about this. 'Do you know how Leslie Walsh died?' Meabh shook her head. 'He threw himself from the Elysian, the glass tower beside City Hall. Apparently he had an apartment there.'

Meabh examined the box and medal. 'Suicide?'

'It seems so. Why do you want to go to the month's mind?'

'Because of what we talked about last night. Robert Donnelly will be there. There will be others too.'

Noelie looked at the time. Glenville was about a forty-minute drive away and it was already close to noon. He explained his dilemma, about his planned meeting at the train station with Hannah at 2.30 p.m.

'Could you call her?'

Noelie showed Meabh his battery-less phone and told her what Casey had said. She suggested he use her BlackBerry. Noelie figured it was worth the risk. He called Hannah's work but he couldn't reach her; he left a message with reception. His plan was to take Meabh to Glenville, drop her there and return in time for the meeting.

They took the Dublin road and, at Fermoy, the road west. There was more traffic than Noelie had anticipated and progress was slow. Noelie asked Meabh about Amsterdam and how she had ended up there.

'Chance really. I wanted to get out of Ireland and I had a friend there. First port of call and I stayed.'

She worked at furniture restoration. She had a degree in psychology but had never worked in the area. In Amsterdam her friend had friends who did period renovations; a sub-speciality was furniture restoration. She had taken it up and liked it. She was now in the final stages of her guild exams.

Meabh asked Noelie if he'd ever lived abroad. He told her about his long stint in the States.

'Why did you go there?' she asked.

'Like you in a way, convenience. I had a social security number from my J1 time there and New York appealed to me. Plus I needed to get away. The eighties were bad. The recession, no divorce, a constitutional ban on abortion. Back then it was even a crime to buy a condom.' But he regretted not finishing his PhD. 'Jacked it in with only a year to go. Crazy. Now I could do with those letters after my name.'

Meabh asked if he had liked it in the States and he replied that he had. 'But I was never going to stay there either. I knew that even before I went. Didn't stop me staying thirteen years though.' He told Meabh about nearly getting married. 'It was going to happen and then her brother got ill and she wanted to go back to Colorado to help him. It was nearly the other side of the States, out in the boondocks as they say over there. I just couldn't go. I stayed on in New York but eventually decided to come home.'

Meabh had been to the Mass Rock as a teenager but she couldn't recall exactly where it was. Finding it turned out not to be a problem. With the crowd attending, there was gridlock in the area. Finally they saw a sign, Carraig an Aifrinn. People were parking on the roadside verge so Noelie did too. He pulled in a short distance from the site. He was worried about how he'd get out again. They sat in the car for a moment.

'Yesterday, in the pub, I asked you why you were involved in all of this. You didn't answer,' she said.

Noelie looked at Meabh and thought about his reply. 'There's something's wrong, I know that. That's a good bit of it. But I guess I'm tired too. This is my second recession. Our so-called betters have ruined the country again. Now I'm hearing that beautiful refrain, let's just pay the bondholders. It's a case of sweep everything under the carpet again. I just can't be doing with that any more. It makes me very angry.'

They got out. Noelie was still thinking about the question. Some part of him suspected that there was some connection to his nephew's death too. Of course he had nothing go on in that respect – just timing and the comment made by Cronin about 'that crowd'.

He rang Hannah's new pay-as-you-go using his own and got a 'You cannot be connected at this time' message. He looked around. It could just be the poor reception but he realised also that he had made an error. He had left his main phone in Cork without establishing contact with Hannah using the new phones. Shit, he thought and texted, *in glenville by fermoy. walsh month mind. returning asap.* Hopefully his message would get through.

There was a dip in the country road where there was an old stone bridge. It was pretty around here, quiet apart from the sound of the nearby river. Meabh pointed through the tree canopy at a sheer rock face about a hundred metres upriver. There was a steel cross impressed on the stone. Under it lay a natural shelf of rock that was being used as an altar; it was dressed with white and yellow flowers for the memorial Mass. A sizable congregation was already present.

Noelie was torn. He wanted to stay and yet he knew that if

he was going to make the meeting with Hannah he needed to get moving. He tried Hannah's pay-as-you-go again. When he had no luck he asked Meabh to try; she had no success either. Noelie reckoned it was the location. There were hills on both sides of the river.

A narrow gate led to a path through pine woods. A young priest was directing mourners onto the riverside embankment. Noelie was distracted, half listening to Meabh's suggestion that they brazen it out and go in when he saw Inspector Lynch. The senior garda was out of uniform and was coming directly towards them. Noelie buried his head in Meabh's shoulder. 'Someone I know. I can't be seen,' he whispered urgently.

Lynch didn't appear to notice Noelie. He was with a bald-headed man also in civvies. Noelie was reminded of Kojak, the lollipop-sucking New York detective from the TV series of the seventies; this man was smaller but had the same distinctive bald round head.

Seeing Lynch decided Noelie: he needed to stay. As soon as the Mass was over he'd head for Cork and hook up with Hannah then; she would probably still be with the Danesfort contact.

A short distance along from the entrance the roadside ditch had collapsed allowing passage onto the pine-covered hillside above the riverbank. They made their way up this to the crest of the hill. Continuing down the far side, they rejoined the river upstream. They followed it back to the edge of the congregation and very close to proceedings.

Meabh winked. 'Good enough?'

'Perfect.'

The Mass was in Latin; Noelie hadn't attended anything like it before. Three priests celebrated the Mass. Two were in green and white, while the lead celebrant was in elegant red and purple robes. There were lines of chairs on one section of the grassy bank for family and close friends. Noelie wasn't able to see their faces. He spied Inspector Lynch, though, standing on the edge of proceedings, downriver from their location.

Communion started with the priests coming across the footbridge over the river. They took up positions to serve the Host and people formed lines in front of the chalices. The piety of the ceremony in the open-air setting was impressive. The good weather helped too; it was a warm sunny day. Noelie finally got a decent look at the Walsh children; they were all in their thirties at least. A woman that Noelie guessed was Mrs Walsh took Communion. He didn't know her.

He wondered about the significance of Glenville. Was Walsh from the area or was it something else? Eventually he spotted Meabh's mother. She was dressed in a black skirt suit and wore a dark headscarf. She looked as dour as when they had first met.

When Communion ended there was a hiatus. People waited and the priests returned over the footbridge to the altar. Then a group of men, all in long cream robes with hoods and narrow red cummerbunds, came forward.

'Jesus,' said Noelie quietly. 'I haven't seen anything like that for quite some time.' In fact he had only ever seen something like it in Spain.

'My dad occasionally wore a robe like that,' whispered Meabh.

Noelie watched. Each of the men, seven in all, held an offering. These were simple items: bread, water, a Bible, a small cross, some form of a chain and what looked like a staff; two carried this. All the items were handed to the family. Shortly after that the ceremony came to an end.

Noelie told Meabh he was going up onto the riverbank hill to attempt calling Hannah again. She gave him her phone too, just in case. Again, he had no success and returned just as the congregation was dispersing.

'Are you going to talk to your mother?'

Meabh was unsure. 'Maybe.'

'This Let There Be Light, what's the story with them?'

'They support Lefebvre. I think. That was quite a big issue when I was growing up. Lefebvre was excommunicated by the Pope but they stuck with him. To cut a long story short they're the conservative end of the Catholic family.'

Noelie was keeping an eye on Inspector Lynch. He had approached the Walsh family and was standing with them. After that he went over to a man in a wheelchair. He held this man's hand. Kojak stayed with him the entire time.

'The man in the wheelchair is Robert Donnelly,' whispered Meabh. 'My dad's old boss in the gardaí. He doesn't look too good.'

Noelie moved to get a better look. Robert Donnelly looked poorly. There was a blanket over his lap and there was little sign on his face that he had recognised Lynch.

'What about speaking to him, after the cops go I mean? You could say about knowing him and see if he recognises you?'

'I don't think that'll be necessary. Look.'

One of the men in the cream robes was approaching. He was elderly. As he reached them, he lowered his hood and spoke to Meabh.

'Aren't you Sean Sugrue's daughter? I'm Albert Donnelly, do you remember me at all? I knew your father well.'

Albert Donnelly had wavy bright white hair and large dark eyes. He was in his seventies but agile looking. He took Meabh's hand like they were old, close friends and clasped it. Strangely Meabh acquiesced. Albert muttered something under his breath and Noelie realised that he was blessing her. It was an odd moment.

'Your mother told me you were away.'

'I am. But I came back for a few days.'

'To be here?'

'No, for another reason. But when I heard about Mr Walsh I wanted to be here.'

Albert looked at Noelie finally. Meabh introduced them.

'To be honest,' said Noelie, 'it was me who dragged Meabh here. I'm working on a history of Danesfort Industrial School and I figured that it would be a good idea to come here and attend this event.'

'I don't follow,' said Albert curtly.

Noelie chose his next words carefully. 'I understood Leslie Walsh was close to some boys from Danesfort. I wondered would they be here.'

'Leslie?' Albert Donnelly shook his head. 'Leslie was never at Danesfort.'

'But all the same, wasn't he familiar with some boys from there?'

Albert's gaze didn't flinch. He turned from Noelie and looked at Meabh once more. 'It's very nice to meet you again.' He let go of her hand finally.

Noelie decided to go for it. 'One more thing, Mr Donnelly. Your family had land at one time, beside Glen Park, that's in Ballyvolane. Am I right?'

'That's going way back,' Albert replied coldly. He turned and left.

28

They were nearly the last to leave the Mass Rock site. At the stone bridge Noelie enquired again if Meabh intended to speak to her mother. She told him to wait a minute and wandered away in a different direction from where their car was parked. While he had the time, Noelie tried Hannah's number, but still couldn't get her.

Meabh returned with the news that Albert Donnelly was driving an olive Berlingo, a model adapted for wheelchair access; a third man was with the two Donnelly brothers, helping with Robert's wheelchair. She suggested that they follow the Donnellys back to where they lived. Noelie reminded Meabh that he needed to make contact with Hannah. He agreed to go along with the idea as long the Donnellys were returning in the direction of Cork.

They headed back to the car and followed the Berlingo. Due to the traffic it was slow going until they reached the Cork side of Glenville. Meabh was very quiet.

'Everything all right?'

'Albert. He squeezed my hand so hard it hurt.'

'Why didn't you say something?'

Noelie got a withering look. He drove on. Outside Glenville, to his relief, two messages arrived on Meabh's phone. One was personal, from Holland, the second from Hannah. Noelie quickly checked his pay-as-you-go to see if it had received any messages; it hadn't.

'Hannah is asking *Is Noelie with u? Tell him meeting went well. Over now. Talk later.* What will I reply?'

'What about *Met Albert and Robert Donnelly. Much to tell.*

See you later? No, that's too much information.'

'What about *He's with me. Great. Talk later*?'

'Perfect.'

The Berlingo stopped on a narrow section of road on Cork's northside. There was congestion as it reversed through a narrow gated entrance. Noelie and Meabh watched from a distance.

'What area is this?' Meabh asked.

'Sunday's Well.'

'Is the river near here?'

'Very close.' Noelie pointed to the houses on the downhill side of the road. 'Some of those properties have gardens running down to the river's edge.'

They found parking near the Cork City Gaol. When they walked back they discovered that the Donnelly car had gone into a substantial house protected by high walls. The nameplate read Llanes.

Meabh walked on to a junction. Noelie followed.

'This is it. Remember I told you that I came to Cork once looking for the place that my father used to take me to? This is the place.'

Meabh pointed to a church a short distance uphill. It was perched on a knoll and had a slate steeple. The building was made from cut limestone, gothic in style. The gates were closed. A notice announced services on Sundays only.

'I'd like to call in.'

'It's closed.'

'To Albert's, to Llanes, I mean. We often went to a house after the service and that house was near the church. It could've been the Donnelly home.'

Noelie didn't want to.

'Look, I'm leaving tomorrow. I have work I need to go

back to. I'll know once I'm in the house.'

'What will you know?'

'If it's the house ...'

Returning to the junction Meabh crossed the road and went over to Llanes. Noelie caught up with her.

'I think we should wait.'

'You don't have to come with me.'

'It's not that. I'd prefer to hook up with Hannah first. Then the three of us can call in.'

Meabh pressed the doorbell beside the roller gates.

'I'm not going in there, Meabh.'

'I'm not asking you to.'

The gates opened. A middle-aged man with lank hair stood looking at them. He called out before either Noelie or Meabh could react. 'Albert?'

Noelie stared at the man. He had large ears, so large they were difficult not to notice. He remembered Martin's description of the man who had called to his place the evening he hid in the train tunnel.

Meabh said something that Noelie didn't catch. At that moment Albert appeared. If he was surprised to see them he didn't show it. He had changed and was now wearing a white short-sleeved shirt and light blue slacks; his hair was combed to one side. He seemed happy to see Meabh.

'Come in.'

'I'm leaving tomorrow,' explained Meabh. 'I called to the church, on the hill. My father took me there a few times. Then I remembered that you were nearby. I thought it might be an idea to say hello to Robert. I should've done that out in Glenville.'

Albert stood aside. 'What a good idea. He'll be pleased.'

Noelie reluctantly joined Meabh inside the gate. The patio was narrow and then widened out into a generous parking area for two cars. Alongside the Berlingo there was a polished dark blue Citroën DS. It was in pristine condition, a beautiful car.

Albert addressed Noelie. 'I was thinking about what you said. Do you realise that I have films of Danesfort? Home-movie quality. You'd find them interesting, I think.'

Noelie tried to get Meabh's attention. He really didn't want to go in but there was no holding her back. He realised he had to stay.

'I'd love to see them,' he replied.

Albert went ahead up the steps. The entrance was Georgian and in perfect repair. 'Robert's out back, although sometimes we call it the front. It's where the sun is. He likes to sit there.' Conspiratorially, he added, 'It's all he does any more.'

The hall widened into a reception area in front of an elegant curved stairway. Noelie noticed a large portrait of a man in military uniform. An unusual flag hung from a staff beside the portrait: a red St Patrick's saltire on a white background.

'Your father?' enquired Noelie.

Albert nodded but didn't stop. They arrived in a warmly painted room with French windows that opened onto a platform balcony. Robert Donnelly was sitting in a wheelchair with a straw sun hat tied to his head. He appeared to be dozing.

'Robert, we have visitors,' Albert announced loudly. He quickly released the chair's brake and swung his brother around. He adjusted the sunhat then changed his mind and removed it entirely. Robert stared at them blankly. Noelie noticed that his right hand was shaking.

'Remember Sean Sugrue, your great friend?' Albert addressed Meabh, 'They were very close.' He took his brother's hand. 'This is Sean's youngest, Meabh. She's here to visit you.'

Albert put out Robert's hand for Meabh to take and hold. She did as instructed and Noelie watched.

'That car crash was an awful blow. Robert lost his brother but also his closest friend.' He began stroking Robert's hair. 'He's in decline. He was head of the Cork gardaí for many years, can you believe that? Now look at him.'

'Was there ever an explanation for how that crash happened?'

Albert looked at Noelie. 'You know about that too?' Albert bent down and spoke in an overly patient voice. 'Robert, this young man, Noel Sullivan is his name, is very interested in our history. I imagine in yours, Robert. After all you were the star, I was nobody. You could've gone all the way, Robert. We all said it but ... it wasn't to be.' Albert looked at Noelie. 'I made my money in property. Too much of it at too young an age. It ruined me actually. I've never been bothered by ambition since.'

Noelie noticed the man with the large ears hovering just inside the French windows, watching them. He nodded at him. 'I think I know your friend.'

Albert dismissed the idea. 'I'd doubt that. He never steps outside the door. Gardens for me mostly. He's a recluse.' In another conspiratorial whisper, he added, 'He's had lots of troubles in his life.'

Albert pushed his brother's chair over to where a set of steps descended from the balcony to the riverside garden below.

'Do you remember the pond, Meabh?'

There was a circular pond at the foot of the steps, at riverside level. 'There were lilies in it and small frogs too. You loved those lilies. Go down if you like.'

Noelie intervened. 'We only wanted to say hello. Maybe we could come back another time?'

'Nonsense, Meabh's leaving tomorrow,' Albert said bluntly. 'There are pictures I want her to see. Her father is in them.'

He walked away leaving Robert Donnelly on the terrace. 'Come,' he instructed. 'This will interest you too, Noel. We have a room dedicated to our family's history. I'll show you.'

They re-entered the house. Noelie caught up with Meabh. 'Seen enough?' Meabh didn't reply. She was preoccupied and looked unwell.

A short distance along the main hall, Albert opened an ornate mahogany door. He stood aside so that Meabh and Noelie could enter. It was a beautiful drawing room with shelves of books. Albert immediately went to the wall opposite the only window. There were lines of framed black-and-white photos on the wall. In the corner there was a glass case containing a uniform and rifle.

'Our father, Anthony Donnelly Senior, fought in the War of Independence. He took part in a number of flying column operations and was decorated. This was his rifle. Killed a few Protestants, it did. He was very proud of it.'

The pictures spanned the early years of the Irish Free State. They were historically significant and Noelie was impressed.

'My father eventually joined the gardaí when it was set up. Robert, in a sense, followed in his footsteps.' He added, shrugging, 'Robert was the golden boy. But look where it got him.'

Noelie noticed another cabinet. It contained a different uniform, a type he had only ever seen in pictures: a pressed blue shirt with a cross insignia, black trousers and a black beret. The uniform of the Blueshirts. Next to it was a picture from Spain. Noelie realised then. Toner, the elderly historian that he had met on his visit to Ballyvolane, had mentioned that Old Donnelly had lost a leg in the war. Noelie assumed it was the Second World War but of course it wasn't.

'Where was your father injured, in Spain?'

Albert drew back in exaggerated shock. 'My, my. You know about that too? The Battle of El Mazuco, to be precise. 11 September, 1937. He was decorated by Franco, did you know that?'

Noelie shook his head. He added evenly, 'No doubt you were all very proud.'

Albert didn't reply. He appeared to be lost in thought. Noelie looked to see what Meabh was doing and realised only then that she was no longer in the room. He looked around uneasily.

'It was a bad blow,' continued Albert. 'He lost his leg. It ruined things actually.'

In the corner there was a wooden cross. It was a large structure, ornate and partially painted in bright blue. There were sketches near it.

'What's that?'

Albert ignored the question. Instead he went to a wall-mounted glass cabinet. 'There are a number of films of Danesfort. You said you had an interest. There's some of the Ballyvolane farm too. Did you say you were interested in that as well?'

'Well, I've noticed Meabh isn't with us any more. I wonder if we should get her and then we could watch the films together. I think she'd like to see them.'

Albert appeared not to hear Noelie again. He unlocked the cabinet. Noelie saw dates on the boxes: 1960, 1961, 1959. They went up to the mid-seventies.

'A friend of our family, a Mrs Finn, a wonderful woman, was in Spain as a nurse and made a name for herself later on as a journalist there. She was a close friend of my father's. She gave me a Bell & Howell home-movie camera for my eighteenth birthday. 1956. It was a wonderful gift. Just wonderful. For years I was the only person in Cork to have a camera like that. All these films are Bell & Howell double-8 format.'

He selected a box and closed the cabinet. Marching out of the room and along the hall, Albert shouted, 'Tea. In the movie room,' as he opened another door.

Noelie remained at the doorway. There was a projector and a screen already set up. Comfortable chairs were arranged in a semicircle. Albert attended to closing the blinds.

'I'd like to find Meabh,' Noelie repeated.

Albert came over. He looked concerned too. 'I'll put the film on. Take a quick peek and I'll find her ladyship.'

Noelie sat reluctantly. The room suddenly went dark. A small side light was put on and a trolley appeared, followed by the silhouette of the man with the big ears.

'Your friend is using the toilet,' he said.

To Noelie's surprise his accent was American.

'Is that okay?' Albert asked, coming back into the room and taking a seat beside him.

Noelie dithered as the projector whirred into life, shining a white light at the screen. Albert handed him a cup of tea.

'You're in for a treat,' he added, also handing Noelie a scone with butter and jam on it. 'By the way, that jam's home-made.'

The camera panned over the broad vista that was the original Danesfort complex. Noelie recognised it from photos he had seen. The clip was shot from a distance, from one of the fields in front of the school. Noelie noticed crows on the ploughed drills and remembered Black Gary's comment. Eventually the camera found a thin priest with specs standing at the chapel arch.

'There's my brother Tony,' said Albert enthusiastically.

'How was he friends with Meabh's dad?' asked Noelie.

'I'll explain that later.'

The tea was bitter but the film intriguing. It cut to the large military-like square attached to the industrial school. A group of boys, immaculately turned out, were performing warm-up exercises. Noelie felt his eyes wanting to close. A moment later his head fell to one side. As he righted himself he felt the first stirrings of alarm. The film was getting fuzzy too. He thought he heard his name being called. Then for no apparent reason the door crashed open. He thought it was Meabh but he wasn't sure. He fell over as he tried to stand.

29

It was dark and cold. Noelie was lying on an incline. He ran his hand over the surface of it. It felt rough and there were slimy patches. He could hear gurgling noises from time to time.

'Meabh,' he called out, but there was no reply.

He was still wearing his clothes. He had his wallet too. He searched for his phone but remembered that he had left it in his car. Trying to sit up, he hit his head against something overhead, almost knocking himself out. He lay back and put his hand up to feel what was there. More rough concrete. Where was he?

He carefully crawled up the incline but the gap between the floor and the ceiling became so narrow he was unable to proceed. Moving sideways he reached a solid wall. It was rough too, with cracks here and there.

A sudden burst of gurgling followed by the sound of prolonged sucking made him stop and listen. He thought he heard moaning but he wasn't sure. He called Meabh's name again.

Returning roughly to where he started from, he crawled in the opposite direction and reached another wall. Again it was not possible to move up the incline.

He sat for a while. There was total darkness – he had never experienced anything like it. He felt afraid and called again. This time he heard a moan. Crawling down the incline he was eventually able to stand. He figured that he was in some sort of underground cavern. Moving about he called Meabh's name. Eventually he found her lying on her side. He took her hand. It was very cold.

'Meabh?'

She shifted and groaned. 'My head.'

He tried to move her.

'My feet are in water.'

Noelie moved down the incline some more. He felt about. Her legs were on a ledge with water just beyond it. There was a pool of some sort out there in the dark. It was still. He put his hand into the water. It was icy. He couldn't touch the bottom.

He helped Meabh crawl up the slope. 'Where are we?'

'I don't know.'

Meabh sat up. 'My head's really sore.'

He reminded her that the last time he saw her was in the Donnellys' family history room. 'Where did you go?'

'I'm sorry.'

'Why did you go?' he pressed.

'To look around the house. I'm sure that's the place. I went looking for something I would recognise. I'm so sorry, Noelie. That man came up behind me. He hit me with something.'

They were silent for a while. 'I was drugged. I took one sip of tea. I should've known.'

'I want to get out of here.'

'Join the queue.'

'Where are we?'

'I have no idea but what worries me more is that no one knows we're here. Who knows that we even called to Albert?'

They made their way around their cold prison on their hands and knees. Overall, the cavern was about twelve feet wide. At the top of the incline the gap between floor and roof was no more than the width of a body; at the bottom Noelie could stand and just about touch the ceiling with raised hands. The incline didn't extend all the way down the cavern. At the lowest point there was water. They were unable to touch the other side by reaching out and they couldn't see anything either. When they called out their echo returned sharply.

They huddled close against the cold. The gurgling and sucking sounds became more regular. They wondered what was causing them and figured it had to be something to do with the water at the bottom of the incline. Noelie grew more anxious. He was angry with himself too because he hadn't followed his instinct. He had known it was a mistake to go into Llanes.

'Do you think we're still in the house? Or are we under it? Or where are we?'

Noelie hadn't even thought about that or that they could be somewhere else entirely. He had blacked out and had no idea for how long. Spontaneously they began to shout for help. When they stopped, Noelie felt a lot worse.

'We're so stupid,' he said bitterly. 'What the hell were we thinking?' He paused and then began again. 'Hannah would come looking for us if she knew where we were ... But she doesn't even know about the Donnellys.'

Eventually Meabh said, 'I can't sit like this. It's like we're waiting for something to happen and what's going to happen? If they come back it will only be to finish us off. They've already drugged and imprisoned us. I can't see this ending well if we stay put.'

She made her way down to the water and Noelie reluctantly followed. They reached the water's edge much sooner this time.

'That's strange. I thought the water level was further down.'
'It was.'

'Is this place filling up? Is that what's causing the gurgling and sucking?'

Neither of them said anything.

'I'm going to explore.' Meabh took off her jacket and gave it to Noelie. 'Don't worry, I'm a good swimmer.'

'Glad to hear it because I'm not.'

She slid into the water. He heard her splashing but apart from those reassuring sounds she may as well have vanished into an abyss. He couldn't see anything at all.

'Okay?'

Meabh's reply echoed. 'It's deep.' A moment later, 'I'm at the far side. It's not far. Eight or ten feet at the most. But I can't stand.'

There was further splashing and then a long silence. Meabh's voice was strained when she spoke. 'It's eight or nine feet deep. More than I expected.'

'Anything over there? Any way out?'

'Nothing. There's not even something to hang onto. I'm coming back.'

She found where Noelie was sitting and climbed out. She shivered and he held onto her.

'It's river water, I think. It's really cold.'

'The Lee?'

'It must be.'

The incoming water forced them higher and higher up the incline. Noelie had difficulty managing the panic he was feeling.

'Isn't the Lee tidal?' asked Meabh.

'Depends on where you are on it. But yes. If we're still at Llanes, definitely.' He cursed again, adding, as much for his own benefit as Meabh's, 'We need to stay calm.'

Another long silence followed. Meabh said, 'I'm not dying in here.'

'Great,' said Noelie flatly. 'Now there's two of us.'

She ignored him. 'If the water's coming in, there has to be a way out. Our best chance is to find the place. There must be a pipe or something.'

Noelie bit back another negative comment. He was terrified and still angry that he had put himself in this situation. How had he been so stupid?

The water level continued to rise. Meabh declared that she would dive in to get a head start on the depth. Noelie heard her get ready. She went in and there was splashing again. Then it went quiet. When he heard her call again, he was relieved.

'Any luck?'

'I reached the bottom but couldn't find anything. I'll try again.'

Meabh was right, they had to try. Noelie scrambled around feeling along the walls and joins for anything that might indicate an opening but he found nothing. Air was getting in but where?

She returned to the surface gasping loudly. 'I found it. In the corner, to the right. It's an opening, sizable too. I'm coming back.'

She clambered out beside him. 'It's a chance, Noelie. Swim around a little with me. Once you are used to the cold it's a lot easier.'

'I can't.'

'You have to.'

'No.'

Meabh's voice rose. 'There isn't a choice here.'

He shook his head – not that she could see that. 'I can't, I'm not able to. Don't ask me again. I can barely swim. I won't make it.'

There was a very long silence. They could hear water lapping just near them.

'I'll stay here in the corner. I might be able to ride out high tide. It can't be long now.'

'And what then, Noelie? Sit around some more? How long can you hold out? Low tide, high tide, how long?'

He didn't have an answer. Her hand touched his face. It was cold but it was welcome. Her other hand took one of his. 'We'll drown here if we don't get out. Do you understand? There isn't any choice.'

He shook his head madly. 'I'm not able. I can't.'

'You are able,' she said, gripping his hand tightly.

He pushed her away. 'I'm not.'

There was an even longer silence after that. He felt water at his feet and moved further up the incline. It was becoming confined.

'I'll mind you. We can do it. It's likely to be just a length of pipe and it'll lead us out into the river.'

'You don't know that.'

He felt her shivering feverishly beside him. 'You go, Meabh. You get help and I'll hold on here. I will.'

She cupped his cheek. 'Okay. But I'll be back.'

He wanted her to go. Anything to put an end to the idea of him getting in the water. 'Go, get help.'

He heard her gulping volumes of air, filling her lungs again and again with oxygen. She kissed him before she went.

'Going.'

After she got into into the water he called, 'Good luck.' He was crying and couldn't stop. He heard her swimming and then it went quiet.

30

On her second attempt, Meabh made it into the pipe. It was narrow and slimy; further through there was faint light. She reached a barrier and pushed against it. It gave a little. Out of breath, she retreated and broke to the surface once more.

This was their only chance, she reminded herself. She filled her lungs again and again, figuring that she had one or two good efforts in her before fatigue set in. She went down again, kicking with all her strength, and entered the pipe. Pushing against the barrier, she wriggled into a narrow gap, forcing it wider with her shoulders. Panic took hold as she became stuck; she had only seconds of air left. Wriggling forcefully, she tore against something sharp. Reaching forward, her fingertips found a lip. She heaved with all her strength and the sluice gate gave way. She was through.

She came to the surface and took huge deep breaths. She was immediately carried by the river current. She went upstream which meant the tide was still arriving. She swam to the riverbank and found the steps leading to the Donnellys' garden. Huddling there, she shivered violently. She knew she had nearly drowned. Panic coursed through her.

There were no lights on in Llanes and the garden looked quiet. Meabh crept onto the lawn, making for the bushes against the wall with the neighbouring house. She figured the cavern was at the end of the garden but there was nothing obvious to indicate its location. She was looking at a plain, well-cared-for lawn.

There was an odd-looking, solid square of concrete on the other side of the garden. She went over and examined it carefully. Nothing. Returning riverside she took a guess at where the escape pipe was located and found a contraption with a lever in a nearby fuchsia bush. It was very old and rusty. What direction was closed or open? In the dim moonlight the river flow looked almost stationary. She guessed and pulled the lever towards her. The mechanism screeched and she stopped immediately. She waited, afraid. No lights came on. She edged the lever towards her more and hoped it was the right choice. She felt panic again: she knew she was Noelie's only chance

Creeping across the lawn Meabh noticed a metal bar embedded in the grass. It looked like a handle and she tried pulling it but it wouldn't budge. It was in the correct location, directly over where she suspected the cavern was. It had to be the entrance. She dug away the grass and soil around it and uncovered a steel plate a few inches below the surface. She tried to lift it but there seemed to be no way to manoeuvre it. Was it electrically controlled? She looked for wires in the flowerbeds but found nothing. Further up the garden, near the lily pond, she took the path leading to the house. There was an entrance at lower basement level. The door was ajar and she carefully looked in. There were tools everywhere – clippers, mowers and strimmers. Lots of garden chemicals too. The place smelled foul.

Further in there was another door. It wasn't locked either. Opening it, Meabh realised it led into the basement area of Llanes. She saw a table, chairs and a small stove with logs beside it. She went in. In a small room off the living area, a man was asleep on a single bed. He still had his clothes on. He snorted suddenly and shifted. His snoring resumed at a more even pitch.

Meabh looked around. There had to be controls somewhere, but would they be so far from the underground cavern? She went through another door that took her further into the house. Looking down the dark hall she froze: black and white flagstones. She knew for sure now, this was the place where she had been assaulted. Suddenly she felt cold and terrified. She reversed, closed the door behind her and focused on helping Noelie.

Meabh returned to where the garden tools and chemicals were stored. She saw a crowbar and took it for protection. From the doorway she examined the high wall dividing the Donnelly garden from the neighbouring property. Maybe she should try to get over it and alert whoever lived there, scream and demand that they call the cops?

By her foot she noticed a white conduit tube. It went outside and vanished into the gravel path. Tracking it back inside the house, she passed through the area with the table and chairs and entered a small windowless room. Immediately she saw the instrument panel. It was compact and fronted with a bright tablet-size LCD screen. A digital clock ran silently in the corner. Icons flashed: closed, half, open. Making a selection, she pressed enter and ran back down the garden.

She saw the opening in the lawn immediately: about a square metre in size near where she had gouged out the grass. As she stooped beside it she felt a draught of cold air. The water level was right up. She slipped in carefully; the water level came up to her knees. Feeling around desperately, she finally grasped Noelie's foot. With huge difficulty, she dragged him to the opening and got him onto the grass. She pressed evenly and rhythmically on his chest. Eventually he spluttered to life. She quietened him by holding him into her chest while he coughed. The look in his eyes was dreadful.

Meabh propped him against the fence and went back to close the entrance. While she was away, Noelie sat and shivered uncontrollably. He stared across the garden at the dark outline of Llanes.

When Meabh returned she started trying to warm him up but realised that there was no point. 'Unfortunately it's back into the water for us. We must swim and this time I'm not taking no for an answer. I'll keep you afloat.'

'Anything.'

She helped Noelie down to the steps. The lid of the cavern had reclosed. The garden prison was ingenious. In normal circumstances it would never occur to anyone that this picturesque location was home to such a place.

At the river, the tide had turned.

'Go, slide in,' urged Meabh.

Noelie knew he had no choice and slipped in. Meabh followed. They were quickly taken by the current. The water was numbing but Meabh held Noelie. She was elated. They had escaped.

'Am I really alive?' Noelie asked as they floated downriver.

Austerity

31

Lucifer was coiled around a naked light bulb. The glowing filament showed Shane's head and Hannah's hair floating inside the serpent's long intestine. Noelie thrashed with fright.

'Calm,' a voice said. 'Calm, you're safe.'

A cool hand moved across his forehead. He opened his eyes and saw Meabh. She smiled at him. Her hair was wet and she had let it down.

'You have beautiful hair.'

Beside her Martin said, 'What about me?'

'You're beautiful too.'

'Finally he admits it. I couldn't get him to notice me for years, now he's moved to poetry.'

'It's an ill wind,' said Meabh.

Memories rushed back – his watery grave. He remembered waiting for Meabh, then sitting at the side of Albert's garden. It was dark and cold. There was moonlight and he could see the houses along the hillside of salubrious Sunday's Well. Albert with his well-to-do neighbours, Albert the killer. He had nearly got them both.

'Where's Hannah? Is Hannah here?'

Meabh looked at Martin.

'I haven't been able to contact her.' He hesitated. 'I went over to her place earlier. I still have my key but the place was empty. Her phone's switched off too.'

When Noelie and Meabh had emerged from the Lee in the early hours of the morning, they were unable to find a taxi that was prepared to take them given their sodden condition. Hannah's place was the nearest so they walked there. Noelie didn't have his keys any longer and they couldn't get a reply so they had carried on to Martin's.

'What time is it now?' Noelie asked.

'Just gone 10 a.m.'

Noelie sat up and perched on the side of the bed. 'It's not like Hannah not to be in contact.' He was worried. 'Where are my clothes?'

'In the wash. They'll be ready soon.'

Meabh spoke. 'We need to think carefully about what to do next. You realise what's just happened, don't you?'

'You saved my life.'

'Well, I walked us both in there. Helping to get us out was the least I could do.'

Noelie shook his head. 'No, I was finished. I gave up. You saved my life.'

Meabh told Martin and Noelie how she escaped. She realised that Noelie would never have made it through the pipe. She was a very good swimmer and capable of holding her breath for quite a long time.

'I was within seconds of drowning. It was terrible. I'll never forget it.'

She lifted up the hoodie that Martin had loaned her: there was a cut on her side where her ribcage began. Noelie winced. 'Do you think you should get that seen to?'

She shook her head. 'It looks worse than it feels.'

She noticed Noelie's hands. They looked sore. He couldn't remember how he'd hurt them but figured it had to be from the rough surface inside the cavern. As it filled with water, he had been forced to try and maintain his position high up on the incline. His hands showed what an awful struggle that had been. He shivered again, thinking about Albert's deathtrap.

Meabh said she had to check out of her hotel room by noon. It was already mid-morning so she needed to head over there soon.

'What time's your flight?'

'Doesn't matter. I'm not going now. I'll call work. I can squeeze a few more days out of them. Don't look too happy about it.'

Noelie apologised. 'It's not that. Of course I'm glad you're staying. It's just Hannah – where is she?'

'Look, let's try not to worry. Hannah's very smart and resourceful. She can look after herself. Let's get moving and see if we can track her down.'

Martin brought them their clothes and they got dressed immediately. He offered to drive them to Meabh's hotel. It was a short journey. Over on the quayside as they got out, and as Noelie was thanking him for all his help, Martin remembered something else.

'I have other news. I'm afraid it's not good either.'

'What is it?'

'Your punk records … They're gone.'

'What? Where?'

Martin was contrite. 'I spent the night of the blast at Hannah's. The few days after that I was in Kinsale. So I wasn't about much. The landlord's crew were in repairing the ceiling damage.' Martin paused. 'But I don't think it was them. It's only your records that are missing. I wouldn't even have thought to look but I saw that one of my plants had dried out. I was watering it and I noticed that the suitcase with the LPs in it had been moved. Just slightly like. When I checked it, it was empty.'

'Fuck.'

'I'm really sorry.'

'The icing on the fucking cake.'

32

The hotel room was plush and calm. It felt for a moment like an oasis. Noelie was reminded of Hannah. Before the crash they had taken a few city breaks together to places like Prague and Cracow. From the outset Hannah had insisted on splashing out on good hotels. 'At my age, I'm not slumming it any more,' she'd informed Noelie. She would've liked this hotel.

Meabh stood beside him. 'I'm sorry I dragged you in there, Noelie, into that house I mean.' Sitting on the edge of the bed she put her head in her hands. 'He wanted me to visit him. He set me up.'

Noelie didn't follow.

'At Glenville, Albert squeezed my hand in a strange way. It was deliberate, I realise now. He was telling me he knew about what had happened to me in the past.'

She told Noelie about the black-and-white flagging and how she had often seen it in the flashbacks that she had suffered.

'I think what happened to me happened in that house.'

Noelie wasn't surprised. 'That place is hell,' he said. He thought about the sudden attack again: Albert had gone for the kill and almost succeeded too.

Meabh went down to reception to arrange to stay a further two nights. While she was away, Noelie thought about what could've happened to Hannah. He needed to remain calm but he was beginning to feel the same as when he had heard about Shane's disappearance: deeply afraid. The worst-case scenario kept coming to mind all the time.

It was nearly twenty-four hours since he had spoken to her. After their meeting at the *Voice's* office, they had had that single text message from her. That message said that she was fine but if so where was she?

When Meabh returned they powered up her computer and logged on to the hotel Wi-Fi. They got Hannah's work number and Noelie called it using the room phone. He eventually spoke to Hannah's boss.

'She hasn't been at her desk since yesterday around noon,' he told Meabh. 'They haven't heard from her either and she's supposed to post copy shortly. They sounded concerned.'

There was a small desk with a chair beside it. Noelie sat down. 'Hannah said in her message that she had made that meeting at the train station, didn't she?'

'That's what I remember. I can't check. Albert took my phone.'

'Something's wrong. I feel it.'

Meabh asked Noelie more about the Facebook hook-up. He confessed he didn't know much about it or about social media. Meabh logged on to her own Facebook account and found Hannah's profile. They couldn't see much. Meabh wasn't one of Hannah's friends and she had tight privacy settings.

'Her computer might be at her place? If it is, she may be automatically signed in. We could try that.'

Noelie wasn't so sure. 'That laptop goes everywhere with her. But' – he smiled – 'I know her password. We go back a long time. It'll be "lawlibrary80" or "loureednyc".'

The law library password worked. There were no recent updates on Hannah's timeline and no messages from anyone called Caffrey.

'Unless they were in contact by phone?'

Noelie didn't know.

Meabh continued looking and found Hannah's correspondence with the industrial school group. It was all there, Noelie realised, right back to the conversation Hannah had had about meeting up with Black Gary. But nothing anywhere about any Caffrey.

Meabh looked worried too. 'You're sure the connection was made on Facebook?'

'I'm certain.'

'There's no Caffrey or any name like that on her list of friends either.'

Noelie didn't want to say out loud what he was starting to think. He remembered the suddenness of the arranged meeting.

'We could check her email. Just in case.'

'Let's do it,' agreed Noelie.

The law library password worked on that too. There were plenty of new emails but Hannah hadn't replied to any of them. Meabh checked recent activity. 'Her mail was accessed last night and again this morning shortly after 10 a.m.'

'Well, that's something.' He thought about what he had said. 'Or is it?'

'I think it is,' answered Meabh uncertainly.

They decided they would go over to Hannah's. Noelie's main phone was there too. There might be a message from Hannah on that.

Meabh had to phone her work in Amsterdam. Noelie stood at the window again looking out. He heard Meabh speak in Dutch and then the conversation reverted to English. He heard her say she'd stay another two days. He was relieved.

Done with the call, Meabh got ready. He watched her re-plait her hair.

'Why would someone steal my records?' Noelie asked.

She looked at him. 'It does seem a bit odd, I agree.'

'Unless they're still looking.'

'For?'

'See, after I found your dad's statement, I went to see Don Cronin. He's the one had the stuff including my records in his lock-ups. He told me that Branch had taken everything. He made a point of saying "everything". At the time I didn't pay much attention, I was too worried about Shane. It was like "They've got everything now".'

Noelie told Meabh about the slip of paper he found in his LP collection that first day. 'It was like a page from a book. There was a biographical piece about Brian Boru on one side and a typed list on the other. A few things were mentioned – documents, photos, et cetera. Anyway, the point is, there must still be information out there, something they're missing. Why else would they come looking for my records?'

33

Hannah's place was a fifteen-minute walk from the hotel. They stopped on the way to buy another pay-as-you-go mobile for Noelie. As they activated their phones Noelie remembered his appointment at Henderson's. They made a detour to the shop and the technician recognised him immediately.

'The boss hung around all afternoon for you. He struck gold.'

Noelie apologised, passing off the missed appointment with 'something came up' instead of 'I was drugged and imprisoned in a cavern by an elderly gentleman from Sunday's Well'.

'The photo's from the *Bandon Express*. They have a substantial archive and were happy to email us the original as long as it wasn't for publication. We guessed it wasn't.'

Noelie reassured her. The quality of the photo was hugely improved. Each face had been blown up to the size of a passport photograph, and looked clear and sharp. He thanked the technician for all her help.

Meabh paid by credit card. As the transaction was being put through she said, 'I'm guessing everything is digitised?'

'You have a USB?'

Meabh produced one in the shape of a Dutch tulip and the transfer was made.

On Washington Street, they waited near Centra. Meabh wandered up by Hannah's block of flats and returned again; she didn't see anyone suspicious.

Using Martin's keys they went in. The apartment looked exactly as it had when Noelie had last been in it, nearly twenty-four hours earlier. There was no sign of Hannah. Her room was the same as usual. She normally pulled the duvet back and did a quick tidy before leaving for work and that was how it appeared now. He felt the bed. It was cold. Looking on her dresser, he saw lipstick, face cream and a hair brush. There were lots of photos, some framed, some just tacked to the wall. Hannah had a very good friend in Australia and had been out to visit her a few times. There was a wonderful picture of the two women on a mountainside outside Melbourne. Beside them was a photograph of Noelie and Hannah taken near the university's old College Bar. They both looked very young.

Noelie's main phone was dead. Once it was charged and switched on, it would reveal his location but he didn't feel he had any choice. As soon as the screen lit up, messages sailed in, reminders that he had new voice mail. Before it died the phone had logged some missed calls: two from Hannah, one from a number he didn't recognise.

He rang his voice mail. The first message was from Hannah and was time-stamped the previous day at 2.35 p.m. In it Hannah said she was having trouble contacting Noelie on her pay-as-you-go. She was at the train station but no one had showed up. That was it. What concerned Noelie most was the anxiety in Hannah's voice. He replayed the message for Meabh and she agreed Hannah sounded worried. There was something wary in her tone.

The next message was from 2.48 p.m. It was Hannah again but there was only silence. All they could hear were muffled noises. The message lasted four minutes and ended abruptly.

Noelie walked over to the wall and put his head against it. He looked at Meabh. 'Something's happened to her.'

The remaining message was from Hannah's friend, Tommy Keogh. It had come in at 6.32 p.m. and confirmed the worst. Hannah had contacted him sounding distressed. He had tried calling her back but without success. He was worried. Could Noelie call him back?

There were no other messages. Noelie rang Keogh immediately but there was no answer. As he was wondering what to do, Keogh phoned back.

'That you, Noel? You okay?'

Noelie said he was fine. He had mislaid his phone, otherwise he'd have called back sooner. Keogh explained again about the call from Hannah. The message he'd received was spoken in a whisper. In it she said she was with someone but was worried; she hadn't been able to contact Noelie.

He told Keogh about their enquiries into Danesfort and the proposed meet-up with a contact made through Facebook. Keogh was derisive.

'You allowed her to go on her own?'

'The meet-up was at the train station. It's a public area.' But Noelie knew he had made a mistake. 'I should've been there. Something came up.'

The doorbell rang. Noelie went to the window and looked out. He couldn't see who was below. Meabh said she'd go down. Covering the phone's mouthpiece, he whispered, 'Be careful.'

Noelie told Keogh he was going to contact Hannah's mother. If she hadn't heard from her he'd go to the gardaí. They agreed to stay in touch.

Meanwhile Meabh had returned up the stairs with Black Gary. Noelie was surprised and very happy to see him. Meabh looked less sure. Noelie covered the phone's mouthpiece and whispered, 'He's on our side.' He told Keogh, 'I need to go.'

'But what's your take on the big news?'

Noelie confessed he didn't know what Keogh was referring to.

'Where've you been? Don Cronin's dead.'

'Dead? How?'

'It's been all over the news. They're saying it was a break-in that went wrong but my sources tell me it was murder.'

Cronin had done a bunk just as Shane went missing. Later, via Detective Byrne, Noelie had learned that Cronin was holed up in Spain somewhere. Byrne wanted to talk to Cronin about the Dalton affair and the possibility that it was connected to Shane's disappearance, but Interpol hadn't been able to locate him. Now he was dead.

The call ended. Noelie shook Black Gary's hand and then hugged him as well. He introduced Meabh and explained how she had come to be involved with them. Next he told them both about Cronin's death. Meabh was shocked.

'Connected to all of this?' she asked.

'Has to be.'

They explained to Black Gary about the situation with Hannah. Noelie got upset and sat down. Hannah and Black Gary sat beside him. Black Gary knew no one by the name of Caffrey in the industrial school network, although he added that that didn't mean that this Caffrey didn't exist. Black Gary had come up to Cork because of Hannah. A while back she had left a message for him at the Jolly Roger reminding him to check up on the Danesfort photo for her. He confessed he had forgotten about it until then.

'But I've news,' he added. From his backpack he produced a large book with a faux leather cover, *The Rosminian Way*.

'I asked about your Danesfort photo. There's a man in England who could be one of the surviving boys in the line but I don't have contact details for him yet. I'm working on that. But someone suggested this. It's a pictorial history of the Rosminians in Ireland. I have it on loan.'

Black Gary opened a bookmarked page. There was a photo of ten or so Rosminians who had travelled to Cork city in 1963 to see President John F. Kennedy when he visited. All the priests were named in the caption. He pointed at one, 'Is that your novitiate?'

Noelie got the photograph that they'd picked up earlier at

Henderson's. Black Gary was impressed by the quality.

'It's him,' said Noelie.

Meabh agreed.

'His name is Father Boran.'

'Great work.' Noelie studied the faces of the other priests in the picture. 'This contact in England, how would we go about speaking to him?'

'A minute, I haven't explained myself properly. This Father Boran is interesting – here's why. A while back you asked about a republican connection.' Noelie nodded. 'Well, it just occurred to me. The thing about this Father Boran is that he was moved to Northern Ireland in the later part of the sixties. The story is that he was accused of abusing boys at Danesfort. We know the church's MO right? Push the problem onto someone's else turf. Apparently he ended up in Newry. I just wondered ...'

Noelie's face brightened. He clapped Black Gary on the back. 'It's possible, I see. Any idea of Boran's whereabouts now?'

'Well, there's a complication and that's why I'm here now. There's a claim that Boran's dead. A few of his victims did go looking for him, but the story is he got caught up in a fire or died in a fire in Belfast. I'm going to head over to the library to see if I can unearth anything on that. I have a few dates to work with.'

Meabh had gone over to the window. She called Noelie immediately. He looked and then stood back out of view. There were squad cars on the street below. As Black Gary joined them a blue saloon also pulled up.

'Branch.'

'Coming here?' wondered Meabh.

'I'm not waiting to find out.'

They made a quick arrangement with Black Gary. He'd meet the visiting party and later on they'd link up at Meabh's hotel. They gave him the details. As they were going Noelie remembered to collect Hannah's spare car keys.

He hurried down the back stairwell with Meabh and they

exited onto the small riverside deck.

'How did they know we were at Hannah's?' she asked.

'Thanks for the reminder.' Noelie took out his mobile phone and removed the battery; he put the battery and phone back in his pocket.

Noelie had remembered the rowboat attached to the pontoon at the apartment block. It belonged to a neighbour but was rarely used. He undid the bow rope and pulled the boat alongside. They clambered in. Noelie gave the punt a push and nearly capsized them. When they were out a short distance the current quickly took them.

'The river again,' observed Meabh.

'I'm not overjoyed either.'

Looking back at the dock Noelie didn't see anyone. They should be out of view before someone thought of looking. They passed the dole office and went under Clark's Bridge. The current was quite strong. After a sharp bend they went over some minor rapids, reaching the calm of George's Quay.

'Are we going somewhere in particular?' asked Meabh.

Noelie rattled the keys. 'Hannah's car could still be at the train station.'

They reached the junction where the Lee's south and north channels merged. The current was very strong and they were swept further downriver than Noelie wanted. Finally they docked at the slipway by The Last Call pub. Walking back to the train station, Noelie eventually spotted Hannah's white Civic near St Patrick's Church.

He pressed the key fob and the car opened. They checked inside and in the boot but couldn't see anything suspicious. 'No laptop,' he said.

Noelie got in. The car looked and felt abandoned. He was afraid now.

'Where to?' asked Meabh.

'Dineen Slate and Tile.'

34

The hardware yard looked even more deserted than the last time Noelie had visited. The gates were padlocked so they drove to the side lane leading to Ajax's home. An Alsatian on a long leash snarled at them. Noelie and Meabh got out of the car and approached slowly. The dog grew angrier. A young man, who had to be Ajax's son, watched from a doorway and Noelie called to him.

'Is Ajax home?'

'Who wants him?'

'Noelie Sullivan. He knows me.'

Something was said inside the house. 'He doesn't want to see you.'

'Tell him I need his help.'

There was a further exchange. '"Fuck off," he said.'

Noelie and Meabh exchanged glances. Meabh said, 'Could I speak to him then?'

Ajax appeared. He leaned on a walking stick. 'You have some cheek. Didn't I tell you never to show your face here again?'

'I came a while back. I asked your wife to tell you I was sorry for the trouble I had caused. I meant it too. Guess she didn't give you the message.'

'She did but talk means nothing.'

Noelie went nearer; the dog snarled. Ajax was missing a few front teeth. He didn't look in great shape.

'You heard about our mutual friend Cronin?'

'I'm not dancing on anyone's grave.'

Noelie looked at Meabh. 'Listen, I haven't fared well either.

My nephew's dead. I don't know if it's over all this or not. Now my best friend is missing too.'

Meabh added, 'It's only a few questions. Please?'

Ajax didn't anwer but he stayed where he was, so Noelie pressed on. 'Cronin had three lock-ups. He said the cops raided all of them and took everything. Is that true?'

'It is. I heard that everything was taken to the army barracks.'

'Why there?'

'They're hardly going to tell me, are they? But last week they came back. They checked everything and everywhere again. My aunt left me this Volvo too, an old tank. They insisted on seizing that as well. Fuckers.'

Meabh looked at Noelie. 'You're right. They're still looking.'

Ajax shuffled uncomfortably. 'I need to sit. You can come to the door but no further.'

They stood at the entrance to the kitchen. There was a homely smell. Mrs Dineen was there but she didn't make eye contact.

'So, a week ago they just turned up again. Looking for what?'

'Those cunts. They don't do explaining.'

Ajax's son spoke. 'I asked to see ID. They were the Special Detective Unit.'

Noelie sighed.

'Special Detective Unit?' asked Meabh.

'I think Branch have been reorganised since your dad's time. The SDU are intelligence, counter-terrorism, that sort of thing. The elite I suppose.'

'I checked my lock-ups after they had gone too. All the floorboards had been lifted, and not put back properly either. Those sheds got a real going-over.'

Noelie nodded. 'My records were in one of the lock-ups. But there were other items too, right? Mrs MacCarthaigh said.'

Ajax snorted. 'Don't bother yourself. They've been to her as well. Not nice about it either. They got everything back, everything I took into the charity shop as well.'

Noelie had wondered many times about the serendipity of finding his records in the charity shop. 'Do you mind me asking, why did you only take some items into the charity shop? How did you choose?'

'Look, I emptied one shed. I put as much as I could from that into the other two. But I ran out of space. Cronin had so much rubbish. There was even a trunk of women's underwear. I mean lots of gear and he didn't come across as any Casanova to me.'

'So what ended up in the charity shop was random?'

'Completely. But in a bad luck sort of way for me, as it turned out.'

Ajax stood and hobbled to the counter. He pulled open a drawer stuffed with envelopes, bills and newspaper cuttings. He retrieved a copybook and passed it to Noelie.

'It's in there what I took down to her.'

There was just one page with writing on it. Meabh offered to copy out the list but Ajax dismissed the idea. 'Take it with you. It's only brought me trouble.'

Noelie examined the items. 'I'm presuming the cops saw this?'

Ajax nodded. 'I had to show it to them. Miserable crowd. I warned herself as well.'

'Your wife?'

'For fuck's sake, not my wife. Mrs MacCarthaigh. I warned her.'

They found Mrs MacCarthaigh in a back room at the charity shop sorting a huge heap of donations into three piles. She remembered Noelie.

'The man who ripped me off, right?'

Despite everything Noelie was miffed. 'I didn't rip you off. Who said that?'

'A detective. He said I should've been given a lot more for those LPs.'

Meabh intervened. She introduced herself and tried to show Mrs MacCarthaigh the copybook page with the list. The older woman wouldn't look at it. 'They took everything back,' she said gruffly.

'Did you sell anything on then?' asked Meabh. 'Like you did with Noelie's records?'

'I got into a lot of trouble. Mr Dineen said he was doing me a favour giving me that stuff, but it turned into a nightmare. You think a charity shop wants to have Special Branch crawling around its rooms? Hitler outside was right annoyed with me. I'm out here in this smelly room a lot more than I used to be.'

She resumed sorting with her back to Noelie. It was slim pickings.

Outside on Castle Street, they stood in front of the shop window display. Noelie looked around cautiously. How were they going to find Hannah? The Ajax angle had been a long shot. If they found what Branch were looking for it might give them some leverage.

'You think she was telling the truth?' asked Meabh.

Noelie looked at her. 'Never occurred to me she wasn't.'

'Why was she so annoyed then?'

'Me, industrial relations, the state of the nation, the list is endless.'

'She wouldn't even look at the list. There was something ... Maybe we should level with her, tell her what this is really about?'

'We've nothing to lose.'

They went back inside. Mrs MacCarthaigh was having a rest. She looked upset.

'We're in trouble, Mrs MacCarthaigh, that's the honest truth.'

Noelie told her about Jim Dalton, about the death of Shane and how that made no sense. The older woman listened but her expression was implacable.

'It's a police matter so. Speak to them.'

'We don't trust them.'

That was not a winning line, Meabh could see that. She sat beside Mrs MacCarthaigh and spoke directly to her. 'My father was in the gardaí. He was a detective. He believed that some sort of abuser was being protected by the high-ups. Before he could do anything about it he died in a car crash on a perfectly fine day when there wasn't a single other vehicle around. I've never had any explanation, it's never made sense to me. Please help me, help us.'

Mrs MacCarthaigh looked uncomfortable. Eventually she spoke. 'Himself passed away ten years ago last week. I don't have much. Last year, my son took himself and his family to Canada. My grandchildren are over there now which is a lot of good to me. The closest to me now is my daughter in Dublin. I may have to move there, God help me. I only get a few bob here.'

Noelie wondered where this was leading but Meabh had guessed. 'We just want to take a look. Noelie found some papers stuffed in his record collection. We only want to check in case there's anything inside.'

Mrs MacCarthaigh put her hand out for the list. She looked it over and said, 'It's not on here. But there was a sewing box – I took it for myself. I never said anything about it being with Mr Dineen's things and they didn't seem to know. I was afraid anyway. If they found out I took something it would be over for me in here. Anyway, one thing led to the next. I couldn't understand why they were so nasty. Mr Dineen was just trying to do us a good turn.'

'We won't tell.'

'It's beautiful. I know it was wrong but all this austerity is wrong too. Can you believe it, they even want to take my medical card away now.'

Mrs MacCarthaigh lived in The Marsh, an area nearby. She made an excuse and they went with her. The sewing box was in her front room under a cover. It was quite a piece: black-and-red lacquer with mother-of-pearl inlay.

'Mr Dineen actually brought it to my attention. We go back a long way, but I'm afraid to have it out now. I've never taken anything before in my life.'

From a drawer she fetched a square white box. Noelie recognised it instantly. It looked exactly like one of the boxes Albert had in his film cabinet at Llanes.

'It's some type of film. Old though.'

Noelie thanked Mrs MacCarthaigh. Meabh didn't feel that was enough. She hugged her and the older woman blushed.

'I haven't forgotten you ripped me off,' she reminded Noelie as he was leaving. Meabh reassured her once more about the sewing box and that her secret was safe with them.

On Grattan Street they walked quickly. Noelie decided to call Hannah's mother. Using his new pay-as-you-go mobile, he called directory enquiries. He knew generally where she lived and they found the number. He was put through but the number just rang out.

Meabh examined the label on the box. '1962 June/4–2/ Gathering 3'. Noelie told her about all the films in the library at Llanes.

'I bet it's one of Albert's films,' he said.

35

Noelie knew of a shop close by that rented out projectors and film equipment. Eventually they found it. A ponytailed attendant examined the reel for a long moment.

'Haven't seen one of these in a while.' He unwound the strip of film and looked at it against strong light. 'Seems fine.'

'Is it viewable?' asked Meabh.

'It's called double-8 film. Occasionally people call it Zapruder film, after Alfred Zapruder. He owned a Bell & Howell home-movie camera. Top grade for its day. Some of them still about and in working order too. Zapruder shot the famous clip showing the moment that Kennedy was assassinated in Dallas. The name's stuck since.' He added, 'We have a projector out back. You can view it there if you like?'

Noelie and Meabh exchanged looks.

'We want to show it to friends, well family actually. It's of my grandparents. Could we rent the projector for the night?' asked Noelie.

The attendant returned with a neat container about the size of a large hatbox. 'We've only two of these. I need proof of ID and a cash deposit of €100. Charge is €25 per night or €150 for a week. Paid in advance.'

'Deal,' he said to the attendant. 'One night should do.'

They returned directly to the hotel. Meabh examined the projector. It worked on a spring mechanism. When the latch was released it unfolded into its working configuration. All they needed to do was set the reels in place.

They decided to use a wall as their screen. Noelie moved the furniture and closed the curtains tightly.

The camera panned along a country driveway. There were trees on one side, open pasture on the other. The film was in colour but there was no sound. A car came up the drive, a red Anglia. It stopped. The driver waved and the car moved on again. The clip then cut to a different scene: two young men stood outside a country house. It was a plain building apart from its portico entrance; statuettes of golden eagles stood on the front corners of the structure. The men wore overcoats and one also held a hat.

Meabh stopped the projector. She went over to the wall and placed a finger on one of the men in the image. A priest's collar was visible under his long coat.

'Recognise him?'

'Looks like Walsh, the developer.'

Meabh nodded. She pointed at the other man. 'What about him?'

Noelie shook his head and switched the film back on. The men chatted. The rear of the Anglia appeared as the camera panned away. In the background there were more woods and a hill. The camera returned to the men.

Another man joined the group. He wore a priest's collar and was younger than the others. Noelie went nearer to get a better look at him. Meabh paused the film again.

'Could be Boran,' said Noelie.

Meabh found the Henderson profile photo of the novitiate. Placing it beside the image on the wall, she nodded. 'It's a match.'

They continued with the film. The action moved inside to a reception room. There were sofas, a large circular table, two standard lamps and glass-cased bookshelves. The men removed their overcoats: two wore priest's attire while the third was in plain clothes. Whiskey was served from a decanter and they stood at the hearth. Occasionally one would glance at the camera. Abruptly the clip ended.

When filming resumed the location was in a different room. It was bare apart from a metal-framed double bed and some pictures on the wall. Noelie recognised Croagh Patrick and the Lakes of Killarney.

Two young boys walked in in their underpants. One had black, wavy hair and a bad squint. The other had fair hair that was cropped very short; he seemed unhealthily thin. Something was said to the two boys because they glanced in unison at the camera. They both looked afraid.

Leslie Walsh, Father Boran and the unidentified third man came into the room. Walsh stood near the fair-haired boy and held him. A moment later he left, leading the boy from the room by the hand. The clip ended abruptly again.

When filming resumed the camera was positioned at a different point in the same room. Father Boran was in the bed with the other boy. He was stroking the boy's face. At one point the young priest looked directly at the camera and smiled.

Noelie and Meabh watched in silence. The scene lasted about four minutes. As soon as it ended, Meabh switched off the projector and went into the bathroom. She banged the door shut. Noelie sat down. Everything had happened so quickly that he hadn't had time to consider what could be on the film. He understood now why it was so damning.

Was the house in the film the old Donnelly place in Ballyvolane, he wondered? Was there an arrangement and had these priests gone to the farm on more than one occasion? The label said 'Gathering 3'.

He called out, 'Are you okay, Meabh?' There was no reply and he called again. When she emerged Noelie saw that she had been crying.

'Now we know what all this is about. What ages are those boys?'

'Maybe eight or nine. The blond boy looks younger. He's only skin and bone.'

'My father uncovered child abuse, didn't he?'

'That would seem to be the case. And he was killed for it. We have to be careful.'

'We need a copy,' she said. She rummaged in her suitcase and produced a small camera. 'This will do as a start.'

They set the projector running again. Meabh recorded it standing to one side near the wall. As the film ran its course, Noelie thought the boys were probably from Danesfort. When they reached the point where Father Boran was in bed with the young boy, Noelie paused the recording. He peered at the frozen image and then allowed the recording to resume.

The copy was low grade but it was something.

'What will we do with it?' asked Meabh.

'Go to the cops?'

They both knew that was a bad joke. However Noelie wondered about Detective Byrne. If he was going to go to anyone, it would be her. But it would still be a gamble. There had to be some connection between the film and a mole inside the IRA. Why else were Branch so interested? Until they knew or understood what exactly that link was they were walking blind in a minefield. Even if Noelie was prepared to trust Byrne, she would be no match for the intelligence network. It would be foolish to think otherwise.

'Wikileaks?'

Noelie agreed it was a good option. Julian Assange had been in the news recently over the release of footage showing a US gunship mowing down a group of journalists in a Baghdad suburb. He admired the whistle-blowing site.

'How would we contact them?'

Meabh didn't know. 'The nearest internet cafe is probably

the best option.'

Noelie thought for a moment. 'This film may be the way to get Hannah back.'

Meabh looked doubtful. 'That would mean showing our hand and, as you said, we need to be careful. Anyway this, what this film shows, must come out.'

Noelie understood Meabh's point. She was right of course, but at the same time ...

Silence followed. He went to the window again and drew back the curtain. The room was flooded with light once more. He tried to focus. Something else was bothering him. He felt he knew Boran's face. He had no idea how and yet it was familiar.

He told Meabh. After a moment she got out her laptop. 'The internet connection is poor here but we can try anyway.'

He watched Meabh load software – Easy Age. It took a while. 'What's the deal?'

'In the Danesfort photo, Boran's about eighteen or nineteen or thereabouts. What would he look like today? He'd be about sixty-five?'

Noelie was amazed that there was software available that could project ageing from a single photo. He was even more amazed when he learned that it was available for free.

'Don't get carried away,' warned Meabh. 'This software is really basic. There's professional gear out there that's very powerful. The cops and a whole host of security organisations use that kind of thing.' She added, 'Also we're dependent on the quality of the original. It's not superb, let me put it that way.'

Meabh uploaded the Boran image from her USB. A knock on the door paralysed them both.

36

Noelie went to the door but Meabh got there ahead of him. 'I'll answer it. If it's anyone who's a bother I'll say I'm not dressed.' She slipped on the safety chain and called out, 'Who is it?'

'Black Gary.'

They had forgotten the arrangement to meet. Meabh undid the chain and opened the door.

'You looked scared. You too, Noelie.' He saw the projector. 'What's going on?'

Noelie told him about the film. 'One of the abusers, we're fairly sure, is Father Boran. Another is Leslie Walsh.' Noelie explained who that was and his ties to Meabh's family. 'The third man we don't recognise. We think Albert is doing the filming.'

Black Gary had news too. He produced a copy of an article from the *Belfast Telegraph*. The headline read 'Former Rosminian Among Tranmere Bar Dead'.

Noelie was very disappointed. 'So the rumour's true.'

'It seems that the Tranmere Bar was a republican drinking club. The doors were chain-locked and a petrol bomb thrown in through a window. It was a sectarian attack. Three people died in the inferno, two from their injuries later on.'

The article included background information on Boran. The Rosminian priest moved from Danesfort to Newry in 1965. A second move, four years later, took him to Belfast. The Tranmere fire happened in late 1971.

Noelie passed the article to Meabh. 'Seems like he got what he deserved,' she said.

Noelie still wasn't convinced. 'Okay then, but if he's dead why go to such lengths over this film?'

'Well, there's Leslie Walsh,' answered Meabh. 'There's also that other man. Who is he?'

'I can't see Branch would be too interested in Walsh. It must be the third man so. He must be someone important.'

Black Gary asked if he could see the film. Meabh reckoned it would be easier if he viewed the copy on her camera. As he watched, Black Gary's expression turned sour.

'Bastards.' He added, 'The drinks beforehand, the location, the relaxed air ... That's organised.'

'But why film it?' asked Noelie.

'Because they're perverts.' Meabh reminded them of a news story from a few months earlier in which a gang of men were arrested after they filmed each other assaulting a woman. 'That's how some people get their kicks.'

'But it's very risky, surely they'd know that?' said Black Gary.

Noelie told them about the cabinet of films at Llanes. 'They may have felt secure. Maybe their connections, their wealth and the boys too ... We don't know who they are but they could be from Danesfort. In other words perfect victims.'

Noelie went across to the window. There was a boardwalk with cafes beneath them, overlooking a section of the Lee's south channel. Ironically they were nearly directly opposite the Elysian, the tower that Leslie Walsh had jumped from.

It was looking more and more likely that these gatherings at the farm were organised. This whole thing seemed much more widespread and dangerous than they'd realised.

Black Gary came over and stood beside Noelie. 'At Hannah's when the cops arrived–'

Noelie apologised. He was so preoccupied he had forgotten about their abrupt parting earlier. 'What did they say?'

'They were convinced you were there. They looked

everywhere and when they couldn't find you they threatened me with being an accessory to murder. I asked them what they were talking about ... Genuinely I hadn't a clue. They mentioned this Don Cronin guy so when I was at the library I fished out today's newspaper and read all about it. He was some big nob in security here. An ex-cop too. He was murdered yesterday at his home. How could you be involved?'

'I'm not. It's some sort of a stitch-up going on.'

Noelie told Black Gary about Glenville and about what happened with Albert. Black Gary was incredulous, though not about Albert.

'I said to you about him. I'm not afraid of many people but he's different.'

Noelie found it difficult even thinking about Albert and what had happened at his house. 'The point is I was nowhere near Don Cronin's place when he was done.'

He went over to Meabh. She was looking at an online report about Cronin's death. Noelie glanced at it.

'I think we have to use the film,' he said. 'Let it be known that we have it. It's the only way we'll find out where Hannah is.'

Meabh shook her head. 'No, I'm against it. I'm not trading the film.'

'I'm not saying that.'

Meabh appealed to Black Gary. 'I think we have to proceed very carefully. And since we don't know yet how big all of this is we have to be doubly careful.'

Noelie swore under his breath. Black Gary came over. 'Let's not forget one thing – we're very close.'

'I think Jim Dalton either recognised or found out something about someone from his past,' said Noelie. 'It has to be a person of some importance. Dalton was in Sinn Féin but on the periphery. It could've been someone significant in that organisation. That's one side of the equation – are we agreed?'

Meabh looked unconvinced. 'Go on.'

'If you've a nasty past, it's a problem. Father Boran left Danesfort under a cloud. He was an abuser. The Rosminians sent him to Newry. Remember, in the sixties the North was like another continent. As was the norm, the Rosminians didn't warn anyone. They sent him there and promptly forgot all about him. Say Boran gets on with his life there and in due course he moves to Belfast. Except the Troubles are beginning.'

Meabh picked up the *Telegraph* article. 'Noelie,' she said slowly, 'Boran's dead.'

'If it's not Boran then it must be something like what I'm describing. There has to be a tie-in with the republican movement. And it goes back to Danesfort. Boran fits the bill, that's what I'm saying.'

There was silence again.

'Let's look at it from another direction.'

'What other one is there?' said Meabh tersely.

'Jim Dalton's. I wonder now was he abused. If he wasn't personally, perhaps he knew about a case at Danesfort. Perhaps he knew the abuser's name. In any case it's something that was well in the past for him. But then one day, out of the blue, he sees the abuser. Is it at a Sinn Féin meeting or something? Just supposing it was. Now he's thinking,"Hey, what's this man doing here in this organisation with the past he has?" He decides to do something about it. But he doesn't know that this man is also a mole inside the IRA, protected by Special Branch.'

Black Gary spoke. 'There's a lot of sense in what you say, I'll grant you that.'

'Maybe there's another priest so,' said Meabh. 'Someone with a similar profile to Boran's?'

Noelie shrugged. 'The Catholic Church has always had strong links to Irish nationalism. But for a priest to move from priesthood to activism inside the IRA or Sinn Féin wouldn't be the norm.'

'The point is lightning doesn't usually strike twice in the same place.'

Meabh looked annoyed. 'What does that mean?'

'The Boran situation is specific,' said Black Gary. 'I think that's what Noelie's getting at. It's not just the link to Sinn Féin or with the North. It's also Danesfort. This is about Danesfort and nowhere else because that's where Jim Dalton ended up. Could there really be another person who ticked all these boxes?'

Meabh sighed. 'Fine. So bearing in mind all of that, would you mind telling me how you propose to deal with the fact that Boran is dead?' There was a long silence. Meabh shook her head. 'Exactly, I think we should focus on something that's tangible. Let's try to identify the boys in the film.'

'And I'll be able to help out from Limerick prison too,' added Noelie sarcastically. 'While I'm being knifed like.'

Meabh looked askance at Noelie. For a moment he thought she was going to clock him.

'Be serious.'

'Meabh has a point, Noelie. There's a network of ex-industrial schoolboys out there. It's extensive and committed. Honestly, I'd be very surprised if we didn't get one or both of those victims identified. In a few days at most.'

Noelie was upset. 'We don't have any fucking time. Don't you realise? Where is Hannah? Seriously, where is she?' There was silence. 'Am I the only one worrying about her?'

Black Gary was taken aback by Noelie's comment. Meabh shook her head too. Her laptop pinged. She called them over and said calmly, 'Let's take a moment. Have a look at this.'

Noelie stood by the laptop while Meabh explained to Black Gary. 'We had a digitised image of Boran. Came from the Danesfort photo. He's young in it so I thought it would be worth a shot to see what he might look like when he was older. Mind, this was before you said that he had died. Option 1 puts him at thirty-five years of age and option 2 shows him at a projected age of sixty-five, which is what he would be around now.'

The facial simulations were strangely artificial creations, quite like police Photofits. They didn't look normal at all really.

Noelie put his finger on the older profile. 'He's familiar.'

Black Gary shook his head. 'Not to me.'

Noelie was sure. 'I'm certain. I've seen him around, somewhere.'

'On TV or something?'

'I don't know.'

37

Noelie assembled his old phone, noted Tommy Keogh's number and removed the battery again. He called him on the hotel landline. Keogh eventually answered.

'I need your help,' said Noelie.

'To do with Hannah, I hope. I just spoke to her mother and Hannah has not been in contact. The woman's out of her mind with worry. Honestly, you've fucked up here.'

Noelie took a deep breath. He didn't need a lecture about what had happened. 'We're all worried. Unfortunately there's no trace of the person she was supposed to meet either.'

'How could you be so stupid?'

Noelie ignored the jibe. 'Something else has come up. We're sure it's connected to Hannah's disappearance. I thought you might be able to help. Could I come to see you? Five minutes of your time. Then we'll talk about Hannah.'

There was a long pause. 'Okay.'

Noelie explained to Black Gary and Hannah who Tommy Keogh was. 'Apparently he has a lot of inside knowledge on the IRA. He might be able to help us with the photos, point us in the right direction.'

Meabh looked doubtful but she didn't object. Black Gary asked if he could come along too but Noelie had another idea. 'We need to make a good copy of the double-8 film. Martin has the sort of camera that would do the job.' He asked Black Gary if he'd link up with him and get a copy made. Black Gary agreed reluctantly.

Noelie drove. There was only light traffic. He thought about Hannah's disappearance again. It didn't seem plausible that she would be taken in broad daylight from a public area.

They arrived at Church Bay. The sun was setting and an orange afterglow was spreading on the horizon far out at sea. Before they got out Noelie explained about Keogh's loyalties.

'He's protective of his Sinn Féin links. Maybe it's to do with the book he's writing and his need to stay on good terms with them. But the thing is, if we spot a match in any photos that he might have, we might have to pull out. He may not want to help us.'

Keogh was in his sunroom. He was wearing a checked shirt with jeans and slippers. He was reading the newspaper and appeared not to hear them. Noelie knocked on the window and Keogh came to the door. Noelie introduced him to Meabh.

'Sean Sugrue's daughter?'

Keogh looked genuinely impressed. Shaking her hand he described her father as a dedicated policeman and said he was delighted to meet her. He invited them to sit around a glass-topped wicker table. There were newspapers strewn everywhere.

Keogh handed Noelie the *Echo*, Cork's local daily. The front page article showed a photo of Cronin's home in Montenotte with crime-scene tape stretched across the gated entrance. The headline read 'Butchered'.

'Apparently he had a lot of enemies. I guess you were one, Noel.'

The comment annoyed Noelie. 'He had my record collection. It's hardly a reason to hack him to death.'

Keogh suggested tea. Noelie declined but Meabh said yes. While he was away Noelie read the article on Cronin. It said that the security boss had been in Spain for the past month. He had been back in Cork to attend to personal business. His wife contacted the gardaí when she couldn't get in touch with him. A squad car was dispatched to the house and that was when the bloodbath was discovered. The article mentioned that the gardaí were following a definite line of enquiry. Robbery was not thought to be the motive.

Keogh returned and put a tray on the table. Stirring the teapot, he said, 'I'd like to talk about Hannah but you said you had something to ask me.'

Noelie told Keogh about his theory that Dalton was killed to protect an abuser in Sinn Féin. 'The organisation probably didn't know about this individual's past. The important point is that the abuser was an informer. He was press-ganged into service in the knowledge that if he didn't do as instructed the truth about him would be revealed.'

Noelie paused to see how Keogh was taking this information. He got a 'Go on.'

'We think Dalton recognised this figure and, aware of his past, let it be known that he was going to report him ...'

'And the gardaí, fearing the worst, stepped in and topped him.'

Noelie hesitated. 'That's what we're thinking, yes.'

Keogh addressed Meabh. 'Do you subscribe to this too?'

'In his statement my dad suggested–'

Keogh shook his head in disbelief. 'His statement? You really think he wrote that?'

Meabh was surprised. 'I never doubted it. It struck me as honest.'

Keogh smiled. 'You're well matched. Noelie swallowed it as well. But most people I've spoken to, and that includes a number of people in the gardaí, don't believe a word of it. My sources tell me Cronin was behind this. He was deep into a difficult connection with a major drug operation in Europe–'

Noelie interrupted. 'How could Sugrue's statement about Dalton's execution be connected to a drugs operation on the Continent?'

'People spin webs. It helps hide what's really going on. Look, Inspector Lynch has been leading the fight against drugs in Cork for over a decade. And he's been successful too.'

Noelie guffawed. 'You are kidding? Successful? Cork's awash with drugs. There hasn't been a big bust in the city in years.'

'There have been interceptions.'

'On the coast, to do with drugs going on to the UK. But within the city itself, very little.'

'My point is, Lynch's good work directly affected Cronin and his paymasters. What better way to get back at him than to divert attention onto his past? Muddy his name with all this Jim Dalton rubbish. And who better to use than your father, Meabh?'

'Why my father?'

'I dislike being the one to have to tell you this but sources have confirmed to me that there was huge animosity between your father and Inspector Lynch. Your father was sidelined by the time the peace process came along in '94. He had won the Scott Medal for bravery but his career tanked afterwards. Whereas Lynch went on to better and bigger things. Your father had it in for his ex-colleague. Cronin saw that and realised that he could use it. Hence that statement that Noel conveniently found.'

Noelie nodded his head slowly. 'Ah, so I'm being used too. I see now. I'm a real idiot.'

Keogh turned his attention back to the teapot, stirred the contents once more and poured a cup for Meabh.

'I hope I haven't offended you,' he said.

Meabh laughed. 'Me? Of course not.'

Keogh offered them cake; they both declined.

'You said there was something specific you wanted to ask me?'

'We have a photo. It's a decent image, not perfect mind, but we're wondering if you can help us identify who it is.'

Keogh looked at them. 'What makes you think I can be of help?'

'The individual we're looking for was probably a priest at Danesfort Industrial School. He had a reputation there.'

'A reputation?'

'For abusing boys.'

Keogh nodded. 'And now?'

'Well, we're wondering if he could be associated with Sinn Féin in some way. No one would know about his past. He probably has a different identity entirely.'

'Okay, I'll help – but before you show me anything, let's be clear. I'm not going to point the finger at anyone without solid proof. And I mean solid. A photo's grand but cast-iron proof is something else entirely.'

'We have cast-iron proof.'

Keogh looked at Meabh. 'Really?'

'Really.'

Noelie was afraid Meabh was going to mention the film. 'We don't need to go into that right now,' he said quickly.

'I'd rather we did actually. I mean if it's cast-iron information I'd be a lot more inclined to help, really help that is. What is it?'

Keogh stared at Meabh as a phone vibrated. It was on the windowshill beside Meabh. She reached over to get it for Keogh but he got there first and silenced the call.

'Well, let's see the photo anyway.'

Before leaving the hotel Noelie had asked reception to print him a copy. He retrieved it from his satchel.

Meabh stood suddenly. 'Could I use your bathroom?'

'It's a bit of a mess, I'm afraid, I'm getting work done.'

'I don't mind.'

Noelie looked at Keogh who looked at Meabh.

'I've had builders in,' explained Keogh. 'There's plaster everywhere.' Suddenly he changed his mind and pointed in the direction of the kitchen. 'Go ahead so. Through there.'

Noelie noticed that Meabh seemed to have left in a hurry. He got up – something was wrong. 'Maybe I should–'

Keogh put a hand on his shoulder. 'I'll check on her, don't worry. See that she ends up in the right place.' He nodded to a different door. 'My office is through there. Take a look if you like. There are photos on the wall. I'll be right in after you.'

Keogh left. Noelie hesitated. Outside, it was getting dark. He could just make out their car. It was where they had left it. Everything looked fine.

Keogh's office was chaotic. There were documents, stacks of newspapers, half-open books, photos and old cups of tea on every surface. At the back a computer screen was showing nature pictures.

The photographs on the wall were interesting. The famous faces of the republican movement were well represented.

Noelie spotted a young Martin McGuinness talking to someone who looked like Keogh. Keogh had no beard in the photo, just a moustache. Another picture showed Keogh with Galway gunrunner, Ciarán Corrigan. Noelie recalled Hannah's observation that Keogh could well have been in Sinn Féin at one time. Maybe it was true.

He heard a noise behind him. Keogh was at the door. He came and stood beside Noelie and looked at the Corrigan photo. 'Figured it out yet?'

'Hannah told me that she thought you were in Sinn Féin at one time. Early days, I guess. Didn't figure it could be true myself what with you being a journalist and all. Was I wrong?'

Keogh indicated another picture further along. The setting was iconic in terms of the republican movement's past.

'Milltown Cemetery, Belfast?'

'Bobby Sands' funeral. That's me there.'

It was Keogh. He was bearded in this photo. Keogh was only a few rows back from the pallbearers which was not a place you ended up in by accident.

'So it's true?'

'Was and am.'

'Am? What about objectivity and so on? With your book I mean?'

'I keep quiet about it. Look, my membership helps. I have access and access is vital – if you want the real story.' Keogh went to his desk. He picked up a tattered folder. 'There are good photos in this.'

Noelie stared. On the desk beside the mouse, there was a ring with an irregular amber stone on it. A thread of cream ran through it. Hannah had one like it. He moved closer but as he did an electrical current burned into his ribs. He shuddered and collapsed.

38

Noelie struggled but his head was yanked back and slammed against the floorboards. He felt lighted-headed and remained still. His feet were wrapped together and he was dragged from the office into the hall. Albert Donnelly stood observing him.

'You must have a death wish, Noel. You walked into my arms once and escaped; now you're back again.'

Noelie wasn't able to speak, there was a gag in his mouth. He was pulled along and put in a different room. Meabh was already in there, tied up in a corner. She was gagged too and there was a wild look in her eyes. Looking to see who was manhandling him, Noelie recognised the figure with the large ears. Albert addressed him as Paul.

The room was decorated with ugly maroon wallpaper. There was an empty display cabinet and a long sofa pushed against the wall. The window was large and looked out to sea. It was dark outside now. Meabh nodded her head vigorously and Noelie realised that she was trying to tell him something. From the position he was in he couldn't see what it was. He attempted to move but fell over. Keogh came in holding a kitbag and some grey sacks. He placed one sack on the floor and straightened it. There was a zip down its middle and plastic handles at each of the corners. He pulled the flaps wide and drew a length of chain from inside.

Big Ears was standing at the door. He went to Meabh and draggged her to the open sack. She resisted but he struck her viciously and she went still. Noelie screamed through his gag. They laid Meabh in the sack and Big Ears pulled the zip up halfway while Keogh worked at wrapping the long chain around Meabh's neck, under and around the outside of the sack, back and forth, occasionally threading it through the handles as well. Keogh tested the shackle by pulling it roughly and Noelie saw Meabh wince.

Big Ears took a lock from the kitbag and Keogh secured the ends of the chain with it. Dumbbells were produced but Keogh hesitated. 'We'll put them in later.' Looking at Noelie, he added, 'We're taking you all for a boat ride, your final voyage.'

Noelie tried to speak but couldn't. Keogh took the gag from his mouth as Albert came in. He surveyed the prisoners and left again. Keogh pulled Meabh closer to the door. He cleared space for Noelie.

'You're Father Boran.'

'You think so?'

'You're the right age, over sixty, you know Albert and you're in Sinn Féin. I can't really see the resemblance but ...'

Keogh came closer, squatting near Noelie. 'My eyes are the giveaway. When I was young I was told I had quite the stare.'

It was possible, although Noelie wasn't sure. Keogh's brows and nose looked different to those of Boran; the shape of his face didn't even look the same. A complicating factor was Keogh's beard. The photos of Father Boran showed a clean-shaven, youthful priest. In contrast Keogh sported a full beard, groomed and grey now.

'How did Dalton work out who you were?'

'He didn't. He saw me with Albert. It was Albert he recognised. I had changed my appearance. The people who wanted to use me had to help out so they paid for a plastic surgeon. I attended for years, on and off, all at the taxpayers' expense. A nose job, brows, a chin lift, implants. Everything helped. Anyway, none of the Danesfort boys had laid eyes on me since way back so I had that on my side too.'

'And you were dead.'

Keogh laughed. 'You're right. When word goes out that someone has died, I suppose people switch off. It put the brakes on anyone with a grudge coming to find me. It was a smart move.'

Watching Keogh, Noelie realised that some part of him had probably enjoyed the deception. He had ditched his abuser–Boran identity and become a personable journalist.

'Unfortunately,' continued Keogh, 'Albert looked just like he always did. Older but the same. We only met occasionally, once or twice a year. So for Dalton to see us together was bad luck – for us, and for Dalton, as it turned out. I don't know what made him suspicious but later on I found out that he had followed me and discovered where I lived. This was the late eighties. He watched me for a while, I think, and then went to the gardaí and made a complaint, saying who I was and what I had done. Things were beginning to change in Ireland then and the police could no longer ignore allegations like that. Dalton didn't know what he had got himself involved in though. If his complaint was followed up, it was going to cause a lot of trouble. So, he had to go away. But a lot of what went wrong after stemmed from our unlucky, chance encounter with Dalton.'

Meabh wriggled and Keogh stared at her.

'Although not her. She was a different complication.'

'What do you mean?'

'Albert hated Sean Sugrue. He was too close to his brother Robert and he was a decorated cop. A high-principled Catholic to boot. All the things that Albert actually wasn't.' Keogh lowered his voice, whispering, 'Albert's a nasty sinner, not that you can ever tell him that.'

Meabh was listening, looking at Keogh.

'Sugrue would bring his daughter to prayer meetings at Llanes. Not that wise. There was trouble in that organisation of theirs, in that house too.'

'Let There Be Light?'

Meabh rolled slightly on the floor, trying to move, but Keogh seemed to lose interest and returned to arranging a sack for Noelie.

'Branch underestimated you,' he said, looking at Noelie. 'Albert too. You've really upset things around here.'

'Where is Hannah?'

'The pipe bomb should've been the end of you. When it failed to do the job Hannah did us all a favour by presenting herself on Facebook. It was too good an opportunity to miss. The idea was I'd meet you both at the station. It would be accidental and I'd lure you away.' Keogh nodded at Meabh. 'Instead, you suddenly went to Glenville with that bitch. The decision was made to take Hannah anyway. It wasn't difficult. She didn't realise until it was too late. And of course, she was perfect bait. Inevitably you were going to come looking for her and you did.'

'Where is she?'

'It doesn't matter.'

'It does matter,' screamed Noelie. 'Have you harmed her? Where is she?'

Keogh frowned. 'The strange thing is, Hannah has gifted Albert something that he was always after. The man paying for Egan's headstone. You know who I'm talking about, right Noelie? The mysterious benefactor, ready to shell out a tidy sum for that large cemetery plot? We know you looked into that too. His name is Irwin and he's coming to Cork tomorrow. Somehow Hannah managed to make contact with him. He thinks he's going to meet you and Hannah but we'll be waiting.'

Producing a second chain, Keogh untangled it and laid it along the sack. Noelie realised he had to keep Keogh talking. It was their only hope.

'You've been a rat for what, nearly forty years? Making friends, betraying friends.'

Keogh stared. 'I never wanted this,' he said coldly. 'In fact

I was trying to get away. I was born a Rosminian, didn't you know that? They raised me, schooled me and when I was just a teenager they offered me a place as a novitiate.'

'You were abused, I bet.'

Keogh dropped the chain and came over beside Noelie. He stood looking at him. 'By 1969 I had had enough. I was out of the order and had changed my name too. I took the name Keogh and I went to live in Belfast. Sure people knew I was a former priest but that hardly went against me. When the Troubles began I got involved in things in Belfast. I had to really. The Catholic community was taking a pounding. At first I just helped out. Then I was asked to join Sinn Féin. I did but I stayed out of the limelight. It suited me. I actually felt safe in Belfast and I would've stayed there if it had been up to me.'

Noelie laughed sarcastically. 'So you were reformed, is it? You expect me to believe that. Look, you abused boys at Danesfort. It's well known. You were a nasty bit of work. Leopards and their spots and all of that. Do you really think I believe you went to Belfast and were transformed. Fuck off.'

Albert had been standing unnoticed at the door. He had a blackthorn stick in his hand. Clearly he had heard the exchange. He came into the room.

'Father Brian had changed, even I saw that. He may well have stayed there in Belfast except something happened. He had to come back to Cork to help me. That's when everything changed, not just for me but for Father Brian too. My brother Robert abused the trust I had in him. It was Robert who created the mole, Brian Boru. Father Brian had no choice but to go along with that plan.'

It was strange hearing Albert refer to Keogh as Father Brian. Noelie wondered about the two men and the extent of the bond between them. In the double-8 film clip, Albert and Boran were young men, Boran only about eighteen. So were they brothers in crime or was there more to it?

Meabh had worked open a part of the body bag zip with her chin. She made muffled noises. Noticing her, Albert went over and punched her hard in the face. Meabh went still.

'You sadist,' roared Noelie.

Albert spoke to Keogh. 'Paul has gone to check on the boat. Don't waste any more time. Be ready.'

After he left, Noelie looked at Meabh. She wasn't moving and her face was covered in blood.

'Let me help her,' he pleaded.

Keogh shook his head.

'Why did he do that?'

'I was forced to return here to Cork to be Robert Donnelly's mole inside Sinn Féin. For a long time I was just that. But, after the hunger strikes, as the eighties progressed, Sinn Féin started to become a real force. I was the ace card that no one knew about. Inside Sinn Féin no one ever suspected anything. I was thoroughly enmeshed. I had been in the organisation from the beginning, from the early months of 1970 in Belfast when it was hell, and that stood to me. My value began to increase but that led to Phoenix Park taking more interest in me. Eventually control over me was wrested from Robert and formally moved to Dublin. That led to even more trouble between Albert and Robert. Branch were increasingly wary of Albert, that he would jeopardise everything, even my identity. Albert's one of a tiny number of people who know the full story.'

'Why didn't they just get rid of him? Isn't that what they do with complications? That's what they did with Jim Dalton.'

'Albert's too much of a danger.' Keogh shook his head, dismissing the idea. He continued, 'By the late eighties the first rumours of a possible peace deal were being mooted. They were keen to get any information that I could give them. Admittedly it was all low level but useful nonetheless – who was allied with whom inside Sinn Féin, what factions were on the rise, who had the initiative, that type of thing. In the years leading up to the peace process I was their eyes and ears inside the party. Think about it – that was a huge advantage and Branch appreciated it. MI5 too. Albert really was the only complication. He resented what had happened to me, what his brother had done. In turn Branch resented him. It's been an uneasy peace.'

Someone shouted from elsewhere in the house and Keogh left. Noelie immediately attempted to free himself but his hands were too tightly bound. He called to Meabh. He could see that she was breathing but she did not move.

Keogh returned with Big Ears. 'Your transport is here.'

'They say abusers never stop until they are made to stop. So where did you party all these years?'

It was the wrong thing to say. Keogh picked up the spare end of chain and whipped Noelie viciously across the shoulder until Big Ears restrained him. When Noelie finally looked up, Keogh hit him again. He felt dizzy and couldn't see for a moment. He heard Albert speaking.

'We'll take your friend first, Father Brian.'

Noelie watched Keogh pull the sofa aside and understood. 'Is Hannah here? Where's Hannah?'

Big Ears yanked Noelie by his hair. As he rose Noelie used the opportunity to lunge at him. The two men stumbled off balance past Keogh and crashed into the display cabinet. Shards of glass splintered around them. Noelie saw Albert standing over him. He hit Noelie with the blackthorn stick.

'Getting that Danesfort feeling, Albert?' shouted Noelie. 'Good to hit people, is it?'

Big Ears was injured. Blood poured from a cut on his wrist. Keogh examined it and fetched a towel. He pushed Noelie onto the sack. Noelie knew they had just one last chance.

'We found the film.'

Albert, Keogh and Big Ears immediately stopped what they were doing. It was like Noelie had fired a shotgun. Albert approached and hit him again, this time with the knob of the stick. Noelie's head went light. He tasted blood in his mouth. Spitting it out he managed to say, 'Keogh's in it. It was another of the items from Cronin's lock-ups. Your friends in Branch or army intelligence or whoever the fuck is protecting you have been wandering around Cork like headless chickens trying to locate the film clip but we have it now. It was Sugrue's trump card all along, right? Does double-8 film ring any bells, Albert? Bell & Howell cameras? One of your movies, Albert, I'm guessing. Shows you with a young boy, Keogh.'

The ex-journalist looked very unhappy. Albert reacted by pushing the point of the blackthorn stick into Noelie's neck and leaning on it. Noelie couldn't breathe and his head swam with pain. Keogh intervened and Noelie spluttered to regain his breath. He couldn't speak for a moment.

'Don't like hearing the truth, do you? Well, I can prove it. There's a picture of the Lakes of Killarney in the room and another of Croagh Patrick. Now do you remember? Was that the old homestead in Ballyvolane, Albert, the one you had razed to the ground? Was that where it all went on?'

Noelie saw they were rattled. He guessed that with all that had been going on that they hadn't actually considered that the film could turn up. Clearly they knew about it though. His only hope was to panic them even more. It could give them a chance to get away.

'You're done for, Keogh. It won't take much to identify that it was your old place either, Albert. By the way Walsh is in the clip and someone else too. The Anglia car, remember the red Anglia? The minute that film goes out the cops are going to have to act. They may not want to but they'll have to. It's scheduled to go on the internet later. It may even be up already. You really think we came down here without making any provisions? You think we're that thick? You sick bastards. The Provos will have a bullet in you, Keogh, faster than you can say Gerry Adams for taoiseach.'

Keogh and Albert left the room. Noelie could hear them talking in the hallway. He told Meabh to hold on. He hoped she could hear him. 'They're worried about the film. We may get a chance yet. If any opportunity comes, run for it. One of us must get out.'

Noelie tried to free himself again but he had to give up. He didn't know how his hands were tied but it was with something very strong. He attempted to wipe blood from his face with his shoulder. As he did, he saw the shape of a body on the floor over by the sofa. It was still and flat and was wrapped tightly in black plastic secured with duct tape.

Albert returned with Keogh.

'Is that Hannah?' shouted Noelie.

Keogh stooped. 'Where's the film, Noel?'

'You bastards – what have you done to her?'

'Paul?'

Big Ears' wrist was bandaged. He held pliers in his good hand. Albert took them. 'Where's the film?'

'Let Hannah go and I'll tell you.'

Keogh grabbed Noelie by the ear. 'We're not doing any deals. You'll tell us where the film is or I'll pull every nail from every finger on your hands. Then I'll pull them from every toe on your feet. And if you haven't talked by then I'll find something else to pull off or out. What about your eyes? Do you think you need those any more?'

Noelie swallowed.

'We'll take you apart bit by bit,' added Albert, 'and you will tell us. We have the time. You're all alone here with us, understand?'

Big Ears moved a chair alongside Noelie for Albert to sit on. He cut the restraints around Noelie's hands and forced his left hand onto Albert's lap. Albert immediately stabbed the tip of the long-nosed pliers under Noelie's smallest fingernail. Noelie screamed and fought back but Albert waited patiently until Noelie was subdued again by Big Ears. When Noelie finally looked at him, Albert wrenched the fingernail away. The pain was immediate and excruciating. Noelie half-stood, screaming. He was returned with force to a sitting position. Albert held the nail in the pliers' jaws in front of Noelie.

'Where's the film?' Albert asked calmly.

'Something's burning,' said Big Ears.

Albert looked surprised, Keogh too. But a moment later, they caught the smell of burning, and so did Noelie.

'Go and see, Paul,' instructed Albert.

Keogh took charge of restraining Noelie.

'Who has the film?'

Albert was pushing the pliers under the nail of Noelie's middle finger when the big window beside them shattered. Big Ears had just come back with news that there was a fire near the back door. The projectile that broke the window hit him directly in the face and he fell. It was half a concrete block. Another large item flew in, narrowly missing Keogh.

There was no doubting now that there was a fire in the house and that it was close too. Black smoke was billowing in from the hall.

Big Ears got to his feet and was struck by yet another missile. He staggered backwards and fell again. Keogh made his way out into the hall. Albert followed.

Noelie lay down. The pain in his hand was searing. He heard loud cracking noises and guessed the fire was taking hold. Keogh's seaside home was largely wooden and it would easily go up with all of them still in it. He tried to stand.

'Noelie?' he heard.

At the window, a coat was thrown over the shards of glass still in the frame. Black Gary poked his head in and looked

241

aghast. Noelie's face was bloodied and red. His hand looked like it had been through a mangle.

'Jesus Christ.'

'They have a chain around Meabh. It's locked. Help me get her out. Hurry.'

Black Gary moved quickly. He climbed in and freed Noelie's feet. There was smoke everywhere. As they lifted Meabh, Martin appeared at the window and they managed to transfer Meabh to him. Torchlight broke up the darkness outside and Noelie could hear voices. A woman appeared and helped Martin to carry Meabh.

Noelie ran over to the body wrapped in black plastic. The smoke was choking him. He tore away the plastic. It was Hannah.

'Oh Jesus,' he said. 'Let's get her out.'

Noelie and Black Gary lifted her through the window to Martin. Neighbours were milling about. Noelie looked back as he climbed out. Big Ears lay on the ground by the door. There was no sign of Albert or Keogh.

Outside, Noelie raced over to Hannah. One of the neighbours had a torch and was examining her. Hannah's sunken face stared back at them. 'No,' Noelie said. He ripped more plastic wrapping from around her. She was wearing the green cardigan and black jeans she'd had on when he last spoke with her at the *Voice*. All her jewellery had been removed.

The neighbour rechecked, looked at Noelie and shook her head.

'No,' he screamed. Black Gary was close by and tried to hold Noelie. He shook himself free. He put his arms around Hannah. She was lifeless.

'Not this,' he said. 'Please, not this.'

Song for a Poor Boy

39

Albert held Keogh by the shoulders.

'We need to go.'

They were in a narrow lane at the side of Keogh's house. The glow of the fire lit their faces. People were emerging along the road, from the nearby holiday estate and from other homes overlooking the sea. They could hear a siren.

Keogh didn't move. His face was blackened and his beard singed. He looked drained and defeated. He had fought the fire for as long as he was able but there was no hope now. A sudden sharp crack saw flames break through the roof and send a shower of sparks skywards.

A neighbour hurried towards them, calling out. Keogh didn't move. Albert turned and walked quickly along the lane as far as the junction with the main road. At the corner, there was a gap where steps descended to the shore below; he nearly fell. He was afraid. There was no handrail and little moonlight. He could hardly understand the sudden turnaround in their fortunes. He made his way down the steps slowly and carefully.

On the shore below he walked towards a flashlight that moved slowly from side to side. He could hear waves breaking. Two men approached. Both wore dark sailing jackets, trousers and baseball caps. Beyond them in the swell, a long rib floated. A man, silhouetted at the helm, was ably maintaining the boat's position. The transport intended to take Noelie, Meabh and Hannah to their deaths would now save Albert.

'What happened up there?'

Albert didn't answer. 'We must go immediately.'

'There's no one else?'

'No.'

There was hesitancy, Albert sensed it. Although it was nearly impossible to see the expressions on the faces, Albert knew these men well. They were conservative in manner and they avoided danger, but they understood self-preservation.

They moved to the water's edge. The rib nosed forward, retreated and nosed forward once again. The pilot was adept. Eventually, he held the rib steady and Albert and the others boarded.

Above, on the cliff, the fire brigade had arrived. The blue emergency lighting rotated eerily in the dark. Suddenly a powerful beam of light lit up the shore in front of them, momentarily panning over the rib. The light settled finally on the burning house, which was now shooting flames into the night. Other emergency vehicles arrived.

The engine on the rib accelerated. Reversing perfectly, the boat suddenly lurched and turned sharply, almost ditching Albert overboard. Repositioning himself he stared at the glow up on the cliff. Soon there would be nothing left of Keogh's place. One good thing anyway, Albert thought ruefully.

What was wrong with Keogh? More than anyone he had the most to fear by remaining. He could've come. With his connections Albert would've been able to get him away. But Albert had noticed a torpor about his friend of late. Keogh had confided to him only recently that he had come to believe that he would never be free of Special Branch. Repeatedly they had broken their promises to him. Albert wondered if this was the real source of his friend's malaise. Had he finally given up?

They passed outlying rock. The water was surprisingly calm. To the west there was a headland and the rib appeared to aim for the tip of this. But, in between, the outline of a sailing yacht at anchor was visible – their destination. Gaining speed the wind gusted in Albert's face and he calmed down. His fear vanished and, as often happened with him, the thrill of the escape turned him buoyant and optimistic.

He called out then above the din of the engine, 'Did you know I came to Ireland by boat? I was only two years of age. Across the Bay of Biscay. I remember it too. They say you cannot remember things at that age but the Lord Jesus blessed me with a good memory and I remember it all. I was happy although I didn't know that I was arriving in hell.'

The others in the rib made no comment. The man closest, sitting alongside Albert, didn't even look at him.

40

Noelie and Meabh were taken by garda escort to Cork University Hospital where they were checked and X-rayed – neither had any broken bones or fractures. The interlude at the hospital was a much-needed respite. Noelie was sore, angry and broken-hearted. Word had proceeded their arrival that they had been the victims of multiple assaults and that one of their number had died. They were treated sensitively. The hospital wanted them to stay overnight but they refused. Noelie knew that a confrontation with the gardaí was inevitable and he wanted to get it over with.

On discharge, they were met by detectives and brought to Anglesea Street Station. It was agreed that Meabh would accompany him and wait in the station's foyer. If Noelie was charged with any offence she'd call a lawyer immediately.

Cronin had been attacked in the early evening two days earlier. He had been beaten extensively over a number of hours. The direct cause of his death was a blow to the head. The murder weapon had been located – a metal poker – and it had Noelie's prints on it.

Simultaneously a car had been reported abandoned near the Lough, a suburb on Cork's southside. This was identified as Noelie's Astra. Blood on the driver's seat had been identified as Cronin's.

Noelie explained that the poker had disappeared from his flat during the break-in on the eve of Bonfire Night. He had left his car near the Cork City Gaol a couple of days earlier, shortly before he and Meabh called to see Albert at Llanes. He hadn't been back to retrieve it.

Inspector Lynch asked for more details but Noelie said that he didn't know anything more. He repeated that he'd had nothing to do with Cronin's death and added, 'We found the film.'

If Lynch knew what Noelie was referring to, he didn't let on. 'What does that mean?' he asked.

'Don Cronin's lock-ups in Dillon's Cross, ring any bells? Know what I'm talking about now?'

Lynch looked annoyed. 'Get something straight – I'm asking the questions around here.'

'There was something else besides the Sugrue statement,' continued Noelie. 'A home movie recorded by Albert Donnelly at the Donnelly farm in Ballyvolane some time in the early sixties. It shows boys being abused.'

Noelie stood up, startling Lynch.

'Sit down,' the inspector ordered. A uniformed garda immediately entered the room but Noelie was already over beside the internal window. He thumped the Plexiglas mirror, shouting, 'The people standing on the other side of this window know all about the film and this sordid business.'

Noelie was restrained and returned to his chair. Lynch eyeballed him. Pityingly he said, 'You've lost it.' He told the garda to leave again.

'Father Brian Boran, Tommy Keogh, know those names? Brian Boru? Earlier tonight Tommy Keogh confirmed to Meabh Sugrue and myself that he was and is a paid informant handled by Special Branch. He also confirmed that he's a member of Sinn Féin and has been since the early seventies. He admitted to being blackmailed and that he was forced to inform on the activities of the party, giving details about the inner working of the organisation. Boran's own story is sordid. As a Rosminian priest he abused boys at Danesfort.

He later moved to Newry, left the order and changed his name. In Belfast he got involved with Sinn Féin and has been associated with them since. Ring any bells now?'

Lynch only stared.

'Jim Dalton was at Danesfort Industrial School. He was abused there. Like other victims, he couldn't forget. A while before he disappeared he saw the man who abused him here in Cork. He couldn't understand it because he had heard that Father Boran was dead, that he had died in a fire in Belfast in 1971. In fact there is a record of a Father Boran dying in the North at that time. According to Keogh himself this was a smokescreen aimed at securing his new identity. Branch knew that it was possible that some of his victims would come looking for him. Jim Dalton was sure though. He did some digging of his own and eventually realised that the man that he had in his sights was his old abuser, Father Boran. So he went into a garda station here in Cork and filed a report. But what he didn't know was that the man he was making the complaint about, Tommy Keogh, also known as Father Boran, was working for Special Branch.' Noelie paused. 'In addition, for your information, this film also features the late Leslie Walsh, the property developer. You know him, don't you? You were at his month's mind; I saw you there.'

Lynch looked uncomfortable for the first time. 'If such a film exists and it's a record of a crime, it must be handed over to the gardaí immediately.'

Noelie laughed. 'So you can destroy it? We intended to hold a press conference in the morning. On the other hand if, as seems likely, I am to be charged with murdering Don Cronin, I think I'll ask Meabh to defer the event until I'm brought to trial. I'm fairly certain I'll be able to use the ensuing media circus to my advantage.'

There was a long silence. It seemed that Lynch was finally about to speak when a sudden rap on the door halted him. He went over. At the door he spoke to someone and left.

After a while Noelie went over to the door and opened it. He asked the uniformed garda outside if he could speak to Meabh. She was allowed in.

'You look bad.'

'You don't look too good either.'

They embraced. Noelie held on to Meabh. Although he had acted defiantly in front of Lynch he felt empty inside. Hannah was dead. Only anger and adrenalin were keeping him going.

'I've been thinking about what my father must've gone through.'

'Hell, I'd say.'

'Sitting on all of this, not knowing who to turn to or what to do. Afraid.'

'He must have known his life was in danger for some time.'

They sat. Occasionally other noises from the station intruded. Eventually Meabh moved nearer and whispered, 'Martin sent word that a copy has been safely put away.'

It took Noelie a moment to understand. He nodded. The film was now their insurance; it was everything.

He still didn't know yet how Martin and Black Gary had turned up in Crosshaven. He enquired if Meabh knew but she didn't. He remembered another thing.

'When we were at Keogh's, before all the trouble began, I saw you look at me strangely and then you suddenly wanted to go to the bathroom. What happened?'

'When Keogh's mobile rang, I saw the caller ID as I reached to get it for him. It said "Albert". Everything fell into place then. Before that, I had been looking at Keogh and it had crossed my mind that he looked a little like the guy in the Photofit. He was going on about my dad too, remember? I thought that that was quite weird. So when I saw the caller ID I knew. My idea was to go into the bathroom and phone for help but Keogh guessed I'd worked it out. He followed me. Albert and that other animal, Big Ears, were already there, waiting. They had just arrived.'

Lynch returned. He made no comment about Meabh's presence and sat down.

'The charges can be put on hold if you hand over all copies of the film.'

Noelie put his wrists together on the table. 'Let's go.'

Lynch held Noelie's stare.

Meabh spoke. 'My father was murdered to protect a child abuser. Let's not mince words, that's what he was. You aided and abetted the cover-up around Keogh and my father's death and now you dare, you fucking dare, to ask us to hand over the evidence that proves what was going on. I'd shoot myself first. Actually, if it was up to me, I'd speak out about this right now. I feel sick even knowing about what happened, about participating in any way in not bringing the entire matter into the public eye immediately.' She looked at Noelie. 'He feels the same. A child abuser and a murderer protected by you and your colleagues, for what?'

Lynch looked at them coldly. 'We're still investigating Don Cronin's murder. For now you're free to go. I would suggest, in respect to what happened at Church Bay, that you both need to make statements as soon as possible. I'd advise you to do it now or first thing in the morning. You can make appointments at the desk outside if you wish.'

Lynch collected his paperwork.

Noelie looked at Meabh and spoke again. 'Keogh told us that Dalton identified him. He saw him with Albert and realised that he was Father Boran from Danesfort. According to Keogh that was the reason why Jim Dalton was killed, to protect Keogh's identity.'

'I don't know anything about that.'

'We don't believe you.'

Lynch put his face close to Noelie's. 'I don't give a fuck what you believe.'

Noelie smiled. 'Well, let's see about that then. Jim Dalton's remains? I think you know where they are. You come up with them or their location or we'll publish the film. Do you understand what I am saying?'

Lynch looked at Meabh and at Noelie once more. He walked to the door. Noelie followed.

'You have forty-eight hours. Tell the Dalton family what they want to know or it's all out in the open.'

Meabh was standing over beside the internal window. 'I assume you heard that too,' she said to the mirrored glass.

Outside the station the streets were quiet; it was the early hours of the morning. Noelie and Meabh walked in the direction of Martin's place. Things had gone better than he'd hoped at the station. They had faced down Lynch and Branch and that was no small achievement. They had also taken the initiative with the ultimatum. Lynch had looked rattled. Yet Noelie only felt sadness. When they reached the south channel of the river, he stopped and began to cry.

'What have I done?'

Meabh stood beside him at the quayside railing. She saw him shudder and held him.

'You didn't cause this,' she said eventually. 'You must never believe you caused any of it. It's like me saying that I caused the attack on myself or that my dad brought about his own death.' She made Noelie look at her. 'Do you understand? It's not true.'

Her words made no difference. Noelie turned away and wiped his face with his good hand. He stared into the muddy river.

41

Black Gary and Martin were waiting for them at Martin's flat. Meabh hugged them immediately and Noelie did the same. Black Gary and Noelie held each other for a long time. They had been through a lot together. Black Gary was a survivor and in spite of everything he was still fighting. Now Noelie had some sense of what that had cost him.

'You saved our lives,' said Meabh.

Black Gary smiled. 'Our pleasure.'

While Martin put on tea they settled in the semi-dark in the cosy sitting room. Noelie felt a little better. In part it was the company but it was also because he felt safer.

Meabh gathered their phones, placed them in the bathroom and closed all the doors. Martin put David Gray on his sound system at a low volume.

Black Gary explained how they had come to be at Church Bay. As planned he had made contact with Martin. They had made a digital copy of the double-8 film and then dismantled the projector. Downstairs in the hotel foyer they were preparing to separate when Black Gary saw Albert.

'I hadn't seen him for forty years and yet there he was at reception. I realised immediately that his being there had to be connected to you two.'

'And,' added Martin, 'the guy with him was the one who called looking for you that evening you hid in the train tunnel. The one with the large ears.'

'We watched them. They were in no hurry until Albert took a phone call. Immediately after that they left. We decided to follow them.'

'If it hadn't been for you we were finished,' said Meabh.

'We weren't sure of where we were going down at Church Bay,' said Martin. 'I didn't realise that there's only one road into the area. We nearly collided with Albert in the dark. I hit reverse and we got out of there. We parked the car out along the road and returned on foot. That turned out to be handy later when we wanted to get away again. Anyway we looked around and eventually found Hannah's car. We knew we were in the right place then. But there were others there too, with Albert. A few men. They talked for a while and then these men left again.'

'Cops?' asked Noelie.

'Don't know,' replied Black Gary.

Martin shook his head. 'They looked too old. Okay, one was about fifty but another was easily in his mid-sixties. I don't think they were police.'

'We went in a circle to avoid being seen, going through a few gardens to get back to Keogh's place.'

'As soon as we saw Albert taking the pliers to you we knew we had to act. We set the fire to panic them, to panic everyone. We didn't plan on the whole house going up.'

'I'm not complaining,' said Meabh. 'Whoever threw the block through the window did a great job too.'

'That was me,' admitted Martin proudly.

Noelie nodded. 'Well, Big Ears copped it right in the face. I don't think he was thinking straight afterwards. Last time I saw him, he was lying on ground and it didn't look as if he was going anywhere.'

Noelie asked if anyone had heard anything since about where Albert or Keogh were. No one had.

'There was a report on the radio,' said Martin, 'about a major fire in the Crosshaven area that had resulted in a number of deaths. They interviewed a few people down there too. I think there was some fear that other houses close by could catch fire. Thank God they didn't.'

Noelie asked how they had fared with the gardaí. Black Gary described the chaos at Church Bay and around the inferno. 'We mingled with the neighbours and when the opportunity arose we slipped away. I didn't see any point in hanging about. We passed some cop cars on our return trip. I was paranoid we'd be stopped as I had the film on me the entire time. But we made it to town safely.'

Martin spoke. 'I went to an internet cafe and duplicated the good digital copy of the film. I uploaded one to Wikileaks and they confirmed receipt of the footage immediately. They said they'd hold it pending instructions. A second copy is in an online filing system I've access to. It'll be safe there for the moment.'

Black Gary produced the film reel. It was tightly wound, with a piece of Scotch tape holding the end in place.

Noelie and Meabh told Black Gary and Martin about what had happened at Keogh's place and what they had been told; it was information that was probably meant to go with them to the bottom of the ocean.

They now knew all about the conspiracy around the identity of Brian Boru and about the murder of Jim Dalton. They also knew that there had been serious conflict between Albert and Sean Sugrue inside Let There Be Light. Noelie wondered whether the organisation was more significant than they had realised.

Another interesting thing that they had found out was that Albert and Special Branch were at loggerheads. Albert wasn't trusted by Branch but he appeared to be untouchable also.

'The question is why,' said Noelie.

'There are few enough people that Special Branch are afraid of,' remarked Black Gary.

Noelie mentioned to the others about the odd comment that Keogh had made about the Rosminians. 'He claimed that his move to Belfast was his route out of the order and to freedom. The way he put it was that he had been "raised" by them, whatever that meant. But he didn't seem to like them either. I wonder was he abused too?'

'Keogh's story isn't that unusual,' said Black Gary. 'Some orders took children straight from the crib and raised them as their own. Particularly bright kids. But they were often preyed on just as much as any of the others. The odd thing is that these abused kids sometimes turned into abusers themselves.'

Meabh told them that before the rescue, while lying on the floor, she could hear what was being said to Noelie. She could also see Albert and Keogh's faces. 'When you mentioned the film, Noelie, it was like you had shot them.'

'Keogh probably knew that the film spelled the end for him. If they could get their hands on it, they were safe, but if it fell into the wrong hands then they were done for. At Anglesea Street Station it was the same,' Noelie added. 'One minute Lynch was talking to me like I was going down for Cronin's murder. The next it was "Oh, we're only gathering information, you're free to go if you like."'

He told the others about the ultimatum delivered to Lynch. 'I think it's the only way we'll get justice for the Daltons. If they do provide that information, it will verify what Sugrue's statement alleges. It will be proof.'

'And if they don't?' asked Meabh.

'We should publish anyway.'

Black Gary nodded. Martin too. Meabh looked less sure.

'What is it?' Black Gary asked her.

'I've been thinking, I suppose. If there are more people involved in this, who are they? Also, are there more films? If we publish now they'll go to ground. I'd prefer to gather more information quietly. I think we need to do that.' She went on. 'There's something else. What about the boys themselves, the victims? We need to think about them. We don't know

259

where they are now or how their lives are. We can't put a film like that on the web without trying to find them first.'

There was silence.

'Meabh's right,' said Black Gary.

'On both counts,' added Martin. We should proceed carefully. 'This is not straightforward.'

'I don't think we'll be publishing, Meabh,' said Noelie, 'I really don't. Branch won't want to risk an open viewing of the film. It's explosive material.'

'Don't get me wrong, by the way,' added Meabh. 'I want to publish but I think there's a right way and a wrong way to do it. There's a right time and a wrong time too.'

They agreed to keep an open mind until it got closer to the deadline. Finally they discussed how to protect the hard copy, and how they would keep a channel of communication open with Wikileaks.

Martin reckoned that from now on everything any of them did online would be scrutinised. 'I don't know much about encryption but I guess I had better learn the basics. We all had.'

They settled for the night on some mattresses on the floor. Noelie lay awake for a long while, unable to sleep. He thought about Hannah. She had worried about him staying safe but he hadn't been as vigilant about her. And he had underestimated the danger they were in, whereas she had been much more aware. He recalled their conversation in the car at Upton and how they had both acknowledged how close they had become. He felt they would've got together, that that was what they had both been saying in a roundabout way. It was too sad. He fell asleep with anger and sadness mixed up inside him.

42

Meabh went to get coffees while Noelie waited at the Arrivals gate. The *Echo* was carrying a full front page report of the fire: 'Bodies Found at Fire Scene'. The article described how a number of people had been rescued from the blaze at the cliff-side home. Two bodies had been recovered. One of the dead was understood to have been a victim of the fire, but the other death was believed to have taken place before the fire broke out. The owner of the house, retired journalist Tommy Keogh, had been observed leaving the scene of the fire in a disorientated state. The gardaí were working on the theory that he could have fallen and injured himself somewhere along the cliff face. A number of people were also helping the gardaí with their enquiries.

Noelie folded the newspaper. He watched a bleary-eyed man in his late thirties coming through the Arrivals gate. He was met by a gaggle of excited family members: parents, siblings and a recent newborn. Noelie heard Canada mentioned and guessed that the man was one of a wave of new Irish migrants that had gone over to those shores. An elderly man followed next. He had wispy, grey-white hair and a tanned face. He looked smart in cream trousers, black shoes and a dark olive shirt. Noelie approached him.

'James Irwin?'

'Noel Sullivan?'

Noelie offered his hand to the older man but Irwin drew back in shock. He stared at Noelie's battered, swollen face. There were tears in his eyes. 'I should've come forward sooner,' he said.

A young man was with Irwin. He had a head of bleached hair and a smattering of freckles on his cheeks and across his nose. He struggled with a large covered surfboard and the luggage.

'This is my bodyguard, my grandson Garret.'

Noelie had managed to get in touch with Irwin a few hours earlier, while he was on his layover at London Heathrow. They had had a long conversation and Noelie updated him on events and told him of Hannah's death. Although he didn't tell Irwin that Keogh and Albert had planned to meet and kill him, he did warn him that the situation could still be dangerous.

Noelie shook Garret's hand. He was no more than twenty. Meabh arrived at that moment with some coffees and Noelie introduced her to Irwin and his grandson. She didn't look in good shape either; the bruising on her face was just turning purple. Irwin kissed her gently.

'I owe you all so much,' he said. 'We all do.'

Irwin had booked a room at the Imperial Hotel in the centre of Cork. He told them that, back when he had worked in Cork – before he left for London – he had once made a delivery to the hotel.

'It's different,' he conceded, looking around.

Noelie figured The Imperial had been through a substantial renovation in the nineties when a restaurant was added to the downstairs area.

Irwin stood on the main stairwell. 'I think these stairs are the same.'

While Irwin and his grandson got settled, Noelie went to the bar with Meabh. She had decided to return to Amsterdam the next morning, providing there weren't any legal objections to her departure. When she told Noelie her plan he had jokingly said, 'Can I come too?' Her response was immediate.

'Why not? In a while, even next week, you should come.' Since the exchange, he had found himself thinking more and more about the idea. Getting away from Cork, even for a short while, was what he needed.

Earlier in the day, they had returned to Anglesea Street Station to make their statements. Byrne, the detective who had investigated Shane's death, had presented herself and suggested that she smooth the process and act as a liaison. Noelie was glad to see her and immediately agreed; they definitely needed an ally.

Byrne had some news about their case too. The gardaí had gone to Llanes in the early hours of the morning. There was no sign of Albert or Keogh at the house. Robert Donnelly was being cared for by a nurse who had informed the gardaí that she had been contracted over the phone to mind him shortly after midnight; she had been engaged in that way before and didn't suspect anything. Albert was not at Llanes when she got there.

The other information that Byrne had was confirmation that the second body found at Church Bay was that of an adult male. Noelie suspected that this was Big Ears. His identity wasn't yet known. Noelie told Byrne that he had heard him being addressed as Paul by both Keogh and Albert, if that was of any help.

Just after they finished making their statements, Hannah's mother arrived. She was a thin woman in her mid-sixties with the same dark-brown eyes as Hannah. After her husband died, she had returned to college as a mature student and got a degree in social studies. She was retired now but still worked in that area in a voluntary capacity.

She held Noelie for a long time. He understood that she was numbed by the terrible news. It was very difficult to look at her and see her pain. Noelie knew that mother and daughter were close. Hannah's brother lived and worked in Manchester and was still trying to get a flight to Cork. Noelie attempted to apologise but Hannah's mother would not entertain it; she did not blame him in any way.

She asked him to accompany her to the morgue and Noelie agreed. However, Hannah's brother then got in touch to say that his flight would get in at around noon and she decided to wait for him so that they could go together to make the formal identification. Noelie would meet them later at the apartment.

When Irwin had settled in he invited Noelie and Meabh up to his room. There was a table by the window and they all sat around it. Some tea and food had been ordered but it hadn't arrived yet.

Irwin took in the view. Cork's South Mall was a wide, tree-lined street long associated with the city's commercial and legal affairs. In Irwin's opinion it hadn't changed a great deal in the forty or so years since he was last in Cork.

A summer downpour brightened his mood. 'One of the things I miss in Australia is the rain.' He looked at an incredulous Noelie and laughed. 'I see you'd like me to begin.'

There were four of them, all ex-Danesfort boys. They had met in London. Two worked in the building trade – Michael Egan and Alan Copley – while Irwin had a job in London Transport as he had a decent Inter Certificate from his time at Danesfort. The fourth man, Peter Spitere, worked in Cricklewood as a barman. Irwin's dream was to eventually go to Australia or New Zealand. He was saving for that when disaster struck.

'When we got together we'd often talk about Danesfort and our time there. Therapy, I guess. Copley often talked about a boy at the school who went missing. A lot of us were loaned out to local farms to work for free. One of these arrangements was with the Donnelly place in an area called Ballyvolane.'

'We know it,' said Noelie.

'It was a harvest-time posting mostly. A bunch of us would be sent there in a lorry and we'd stay for a week or two at most. We were put up in outhouses.' Irwin paused. 'But there was another arrangement too. These visits lasted for an extended period and usually involved just one or maybe two boys at a time. Troublesome kids were often picked. It was seen as punishment and you were worked hard, day and night.' Irwin paused. 'This boy that Copley knew of had been one of those kids. He was from Youghal, as was Copley. It turned out that this boy's sister had heard about Copley and that he had been to Danesfort. She had made contact with him to ask about her little brother, if he could help with tracing him. There were rumours. One had it that the boy had run away. The Donnelly farm was big so it was easy enough to get out of view, if you wanted to. The story went that the kid had made good his escape, left Cork and never looked back. Another version claimed that Albert had caught him after he attempted to escape and had beaten him really badly as punishment. Some said the boy died from his injuries – which would explain why he was never seen again.'

'This was when, roughly?' asked Meabh.

'The boy's sister had been in an institution herself. So it was quite a bit later, 1967 or '68 or thereabouts that she was in contact. I think the boy went missing long before that, more like the early sixties. Not that long after the family was broken up by the courts. But I'm not certain.'

Meabh and Noelie exchanged looks.

'In 1970, Copley returned to Cork without telling the rest of us. Building work had been going on in an area not far from the Donnelly farm, on the edge of Cork. The Glen as it is known, I believe. Human bones had been found. Copley was on it like a hawk, suspicious immediately. Later he admitted that he had visited the Donnelly farm. Basically he broke in.

Albert had always been open enough about his movie camera interests. In those days it went everywhere with him. He filmed us at the farm and he regularly filmed events at Danesfort. Occasionally, if he was in good form, he would even arrange for us boys who went to the farm to view the films. All above board now. It was actually nice. Films were an incredible novelty back then.'

Irwin continued, telling them that Copley had stolen a few of Albert's films. 'He used to say later that it was just an opportunity presenting itself but Copley knew that Albert loved his films. In other words it was a way of sticking it to him. So he took some films at random. One turned out to be *féis* day at Danesfort. Another was of Cork. In one part, there was a motor car race out on the Straight Road, if that's still there?'

'It is but there hasn't been a speed car race on it for decades,' Noelie said.

Irwin looked out the window. The sunshine outside was bright on his face. However his mood had turned sombre.

'The third film was very different. Even now it makes me shiver. It showed a couple of young boys naked with a group of men. I remember a boy was crying.' Irwin hesitated. 'I'll never forget the helpless look on the little fellow's face.'

Meabh interrupted to tell Irwin about the film that they had found. Irwin nodded.

'We all got a right shock when we saw that film. There was a priest in it as well. The men were on the young side. Early twenties I'd guess. There was one elderly man. He could've been in his fifties. That's about all I remember.'

Noelie asked Irwin if he had ever heard rumours about goings-on at the Ballyvolane farm. Irwin shook his head.

'We weren't innocent, mind. We had made it in London the hard way. We weren't unaware of what went on. There was quite a scene around Paddington where vulnerable boys just off the boats or those in from the borstals were handed about and used. It was widely known that wealthy people were involved. But we were shocked at the same time. Holy Cork and all that.'

'What did you do?'

'For a while, nothing. We considered going to the police, in London that is, but realistically that wasn't going to happen. We didn't trust anyone in authority. I never have and I still don't.' Irwin's expression turned grim. 'When we finally did do something we made a big mistake.'

'How?'

'This was 1970 and the film was from early in the sixties. There were five or six men in that film alone. If we had stopped to think we might have realised that the film probably wasn't a one-off, that it was likely that there were more films and more people involved. And we didn't give a thought to the boy from Youghal who had disappeared. If we had thought about any of this, we might have realised that there could be quite a few people around Albert with lots to hide. None of that crossed our minds though.'

Meabh looked at Noelie once more. This was what they were thinking, that there could be a lot more to all of this. Noelie thought of Cronin's reference to 'that crowd'. Were these the people that he was alluding to?

'Copley got it into his head to blackmail Albert. I was against the plan from the beginning. I knew it was too dangerous. I should've objected more strongly. It might have saved all of us from what was to come.'

Irwin moved from the window. He lifted one of the complimentary bottles of water, opened it and took a drink.

'It was hard to stand up to the others. And there was the prospect of money. We viewed it as a type of compensation. When we were at Danesfort there was never any idea that one day we might be due something, even for all the work we did for free on those farms. So this was our due, we felt. Although that wasn't what motivated Copley. He just hated Albert. The idea that he could get at him was irresistible.'

'So you returned to Cork?'

'We came back with this half-worked-out plan to make Albert pay up.' Irwin shook his head bitterly. 'There had been other changes too though. Although the Donnelly place was still in Ballyvolane, the farm itself was in the process of being broken up. I found out later that some of it was rezoned as residential land and that they made quite a bit of money out of that. Albert was no longer farming. He had been taken on at a law office, just up the street from here in fact. So Copley and Spitere arranged to call in there to see him.'

Irwin looked upset and vulnerable. Noelie was about to suggest a break but Irwin continued, 'They were trying to take him by surprise but, looking back on it, Albert was ready. He understood the threat. He knew the film had gone missing and he knew what was on it too.'

Noelie got up now as well. The room was generous in size but it suddenly felt quite confined. He stood beside the bathroom door. 'Copley and Spitere went to visit Albert – what then?'

'I am the only one who survived.'

'What do you mean?'

'I mean I'm the only one of the four of us that is still alive.' Irwin sat down. He looked pale. 'Albert pretended to give in. He said, right, I'll pay up, how much? He explained that it would take a bit of time to get the money. Over the next few days, he prepared. Maybe we were followed. We were sleepwalking really. Copley even had the film with him when he met Albert, that's how naive we were.' Irwin shook his head in despair.

'The meeting was arranged near the Glen. In those days it was a real wilderness. Before we knew it Copley and Spitere were both dead. Albert had at least four others there with him that night. The reason I know this at all is that Egan was on lookout and saw what happened. He was very lucky to get away. If he hadn't got back to tell me I wouldn't be here now either.'

'Why didn't you go to the meeting?' asked Meabh.

'I was nominated as the backup person. Maybe because I was the least enthusiastic I stayed at the bed and breakfast, looked after our van. I don't think we even had a plan other than that though. When I heard what happened I just fell apart. Egan was completely distraught. He was hardly able to function. He had stayed out of view and saw everything. Copley and Spitere were bludgeoned to death. I mean, we never expected anything like that, to be met with that violence.'

Irwin continued, 'We abandoned our van and made our way back to London by a long, circuitous route. We were terrified. We hitched and got off the beaten track. It worked. Back in London we lay low for a long time. I was traumatised by what had happened, I'll tell you that. I decided also to advance my plans and go to Australia as soon as I had the money. I gave myself a month. Then Egan vanished. He literally vanished into thin air. I knew immediately I was in danger. I didn't even dare go to his place I was so scared.'

'How would they have found you in London?' asked Meabh.

'I have a theory. I don't believe in God. How could I, right, after seeing the carry-on at Danesfort? But Egan did. My feeling is that Egan was identified by a priest he knew in London. See Albert and his brothers were all Holy Joes, as you probably know. But there was more to it than that. They had connections. I think they put the word out and that was how Egan was located. He went to Mass regularly, silly man, and I believe that was how they found him.'

There was a very long silence. Meabh looked gravely at

Noelie; he didn't know what to say. It just made sense, that was all that he knew.

There were tears in Irwin's eyes. 'Egan was a great mate. I was very fond of him.'

Noelie asked if they should take a break but Irwin shook his head.

'It took me a day to make up my mind. I dropped everything. I was near King's Cross Station and I saw someone looking at me. I got a weird feeling. I don't know if I was imagining it or not, but I went right then and took all the money I had from the post office and left. I went to Glasgow. I holed up there for a while. I had a very good friend in the shipyards. He was in a working man's club there. They helped me. Got me new papers and a working passage on a ship for Melbourne. I wandered around out there for a good few years. I was sure they were still after me. I completely avoided the orbit of the Catholic Church. I was afraid of them, still am. They have reach, you know.'

Noelie nodded.

'Eventually I felt safer. New name, new identity, and I had to cut off all contact with home. I even avoided the Irish community. I re-made myself. Never told anyone about Danesfort other than my wife, in time. But I even made her swear never to mention it to anyone. I was thorough. I'd go to the library sometimes and look up the newspapers from home, but I never made contact with anyone or wrote to anyone to ask about Albert or any of that crew. I just felt it was too dangerous. I knew that if they knew I was still out there they'd come for me.'

'I worked in mining for a long time and then with AMWU, the Australian Mineworkers' Union. They sent me on various courses to help me. So I got in early on the internet thing and through that I was able to keep an eye on Albert and what he was up to. But I was careful. I always used aliases.'

Noelie explained to Meabh about Irwin and the self-destructing emails that he had used to arrange Egan's gravestone. 'I was shocked when I discovered that the Egan plot could take three coffins. I couldn't work it out but it would have been crystal clear to Albert.'

'I was getting my courage back, I suppose. It was deliberate, a warning to them. I'm older now and it bothers me more than ever that justice hasn't been done.'

Noelie told Irwin that it was Hannah's interest and persistence that led to the move to establish contact with him. 'She figured that something important was behind your reluctance to come forward.'

'She was right.'

The food arrived. It was on a trolley, mainly sandwiches and more tea. Irwin had also ordered cakes. Noelie didn't have much of an appetite. He took tea. After a while, Irwin continued.

'This is 2010. It's been nearly forty years since my friends were murdered. Those murders were never discovered and I went into hiding. There were four men there that night at the Glen and we know there were others, connected to the abuse that was going on at the Donnelly farm. I see it a lot more clearly now. We had acquired a film that had the potential to destroy the reputations and careers of some powerful men.'

Meabh spoke. 'That's exactly it. There's more at the back of this, I think. We don't know who these people are, what power they have or what links they have, but they're there.'

Irwin asked about Jim Dalton and his link to what had happened. Noelie explained about the mole Brian Boru. An unanswered question for Noelie was why Father Boran had returned to Cork in 1970. Albert had implied that it had been to help him. Noelie wondered now if it was to help deal with the threat posed by Irwin and friends? The timing was about right.

Noelie had a picture of Father Boran. He showed it to Irwin but he didn't recognise Boran. Noelie posed a different question. It had intrigued him from early on. 'What piqued your interest in recent events here in Cork?'

'Google's word alert.' Irwin smiled. 'I got to know of it in the early days, again via my union work. I had a bogus name and identity on the net and I set up a system with all the names I was interested in. Copley, Spitere, Egan, Albert Donnelly, and so on. Sometimes I'd get hits but it would often turn out to be someone somewhere else, in California or some place like that. I added overlapping alerts for the Glen, Ballyvolane, 'human remains', Danesfort. I had every permutation covered. One day the garda search in the Glen popped up. I couldn't believe it, I just couldn't. Garret will tell you I was on the computer day and night after that, to check if anything was coming up about it. I mean it could have been anything but I watched and followed. Then I read about the find and about the Daltons and their disappointment. I knew that it could be one of my missing friends.'

Noelie smiled. If there was any brightness in all that had happened, then it had arrived with Irwin and the possibility that he might find justice for his murdered friends. Noelie remarked about the quick ID that the gardaí had made on the remains found in Glen Park. 'Your hand too?'

Irwin nodded. 'I sent information to two places, to be sure. To the gardaí at Mayfield and to Red FM, the radio station. I didn't want it getting "lost". I also did something else that was smart, if I may say so myself. I had the address for the people that Egan was in digs with when we were all in London. Shirland Road, W9. The boy who was in that house when Egan was in digs subsequently became the owner of the house. He remembered Egan. His parents had gone to the cops at the time. They had actually kept a box with Egan's belongings in it. The gardaí were coming down with information in no time.'

'They must've been wondering.'

'They had no way of getting to me though. I had my tracks covered.'

Noelie liked Irwin and his wily tenacity. Hannah would have liked him too. He thought about her and suddenly had to excuse himself. In the bathroom with his back pushed against the door he broke down. She should be here with them all now. What would he do without her?

Irwin and Meabh were chatting quietly when Noelie returned. He had been telling her that he had made contact with a solicitor and was now intending to present himself at Anglesea Street Station the following day to make a full and complete statement about what had happened. He wasn't sure what would be made of such a report but he was now determined to have the murders recorded.

The meeting ended shortly afterwards. Irwin was planning to have a nap and then he wanted to walk around Cork to see how it had changed. Noelie would've been interested to accompany him but he felt they needed to press on. Down in the hotel foyer he said, 'Your mother knows more than she is admitting. I think it's time to pay her a visit.'

Meabh agreed immediately.

43

It was still bright when they reached Mitchelstown. Mrs Sugrue was in her garden at the gable end of the house, kneeling at a flowerbed. She looked up as they opened her gate then looked away. They stopped a short distance from where she was working. She ignored them.

'Can we talk?' Noelie asked.

'I don't want to talk.'

'Children were abused at the Donnelly farm in Ballyvolane. Boys were taken there and assaulted, the weakest, the most vulnerable children. We have proof, we have a film. It's the same film that your husband possessed at one time. It is probably why he was killed. You owe it to him to tell us what you know.'

Mrs Sugrue looked angry; she didn't acknowledge Meabh. 'I owe you nothing.'

She stood up, walked to the back of the house and went inside. At the door she attempted to stop Meabh following. Meabh barged through. Noelie followed.

'What's wrong with you?' shouted Meabh. 'Do you hear me? I'm your daughter, I'm yours ... Why did you never help me?'

Although Mrs Sugrue was standing defiantly on the other side of the kitchen table, she had turned pale.

Meabh shouted once more. 'Why did you never help me?'

'I tried to help, I did my best. I contacted Robert Donnelly. I told him and he listened. At this very table, here in this house. He came all the way here and I told him what you said had happened. He asked me not to let the matter go any further.'

'And you accepted that?' Meabh looked incredulous. 'He did nothing, don't you see?'

Mrs Sugrue didn't reply; she looked very uncomfortable.

Meabh moved closer. 'You make no sense. I'll never understand you.'

Mrs Sugrue appeared to wilt. She pulled out a chair and sat down.

'Did Robert Donnelly accept that something had happened?' Noelie asked.

'Llanes was his home. He lived there with Albert. He said that if an allegation of assault was made, it would ruin him.'

'Which was probably true,' said Noelie.

Meabh glared at him. 'Who gives a shit? Robert Donnelly can drop fucking dead for all I care. What about me?'

'There was more than you to think of, Meabh. There was this family and there was also your father's career. Everything was within Robert Donnelly's gift. You don't realise how it was.'

Meabh shook her head. 'No,' she admitted, beginning to cry. 'I don't.'

'The Donnellys are not what they seem. Albert isn't Robert's real brother. Officially he is. His birth certificate records that he is but he's not and he knows he's not.' Mrs Sugrue paused. 'The two of them never got on. It's a lot worse than that – there's hatred between them. I feel so bad for Robert now that he has ended up in that house under Albert's care. I'm sure Albert mistreats him.'

'Fuck him,' screamed Meabh. 'Do you hear me? Fuck him.'

Noelie went across to Meabh. He wanted her to hold back and allow her mother to talk. He figured that Mrs Sugrue knew quite a lot more than she had let on so far; he wanted to know what she knew.

But Meabh couldn't hold back. She was standing over her mother, crying. 'They matter more than me, is that it?'

There was no reply from her mother.

'Why is the relationship between Albert and Robert so important?' asked Noelie.

Mrs Sugrue looked at him. 'Robert was not his own man. By the time the incident with Meabh happened, he was–'

'It was not an "incident".'

Noelie felt sorry for Meabh. The description, he realised, probably reflected what Meabh's mother thought of what had happened to her daughter. He went to Meabh and tried to put his arm around her but she pushed him away.

'Robert was afraid of Albert. I didn't understand that until he came here that night. Sean had hinted at it a few times.'

Suddenly Meabh left. She turned, went out the back door and down the garden. Noelie saw her at the fence retching. He went out and got her to a garden seat. He explained that he wanted to go back inside and keep her mother talking. She nodded.

Inside Mrs Sugrue was still at the table. She looked miserable.

'Why would Robert Donnelly be afraid of Albert, Mrs Sugrue? It just doesn't make sense. Robert was a top policeman in the city. He wasn't without means.'

'I'm saying he begged me not to take my complaint further. I mean he really begged me. He believed Albert was trying to destroy him.' Mrs Sugrue paused. 'I believed him.'

'Was he physically afraid of Albert or was it something more? Was Albert blackmailing him?'

'If a child is abused it doesn't just stop when you say it should. It would've been a disaster.'

Noelie didn't understand what Mrs Sugrue meant. He waited and then asked, 'Had Robert Donnelly other things to hide? I know your husband was suspicious. Did something happen inside Let There Be Light?'

Mrs Sugrue wouldn't look up.

Noelie continued, 'I want to think the best of Robert

Donnelly. I want to believe that he didn't know that there was abuse going on but I'm beginning to wonder. See, we know there were other crimes. Some people found out that Albert had films showing abuse and they were killed. Did Robert Donnelly know about those crimes? Did he help cover them up too, to save his career maybe? It would make him an accessory to murder.'

Mrs Sugrue didn't react. She didn't look interested either.

'I'm asking again, Mrs Sugrue, did Robert Donnelly cover up crimes at the farm and was that what Albert had over him?'

Without looking at Noelie, Mrs Sugrue nodded.

'Albert had the means to destroy his brother, to destroy all of them, everything. Robert knew it and believed that Albert would carry it out too. Robert didn't want that. No one did. Let There Be Light has done good work. Everyone has put a lot into it.'

'Did you know about the films?'

'There were rumours. I had heard those.'

'Your husband had one of the films. It was part of the evidence he had accumulated, the evidence that got him killed. How did he get it in the first place?'

'Sean was a good man. One of the best. He didn't like Albert, never took to him and he was close to Robert. What happened to Meabh ...' Mrs Sugrue paused for a long moment. 'We had to keep it from Sean. I would never have told him, ever, but Meabh had to blab. Sean was bound to face up to the situation then. There was no other course open to him. But look where it led.' She spat her answer at Noelie. 'To his death.'

'You denied all this when I first came here.'

Mrs Sugrue stood. 'I've lived on my wits for years. I've had to live with lot of things that I've never wanted to have any hand, act or part in. I didn't want to help you either and I still don't.'

Noelie was angry but he didn't want to aggravate Mrs

Sugrue; he wanted to keep her talking. He asked about the Danesfort photo.

'Sean never brought work home. It was a rule with him, to protect us all he said. The night of Jim Dalton's murder was an exception. He was in turmoil afterwards. I remember it clearly. He told me everything that had happened at that house outside Mallow. He never spoke of it again after that night. Jim Dalton ranted in the car on the drive to Mallow. He spoke in Irish. Sean was a fluent speaker and so was Dalton. It passed over Lynch's head. Dalton talked about an abuser at Danesfort and finding him, and being punished for that. None of it made any sense to Sean but he listened and it stayed in his head. It was one of the things he told me that night when he arrived back here. But I knew about Danesfort. I told him about the Donnellys' links to the institution.'

Noelie was surprised. 'But how did you know about those?'

'Because I'm related to the Donnellys. I'm a cousin. Robert and Tony's mother, Clara Riordan, in other words Old Donnelly's wife, died in childbirth with their third child. The child died too. Albert came much later on. I don't know if you know this but Albert came from Spain. He was one of those orphans that they traded from there. It was a very secretive arrangement. I don't know the full story but I understand there is something about his origins.'

'Meaning?'

'He's a child of the war, of what can happen in war.' Mrs Sugrue looked away. 'My mother and Robert Donnelly's mother were first cousins. Robert was always good to me for that reason. It's why I'm close to him. It was partly why he minded Sean too. He looked out for Sean because he was looking out for me.' Mrs Sugrue hesitated. 'Old Donnelly never took to Albert. Robert said he was treated terribly as a child. One story was that Albert was gifted to Old Donnelly for him losing his leg in the war there, but Old Donnelly despised

Albert from the outset.' Mrs Sugrue shook her head. 'I never liked Old Donnelly. A nasty piece of work and a drunkard. Robert would say sometimes that he wasn't surprised by how Albert turned out.'

Noelie joined Mrs Sugrue at the window. Meabh was still sitting on the seat outside. A black cat had joined her and was sitting on her lap.

'So you put your husband on to Danesfort. Then in time he found the Danesfort photo at the Dalton house. He probably recognised Tony Donnelly in it and realised then that what Jim Dalton had told him in Irish was quite possibly true.'

Mrs Sugrue nodded. 'He was upset for a long time over the Jim Dalton matter but he let it go. I think he decided to accept it for what it was, just another of those horrible things that happened because of the Troubles. But when he learned about Meabh everything changed. I knew it would too. I knew he wouldn't let go after that. In a way I always knew how it was going to end.'

Mrs Sugrue met Noelie's stare. He understood then that she had known all along that her husband's death hadn't been an accident.

'The day that Sean died, that afternoon in fact, Special Branch came here. They went through everything and I mean everything. It was all Official Secrets Act with them and they claimed they had the right because of him being in Special Branch all those years. They took the whole lot. I have little of his now, other than photos, which they only returned to me after I complained and threatened to go to the newspapers.'

'But your husband was one step ahead of them. He had made provisions and arranged for the information to go to Don Cronin.'

'He trusted Don Cronin. I never did. He was a selfish, greedy man. But Don Cronin knew what to do. He was no one's fool. He kept the information out of circulation all this time.'

'Did you know what was in the file that your husband gave Don Cronin?'

'No, he wouldn't tell me but I knew it was going to cause him trouble.'

'When did you realise that your husband was steadily gathering evidence about what had been going on with Albert and Danesfort?'

'Not until we went that day to Garda HQ. He told me then. I had read between the lines though. Sean changed a lot near the end. He became secretive and obsessed. He was weighed down by what he had found out. And to add to his problems Robert's health had deteriorated much more rapidly than anyone had expected. When it became clear that Robert's days in the gardaí were numbered and that his illness was worsening, Sean found himself even more on his own. Robert passed some of the information to Sean, I believe, in an effort to right past wrongs. That's possibly how he got the film, but I don't know for sure.'

Noelie also wondered how the map of Egan's burial place had come into Sugrue's possession. Perhaps Robert had had it all along.

'Did you know about Brian Boru?'

'I heard the name mentioned but Sean was careful. There was information that could get you killed and knowing anything about Brian Boru was one of those bits of information. I knew nothing other than that a mole of substantial value existed.' Mrs Sugrue looked at Noelie. 'Our betters have covered up quite a lot to keep that bird singing.'

Noelie felt angry again. 'You could've helped me when I came here. My best friend was murdered.'

Mrs Sugrue looked at him angrily. 'I've done my bit. I paid with Sean's life. I loved Sean. He was everything to me. You don't understand what it meant for him to turn whistleblower. He didn't want to be one. He didn't want to bring shame down on anyone, in particular on Robert who he was close to and who had helped him so much. But in the end he had no choice. So don't lecture me about doing the right thing by you or by anyone.' She paused and looked at Noelie. 'You won't win, by the way. This sort of business destroys everyone and everything it comes into contact with. I knew it would bring us all down and it nearly has.'

'So you accept your husband was murdered?'

'I fooled myself for a while that he wasn't, but the evidence was everywhere.' She shrugged. 'An inquest was held. No one could explain how or why the car hit the wall at that speed. You know Sean didn't have his seatbelt on. Tony Donnelly did though. Yet Sean always wore his belt. Ask Meabh, he was obsessed with those sorts of things.' Mrs Sugrue sighed wearily. 'I had to make a decision. I could have kicked up a fuss but I knew also that I had to go on. I have Tomás, Meabh's brother, to look after. And things did turn around for Meabh, although she'd never admit to that. She went on to college. Our community rallied around me. I was offered help financially. If I was to rail at what had happened to my husband, where was it going it get me?'

'They bought you off.'

'Our family counts. Sean couldn't see that, he was so blinded by doing the right thing. He went to Garda HQ, the highest authority in the police force, and look where it got him. I've decided to turn the other cheek. Call it being bought off, if you like, but I'm still alive.'

On the return journey Meabh asked Noelie to stop outside Mitchelstown where there was a walk that she knew. It was a grassy stretch of riverbank. A passerby gave them a strange look and Noelie realised it was their faces. They both looked like they had gone fifteen rounds with Muhammad Ali.

Noelie watched the river current and remembered the cavern under Albert's garden, how close he had come to death. It was a bleak memory and he moved on quickly.

Meabh spoke. 'I'm glad I faced her.'

'It was the right thing to do. I understand her better now.'

'I never will.'

Noelie moved nearer and put his arm around Meabh. She leaned against him.

'Your father's a man to be proud of, Meabh. I'm not sure he would've been my cup of tea, being Branch and so on, but he stood up when he had to. He should be awarded a second Scott Medal, but I don't think that that will be happening any time soon.'

'He stood up only to be cut down.'

'That's how it is so often.'

She looked at Noelie. 'But you have to, you must stand up. I did and it's the reason I've survived.'

Noelie agreed and thought of Hannah. She had got involved to help Noelie and when it became clear that the situation was dangerous and she was putting herself at risk, she had stayed committed. She believed in doing the right thing, whatever the cost. A lot of people simply weren't like that. Hannah couldn't be any other way.

44

Meabh's confrontation with her mother reminded Noelie that he needed to see his sister. A lot had happened since he had last spoken to her. She would've heard about Church Bay and would know that what had happened there involved him. He needed to explain.

Meabh offered to accompany him but he felt it would be better if he went on his own.

'We're still in danger,' she reminded him. 'I know you have to go but come straight back to the hotel when you're done.'

Noelie said he would.

His brother-in-law answered the door. He made no comment about Noelie's appearance or about what had been in the news. He didn't ask him in, simply called loudly to Ellen that her brother was at the door and walked away. Noelie wondered how Arthur was coping with Shane's death. Maybe it was easier for him to stay angry with Noelie.

Ellen came along the hall. Noelie thought she looked a little better.

'Jesus,' she said. 'What happened to you? Come in.'

They went into the room immediately inside the front door. It was one of Noelie's favourites, bright with a high ceiling and a wide bay window. He sat on the edge of the sofa. At first Ellen stood then she sat too.

'I heard about Hannah. I'm so sorry.'

He met his sister's eyes. He saw her hesitate and then come over. He stood and she held him.

'She was such a lovely person and I know how close you were.'

Noelie nodded, struggling to maintain his composure. He put his head on Ellen's shoulder and she didn't move away; Ellen knew better than anyone how far back Noelie and Hannah went.

'Thank you,' he said.

'They said she was murdered.'

'Yes.'

Ellen grimaced and shook her head. Noelie sat again. 'I owe you an explanation. I want to tell you everything.'

He began at the beginning: finding the records, discovering the statement and the allegations about Jim Dalton's murder, and becoming entangled with Inspector Lynch and Special Branch. It took him nearly half an hour. When he finished, his sister stayed silent for a while.

'When I heard about the bomb in your flat, just after we argued, I knew then that whatever you had got involved in was a lot worse than anything I had imagined. I don't know where I got the idea but I thought you were involved in something to do with drugs or money-lenders or I don't know what.' Ellen paused. 'Byrne had told us a bit about the mole in the IRA story and how she had looked into that in relation to Shane's disappearance. I sort of came to my senses with the news of that bomb. I put two and two together, I suppose. Look, it's no excuse, but things like that are far removed from everyday life, from my life, I mean. I didn't realise it was so serious. Now I'm just glad you're safe.'

She continued, 'We're different, Noelie, and we need to accept that about each other. I need to accept it about you but you need to accept it about me too.'

Noelie nodded. He agreed. They had always been going in different directions. Ellen had never been interested in politics or history or anything like that; she couldn't get out of school fast enough. Noelie was the opposite.

Ellen wasn't finished. 'Part of the problem, a big part, has to do with what's gone on between you and Arthur. He's my husband and you're my only brother. Neither of you think about me in the middle. I need you to make an effort, Noelie – especially now. He's a good man, he's very kind, and I love him. What's happened has broken him, it really has.'

Noelie nodded again. Maybe it was the impact of the grief that he was feeling but he didn't want to cause anyone any more pain. He needed Ellen. If he was going to make that work, he had to get on better with Arthur.

'I'm sorry.' Hesitating, he added, 'I want to sort this out. I know it will take time, I understand that, but you're all the family I've got.'

Ellen nodded.

'Would you come to Hannah's funeral?' he asked. 'We don't know when it will be yet, there's an issue with the police investigation, but it would mean a lot to me.'

'Of course.'

He stood and they hugged once more.

'I miss Shane, Ellen. Coming here, knowing that he's not around any more. It's ... I'm so sorry.'

'I know that.'

45

Noelie slept on the floor of Meabh's room at the hotel. In the morning he walked her to the taxi rank near the bus station, a short distance away. It was bustling around there and he was reminded that life was going about its business as it always did.

There had been further news coverage of the events at Church Bay. Though there was still no mention of Keogh's connection to Special Branch or his unsavoury past, one report had linked what had happened to the murder of Don Cronin. As to where Albert or Keogh were, there was no word yet.

Overnight and during breakfast Meabh had been quiet and withdrawn. Noelie put it down to her confrontation with her mother. Mrs Sugrue was a formidable woman, more stubborn and firmer in her convictions than Noelie had realised. Clearly she knew a lot more than she was saying and even now, with all that had emerged, he couldn't say with certainty where her allegiance lay; certainly it was not with her daughter.

Noelie had also been in contact with the Daltons. After seeing his sister the previous evening, he had visited Mrs Dalton. He told her about what had happened, about what they learned about Keogh and about what could've happened to her husband. Not surprisingly Ethel Dalton had become upset. Noelie was glad to be able to tell her about the ultimatum he had put to Branch – to produce information on the location of her husband's body within forty-eight hours or else. He asked her to let them know immediately if she heard anything.

They found a taxi. After hugging tightly, Meabh reminded Noelie about Amsterdam. He reassured her he would visit and thanked her again for all that she had done.

'Nearly getting you killed, you mean?'

'Then saving my life.'

They both laughed.

'We'll call it quits so.'

Noelie shook his head. Half-serious, half-laughing, he said, 'For me it will never be like that. I'm bound to you forever now. Isn't that what they say about anyone who saves your life?'

Meabh got in the taxi. 'We'll see.'

He went from the taxi rank to Hannah's. Her mother and her brother were there. Eoghan was married with a family in Manchester and, from what Hannah had told Noelie, he was strapped down by a big mortgage. He was obviously shaken. He asked Noelie to explain the background to Hannah's murder so Noelie told him the whole story. He pointed out that Hannah had made the link with Irwin in Australia, and how important that development was to understanding the criminal nature of what had been going on over decades.

It was good for Noelie to retell Irwin's story. In going over it again, he gained a better appreciation of how poisonous the conspiracy was. The accounts of abuse relating to Danesfort also better explained the violence that had been meted out to Irwin's friends and, in due course, to Hannah. Noelie reiterated his view that the single biggest miscalculation they had made was in underestimating how dangerous Albert and Keogh were.

The family had received more details about Hannah's death. She had been strangled and had been dead for approximately twelve hours by the time her body was recovered from the fire scene. CCTV footage showed her meeting one person at the train station; he had since been identified as Keogh. The pair had left the station together and that was the last sighting of them. Gathering further evidence, including forensics, was complicated by the fire at Church Bay which had destroyed the contents of the house. The investigation was ongoing.

Hannah would be buried in Kenmare, the family's home town. No date could be set until the body was released by the gardaí and for the moment there was no indication as to when that might be; it could be a week to a fortnight at least. The family would keep Noelie posted.

They weren't sure about what to do with Hannah's place. Noelie was invited to stay on until something was decided. From a practical point of view he had nowhere else to go, but the flat was full of memories. He remembered that he had come to view it with Hannah, way back when she had first considered buying it. He agreed to stay there for the moment.

Around lunchtime he got a call from Detective Byrne. There had been a development and she figured Noelie would want to come with her to see it for himself.

She picked him up in an unmarked car. She offered her condolences and asked after Hannah's family. After a while, she enquired if Noelie and Hannah were an item and he explained that they weren't but that they were very close friends.

They drove in the direction of Ballyvolane and Noelie wondered if Byrne's news was to do with Glen Park. However they carried on beyond it and into open countryside. He noticed the fancy computer communications system on the police car's dash. Although the tablet-sized screen was tilted out of his view, he saw text flickering down the screen and was reminded of Special Branch and of how long they been watching him and Hannah.

At Church Bay, Keogh had confirmed that Branch were behind the pipe bomb thrown into his Douglas Street flat. At first Noelie had assumed that the same group of people were also down at Church Bay helping Keogh and Albert. Now he realised that that probably wasn't the case. Their age, for one, suggested that they weren't police. There was also the revelation that Albert and Branch were at loggerheads. For the first time Noelie was coming to appreciate that they had been facing two distinct opponents all along. Evidently these two groups had interests in common – in the main around managing the Keogh/Father Boran identity – but they had separate agendas too.

Branch wanted to retrieve the double-8 film because it was part of their means of controlling Keogh. Albert wanted the film because its publication would expose the abuse at the Donnelly farmstead and Danesfort.

There was an important unanswered question though: what was the overlap between the groups? Was it just tactical or was there someone in both camps, someone high up in the Irish intelligence service whose real allegiance was to Albert and his group? Noelie thought about the other unidentified figure in the film, the third man. Who was he and where was he now? Noelie didn't know the answers to these questions but he was sure that information – regular, accurate and up-to-date – had been passed to Albert and his group about what Noelie and the others had been doing. The question was, who was channelling this information to Albert?

Near Whitechurch, Byrne stopped the car suddenly at a division in the road. After consulting a map she took a left along a narrow slip road that eventually led into a builder's quarry. It was desolate.

'Getting rid of me too?'

The detective feigned shock. 'Really, Noelie.' Suddenly smiling, she nodded to the rear. 'I almost forgot, on the back seat, take a look. There's a folder.'

Noelie retrieved it. The name on the front read *Paul Cavanagh a.k.a. Andrew Teland*. Prominent inside was a photo of the man they knew as Big Ears. He was wearing a priest's dog collar. Born in 1963 in Terra Haute, Indiana, he later attended seminary college at the University of Saint Mary of the Lake in Chicago. Later again, he served in the archdioceses of Chicago, Baltimore and Boston before being laicised in 1997 following a conviction for sexual assault on a minor. Approximate date of arrival in Ireland: 1999. According to the file, Teland was still wanted on charges in the States. A copy of a US warrant was with the file.

Byrne spoke. 'What do you make of that?'

'Albert was looking after him, giving him protection?'

'That's how it seems.'

Noelie thought about this. 'Was it known that Teland was here in Cork?'

'It's not clear. That's being looked into, but I've a feeling it wasn't known.'

They reached a wide, open yard. There were some locals standing around. Two garda cars had made a checkpoint but Byrne and Noelie were allowed through. Byrne stopped near two plain-clothes officers and rolled down her window. She spoke to a detective who looked Noelie over. He cut quite a sight, he knew, with his bruised face and stitches. The swelling on his face had gone down a little but he was now various shades of black and blue.

They got out and walked a short distance to an excavated area. There was a heap of gravel that was overrun with weeds. Noelie saw two people in dust suits. One checked that they had permission to continue. They were given the go-ahead. Noelie saw a body lying on the ground; it was covered. Byrne approached and squatted. He followed. She pulled the sheet back and Keogh's dead eyes looked at them. He was staring sideways like something had caught his attention at the last moment. There was a single bullet hole in his forehead and a rat jammed into his mouth. Noelie had never seen someone who had been shot at close range before. The bullet hole was neat. Some blood had crusted on the wound's perimeter. The rat had been stuffed in tail first so that that its head and bared teeth faced them. It was an ugly sight.

'Found this morning. Forensics reckon he's been dead five hours or so.'

'So in the early hours.'

She nodded. 'They lost no time.'

Noelie stared at the corpse. He had very mixed feelings. He knew Keogh would've killed him and Meabh. He also knew that he had killed Hannah. As if that was not enough he was also an abuser. Yet this end didn't feel satisfactory.

'The Provos are crude.'

'You're sure it was them?'

Byrne looked at Noelie. 'This is their trademark treatment for informants and touts.'

'Except that anyone could've done that.'

She shrugged. 'I guess.'

Noelie caught a whiff of urine and wondered if it was from the corpse. He looked around. It was bleak and isolated, not the sort of place he would fancy being dragged to in the middle of the night. As an informer, Keogh must have known that this was how things might end for him. Thinking about it, Noelie reckoned that Keogh must've lived with this outcome as a real prospect for quite a long time. One word in the wrong ear and it was always going to be over for him. And yet he had come across as calm. On the two occasions they met Noelie recalled a relaxed figure, someone sure of himself. Had he made peace with his role or was it that he was aware of his value and the protection that it afforded him? On reflection Noelie could acknowledge what a huge asset Keogh was. Having a reliable informant inside Sinn

Féin over the decades must have been invaluable. Keogh was intelligent too and above suspicion. With the remit that he had, he would've been able to glean a significant amount of useful information about the inner workings of the party and its relationship with the IRA over a very long time. When austerity hit, his position within the party would have been even more useful. There was real concern in some quarters about any Sinn Féin involvement in the government in the South. Their occasional flirtation with Marxist ideas made them the ultimate ogre in some quarters, particularly with a section of conservative Ireland, which for the most part kept itself out of public view.

A garda came towards them. He was clearly an officer even though he was kitted out in tactical garda wear. Byrne stood to say hello and introduced Noelie to Superintendent Kenny. Noelie shook the cop's hand. He was younger than Noelie and had that emaciated appearance that distance runners often have. He enquired about Noelie's injuries and how Meabh was.

Noelie put out his injured hand. 'I always wanted a good manicure,' he said. No one smiled.

Kenny asked if he could have a private word with Noelie.

'I'll wait in the car,' said Byrne.

He walked away and Noelie followed him past a mound of bitumen into a section of yard where a rusting silo was leaning precariously to one side. Turning eventually he faced Noelie.

'It will come out tonight or tomorrow about Father Boran and the Keogh identity. With what's happened, with this execution, it has become possible. We want to draw a line under this entire affair. Senior garda management are shocked by what they have learned. As long as Keogh was alive, it wasn't possible to fully investigate this entire business but now that's going to happen. If anyone has hidden evidence of any crimes or obstructed justice you can be assured they will be held to account.'

He told Noelie that he had also just been apprised of the statement made by James Irwin alleging the murder of three men in the Glen Park area in 1970. It was his intention to appoint an investigating officer to examine all aspects of these claims and to establish if there were links between those events and the matter of Father Boran's identity.

'Mr Irwin is of the view that Albert Donnelly is at the centre of this. We are also concerned about the presence of Mr Teland at the Donnelly property over a number of years. Everything will now be investigated, which leads me on to what I want to ask you. We'd like to view the film you claim to have. Even if you don't want to hand over the original at least allow us to see a copy.'

Noelie wasn't surprised by the request. Decision time was fast approaching and Branch needed to work out their exposure. It was likely that they hadn't seen the film in decades. It could well have been edited or even altered in the interim. They needed to know what they should be afraid of.

Refusing to cooperate could be dangerous. Noelie could be done for obstruction of justice and he was in plenty of trouble already. There was only one other option.

'There's just the one copy now and that's with Wikileaks,' he lied. 'I couldn't retrieve it for you even if I wanted to. See, we entered into a contract with Wikileaks to the effect that they would hold a copy until we instructed them to make it public.' He frowned. 'I imagine you have been informed of other developments. We have instructed Wikileaks to publish the film in its entirely tonight at 2 a.m. unless the Dalton family are informed where Jim Dalton's remains are.'

'What have Jim Dalton's remains to do with this?' Kenny asked coldly. 'We are looking into crimes that took place in the sixties. That is what we're investigating. We need to view the film.'

'It's out of my hands,' said Noelie shrugging again. 'I'd love

293

to help but I can't. On the other hand, if as you say Jim Dalton has nothing whatsoever to do with all of this, then you'll be able to see the film tonight anyway at 2 a.m. Along with the entire world.'

Kenny's stare was icy. 'This is a criminal matter and you are deliberately compromising the investigation. I repeat: I'd like to see the film.'

A garda jeep entered the yard and turned noisily on the gravel. Noelie was glad of the interruption and watched the vehicle. Eventually he looked at Kenny again.

'I think you need to understand something. I'd like to help and I'll try to but the truth is I don't trust the gardaí. Whether it was officially sanctioned or the work of some rogue element, members of your organisation engaged in a criminal cover-up and also killed to cover up their cover-up.' Noelie hesitated. There was a lump in his throat and his anger over Hannah was raw. 'My best friend was murdered. Now I know for a fact that we were being watched from around Bonfire Night onwards by a part of the intelligence community. Meanwhile, Hannah was entrapped into attending a bogus meeting using a manufactured Facebook identity. I believe it was known by the security services that she was going to her death that day. People in your organisation allowed her to be killed.'

Kenny's expression didn't change. He took a cap from his back pocket and unfolded it slowly and meticulously. 'I was warned about your mindset, Mr Sullivan. It will be your downfall.'

Kenny walked away and Noelie watched him go. Sometimes when you said things out loud, they became more real and that had just happened for Noelie He realised now that he would most likely never get justice for Hannah and that those who had sat back as she went to meet her murderer, who had perhaps facilitated all of that, would never be called to account. These people were protected and beyond reach.

That didn't mean he wouldn't try, that he wouldn't cause as much trouble as possible. No way he would ever forget what had happened to Hannah.

At the car, Noelie found Byrne leaning against the bonnet, taking in the sunshine.

'So how was that for you?'

'We're no longer drinking buddies.'

Byrne smiled. 'A word of advice: don't underestimate him. He's a former Ranger, the new breed.'

Noelie was surprised to hear of Kenny's pedigree. The Rangers were the elite army counter-terrorist unit.

'It's a new initiative. The force is stagnating – or haven't you heard? The word cross-fertilisation has been used. And no funny jokes about that please. Back to Cork?'

'If you don't mind.'

They chatted on the return journey. Byrne told Noelie that there were still no leads regarding Albert's whereabouts. Interpol had been alerted to look for him. In his statement Noelie had mentioned the threat to take their bodies out to sea on the night of the confrontation at Church Bay. Byrne said they had looked into this but so far they hadn't been able to identify any vessels in the area that had been acting suspiciously. Noelie wondered. Keogh had implied that there was something untouchable about Albert. How much of an effort was really being made?

As they arrived back in Cork, the detective mentioned that Inspector Lynch was taking early retirement.

'Nice. Hauling a fine fat bonus with him too, no doubt.'

Byrne nodded. 'Correct. With the austerity squeeze, there are lucrative packages on offer, particularly to senior level officers. Considering that his stock has also fallen, it's a good outcome for all concerned.'

'At the last place I worked they liked to use the term a "win-win" situation a lot. Is that what we're talking about?'

'In one.'

'Is it any wonder I'm so cynical?'

'So the new man is Kenny. He'll be deciding how the Cronin case is pursued and if they're going to go after you too. So I hope you haven't pissed him off already.'

Noelie laughed. 'They won't be going after me. Over Cronin? The Keystone Cops would've done better. The entire business reeks of a fit-up.'

'Except the Director of Public Prosecutions may not see it like that. There's the poker and there are forensics from your car too. That's evidence.' Byrne pulled in on Washington Street. 'I'm not trying to bother you, Noel. Just be careful is all.'

He nodded. 'Speaking of unsolved crimes. My punk records were stolen again. Last week. I guess I should put that in the pot too and make a new report.'

Byrne smiled. 'Touché.'

46

Albert was sitting on a bench under some bougainvillea in the monastery at Čapljina in Bosnia-Herzegovina. Travelling as Father James Burke, he had crossed the border into Northern Ireland and flown from Belfast to Stansted and onto Dubrovnik where he was collected and allocated a room at the retreat.

He had been helping in the garden when he was handed the note with the short account of Father Brian's death. Tears came to his eyes. It was a sad end to their long and arduous journey together.

The messenger had not stayed as there was a practice of silence and solitude at the monastery during daylight hours. Albert kneeled, put the piece of paper in his pocket and said the 'Our Father'. Afterwards he went over to the central fountain around which the quadrants of the garden were arranged. It was peaceful.

They used to say about each other that they were chosen men. Born into institutions, uncertain of their origins, they had both been singled out for special treatment.

It took them a while to appreciate their similarities; in particular how isolated each of them was. In time they became very close and came to see themselves as siblings of a special type.

They met when Father Brian was in his first year as a novitiate; he was seventeen then and Albert twenty-one; the year was 1959. Father Brian had come to the Ballyvolane farm with Albert's oldest brother, Father Tony. By then Tony was a rising figure at Danesfort. He had seen the opportunity of free labour for the family farm at Ballyvolane; it was struggling because of Old Donnelly's alcoholism.

That first meeting with Father Brian happened at a particularly important time for Albert. He was finally taking the lead at the farm and was being viewed by his brothers – Tony and Robert – as the one most likely to carry on the family's farming tradition. Long denied legitimacy by Old Donnelly, this role brought him a measure of acceptance. But he harboured only hate and anger for Old Donnelly and for his brothers who had watched his ritual humiliation over many years and who had done nothing to help him.

Father Brian was an elegant, striking young man whose physical beauty was often remarked upon. An abandoned baby, he had been placed into the care of the Rosminians and offered the advantage of a special education. He was held up as an example of a soul whom the Rosminians had rescued from a debauched sinful parentage. He was being transformed and would in time become an officer in God's army, charged with doing his good works around the world.

It was a narrative familiar to Albert. In Spain, at the moment of his birth, he had become the property of a religious organisation, Deum Fidem, which believed that the worst sins of heathenism could only be extinguished by a strict Catholic upbringing. Albert was given to Old Donnelly to be his third son, to be turned into a faithful Catholic. But it hadn't worked out that way.

One day he found Father Brian in one of the outlying sheds at the Donnelly farm with one of the Danesfort boys. Albert had already formed a bond with Father Brian. He liked him and understood him. He saw in Father Brian's situation a way out of his loneliness. He would protect the young novitiate. The remote farmstead was perfect and Albert would be in charge one day.

Now it was over. Albert did not want to dwell on Father Brian's end. He had been expecting such an outcome and knew it was inevitable. He felt empty inside, a feeling that he was unfamiliar and uncomfortable with. He had escaped and he was happy at the monastery – a lot happier than he ever expected to be; it was perfect in many ways – but he was finding it difficult not to do battle with the mistakes he had made; with the threat that Sullivan and the Sugrue woman represented. Over the years he had learnt to be meticulous, dedicated and ruthless. It was an approach that had brought peace and calm to everyone; to himself too. Now this had happened. The future was no longer under his control. He had let everyone down. Perhaps he was weakening? Perhaps it was age or arrogance? These thoughts unsettled him even more.

It was peaceful here, the fountain of water calming. Then he heard a voice, quoting the apostle Paul. It was unmistakably Father Brian, clear and distinct. 'In my flesh, I am filling up what is lacking in the afflictions of Christ on behalf of his body, which is the church.' Albert and Father Brian had argued many times about those words, about their precise meaning, on those occasions when they had walked together around the Lough in Cork. It had been claimed by some that Paul was being heretical by suggesting that his suffering was equal to that of Jesus; he was at the time a prisoner of the Romans and drained of hope. But Father Brian never agreed with that interpretation. He believed that the apostle was coming to an understanding that persecution and misery could be the greatest offering to God. It was salvific and would lead to renewal.

It was clear then to Albert; he was being offered guidance. He put his hands in the fountain's cold water and drew them up to his face. It felt good. They were not finished: Father Brian had left this earth but he had not left Albert. He spoke then, in reply, into the bright sunshine, in bold defiance of the monastery rule, 'I am the good shepherd: the good shepherd giveth his life for the sheep.'

47

There was no one at Hannah's apartment. Noelie went over to the sofa and sat down, his eyes falling on a large wall print that Hannah had brought back from one of her trips to Australia. It was of a sunset at Kakadu National Park in the Northern Territory.

Noelie didn't know what he was going to do. A couple of months ago he had been struggling with boredom and where he was going in his life. Should he emigrate again? What could he work at? Hannah had planted the idea of going back to college. He had been thinking about it.

These were real worries but now they felt insignificant. He had become caught up in something so dark and serious that it had led to the death of his best friend. It was no surprise that terrible things had gone on in the past. Every other year there was some new revelation. If it wasn't to do with a particular Catholic diocese, it was about a mother and baby home or a Magdalene Laundry. But he had never expected to end up at the centre of something that was so ugly. He had uncovered a number of serious crimes that had damaged the lives of lots of people, including his. He just couldn't walk away.

He decided to get out of the apartment for a while. Walking along Washington Street, in the direction of the university, he veered right at the main campus gates and went towards the river and Fitzgerald Park. Passing the bust of Michael Collins he finally arrived at the river, which was at full tide. He sat on the riverbank. Llanes was just across the way.

He understood a lot more now: there were two crimes not one. The first centred around the identity of Brian Boru and initially involved Robert Donnelly. Later on, Special Branch with the assistance of other arms of Irish intelligence and, quite possibly, Britain's MI5 had taken control of the mole. In exchange for turning informer and giving information on the inner workings of Sinn Féin, Father Boran's past crimes were covered up; Boran was also given protection and a new identity as Keogh. As Tommy Keogh, Boran had evolved into a highly valued informer. Over almost four decades his handlers did everything possible to keep his identity a secret. Dalton, Sugrue, Hannah and Cronin had all been killed because of him.

Noelie believed that Keogh's execution was the result of Branch's assessment that his role as an informer was no longer viable; it was safer to close him down. An orderly retreat from the entire mess was now underway; this would be managed and choreographed with the able assistance of the usual sources in the media.

The second set of crimes centred around the organised abuse of boys at the Donnelly farm. It wasn't clear for how long this activity had gone on, nor was it clear who and how many men were involved. In fact the only proof that these crimes had taken place at all was the double-8 film that they had found. They were living at a time when more and more victims of historic abuse crimes were coming forward, but no one had come forward about the Donnelly farm.

The pivotal event linking the two sets of crimes was probably the murder of Spitere, Copley and Egan. Noelie surmised that Robert Donnelly had learned about those killings and, calculating that the furore over the murders and what they were about – the existence of a ring of abusers operating around the Donnelly farm – would destroy his career in the gardaí, had decided to assist with the covering up of those crimes. He saw the potential to use Keogh as an informer and demanded that Albert give him one or more of the films that he had made of the gatherings at Ballyvolane to secure Keogh's agreement.

Father Boran's transformation into Brian Boru had paid off handsomely for Robert Donnelly until Special Branch moved in to transfer control of the mole to Garda Headquarters in Dublin. For reasons not fully clear to Noelie, this change upset the uneasy balance at Llanes, reigniting the conflict between Robert and Albert.

Don Cronin's involvement and untimely death now made more sense. Noelie figured that Cronin could well have been one of the few people not directly involved in the conspiracy who knew its full extent and the degree of criminality involved. With Sugrue's death in 1998, he was handed the poisoned chalice that was the Brian Boru file. He had probably worked out that its contents were far too incendiary to reveal. On the other hand if he held onto the information and hid it securely, it was capable of buying him long-term protection – the route he eventually took until his dispute with Ajax Dineen.

Noelie's accidental discovery of part of the Brian Boru file changed everything for Cronin. With the publication of the Sugrue statement, it became clear to all the interested parties that Cronin had had the Brian Boru file since Sugrue's death in 1998. Branch probably felt that they had scored a significant success when they recovered most of the file following their raid of the lock-ups, but their celebrations would have been cut short when they realised that a key item in the file, the double-8 film, was still missing. When it emerged that Noelie hadn't the film either, attention switched back to Cronin.

Noelie wasn't sure who had murdered Cronin. Branch had motive, means and opportunity. However the murder weapon – Noelie's poker – had probably been stolen from Noelie's flat during the break-in on the afternoon before Bonfire Night.

That break-in was almost certainly the work of Albert and Big Ears, suggesting to Noelie that Albert had been an active agent throughout the period that Noelie and Hannah were looking at Dalton's disappearance.

For Noelie, Sugrue shone brightly, despite his wacky beliefs. As a committed Branch operative he had undoubtedly signed off on many unsavoury activities during the Troubles, but the murder of an ordinary citizen was unacceptable to him, as was the idea of protecting child abusers. Noelie didn't know if Sugrue had worked out the extent of what had been going on at the Ballyvolane farm but he had certainly figured out enough to know that he had to act. To his credit Sugrue probably understood the danger involved in challenging the garda hierarchy and its intelligence wing.

Tony Donnelly's role and motivation was still something of an enigma. Noelie didn't know the exact allegiance of the oldest Donnelly brother; if he was a stooge for Branch or an active member of Albert's circle. It seemed more likely to Noelie that he had been trying to protect Robert Donnelly, or the Donnelly name or even the reputation of Let There Be Light; his motive had simply and conveniently overlapped with that of Branch.

If nothing else, the death of Sean Sugrue did underline the intertwined interests that had made it so hard to get to the truth. Inasmuch as there were two crimes, there were in consequence two groups of criminals loitering with intent, watching developments and assessing how they impacted on their own interests. On the one hand, Branch was protecting its patch; on the other, the group that Cronin had referred to as 'that crowd' was also observing proceedings, looking for any sign that its existence would become known.

Albert was a key figure, if not the key figure. Intelligent, well educated and ruthless, he was prepared to murder to get his way. Although Albert gave the impression of being a genteel, kindly Christian, Noelie knew that he and Meabh had only narrowly escaped death at his hands. Others hadn't been so lucky.

Looking across at Llanes, Noelie's eyes rested on the area of the garden under which the cavern was located.

If Noelie and Meabh had drowned there, Albert would simply have opened the sluice gate a day or so later – their bodies would have floated out into the Lee and downriver. They would have been found close to where Shane's body was discovered.

It had occurred to Noelie that Shane could have encountered Albert and Big Ears at his flat on the afternoon he vanished. Noelie wasn't sure but he thought he might have told Shane that he should come over sometime to listen to the punk collection. It was something that Shane would have done too; the kid loved music. Noelie hadn't pursued that scenario, in part because Shane's body showed no signs of having suffered violence and his death was judged to be by drowning. Detective Byrne's report had confirmed all of this. But Noelie now knew that Shane's death could be consistent with incarceration in Albert's garden prison.

Something else was bothering him. If the break-in at his flat on the day before Bonfire Night had been carried out by Albert and Big Ears, how had Albert found out so quickly about the Sugrue file? How did he know about Noelie's involvement or where he lived? It led Noelie back to his belief that there was someone inside the gardaí passing information to Albert.

Later, at the apartment, they held a wake for Hannah. The Hegarty family were there, along with Irwin, Garret, Black Gary and Martin. They told stories about Hannah and Irwin talked about his early years in Australia and his life there. At one point they talked about Danesfort and listened to Black Gary's accounts of his time there.

Around 10 p.m. Noelie called Meabh to give her an update and to get her final agreement to go ahead with the release of the film at 2 a.m, if there had been no word by then about Jim Dalton's remains. Meabh remained unhappy about the prospect of publication but she reluctantly agreed and told Noelie some news of her own.

'I've been coming and going through Schiphol airport for about seven years. I've never had the slightest problem and it's normally just a cursory passport check. This time, though, I was thoroughly searched. I didn't have a lot of luggage but everything I had was examined in detail. They also insisted on doing a full body examination on me, which was gross I might add.'

She told Noelie that she had kicked up a fuss and asked for an explanation but none was forthcoming.

'I guess we both know why you were searched.'

'I guess we do.'

After the call ended Noelie told the others what Meabh had just told him. It was sobering news, confirmation for them all that behind the scenes a lot was still happening. A while later they ordered pizzas and, as these were being delivered, the call came through from Ethel Dalton.

48

In the late afternoon of the next day Noelie, Black Gary, Martin, Irwin and Garret arrived at woodland near Mitchelstown, on the low slopes of the Galtee Mountains. Noelie had walked in the area a few times and knew that there was a range of trails, for beginners through to advanced hill walkers, at the location.

They drove for a long distance along a narrow country road, eventually reaching a gated entrance into a forest conservation area. Conveniently, a garda car was parked at the turn-off and they were able to confirm that they were going in the right direction. They continued along the track for another two kilometres, finally arriving in a clearing under a canopy of tall pines.

Some patrol cars, two Special Detective Unit 4x4s and a forensics van were parked beside a command centre that had been established in a large mobile vehicle. Noelie tried ringing the Daltons in advance of their arrival but he couldn't get a signal. He approached a garda and was instructed on the route to take, which ran along the side of a steep gully. The investigation site was about two hundred metres in.

'You'll see blue tents below you,' the garda told them.

They walked carefully. There was a strong smell of pine in the air and the ground underfoot was soft. Eventually they came to an older stretch of deciduous forest. Noelie could see up a bare featureless mountainside. A short distance on, by a large lichen-covered rock, the gully abruptly turned at a right-angle and descended downhill. It was inhospitable terrain. The garda tents, two placed side by side, were positioned in a clearing.

A digger had been in use but was now parked beside the covered area. Noelie didn't recognise any of the gardaí; there were both uniformed and plain-clothes police present. At the entrance to the tent he saw a person in a white protective suit.

Ethel Dalton was with her daughters and her son, close to the tents. A temporary rope-aid had been erected to make movement up and down the slope easier. When she noticed them, Mrs Dalton came towards them immediately. She was in tears as she spoke.

'It's him, Noel. Part of his jacket is visible. There's lime in there with him.'

The older daughter came up. She too had been crying. Noelie introduced everyone and they hugged. Irwin broke down and they found him a place to sit for a while.

Ethel told them that she'd been up all night. She had received an anonymous call just after eleven and had called Noelie immediately and then the police.

'He wouldn't say who he was. He was abrupt and rude. "Write down these coordinates," he said. "This is where Mr Dalton is." He described the area generally and that was it.' Ethel took Noelie's hands. 'Thank you.'

Lighting units had been moved into position down near the tents. Noelie watched a contractor running electrical cable up the slope.

'It might be tomorrow before he's out,' Ethel explained. 'They're saying that they want to gather every bit of forensic information they can. It seems the lime is the problem and they may opt to take it away spoonful by spoonful.'

Ethel Dalton's son and younger daughter had arrived up too. There were more introductions. A while after Noelie went down the slope to see what was happening.

It was an out-of-the way place, well away from the walking paths. It appeared that the body was deeply buried; certainly not a job done in a hurry.

Irwin joined him. 'It's the strangest thing to be happy about finding out where someone is buried, isn't it?'

'Very odd.'

'I was the same when I heard about the remains in the Glen. I mean I didn't know that they were Egan's, although I suspected they were.'

'When you suspect someone is dead, I suppose it's different. Then it really is about bringing closure.'

Irwin asked Noelie about Jim Dalton. They talked about the web of deception that had been spun around Dalton – the false information that he was an informer who had been spirited away into a witness protection programme.

'The family never bought that?'

'No, and when I met Mrs Dalton she said something that convinced me too. It was about Jim being an orphan and never having his own family until he had his own children. She said he'd never leave them and I believed her.'

A plain-clothes female detective approached Ethel Dalton and asked to speak to her and the family. Noelie watched from a distance. The Daltons were clearly unhappy about what they were being told but eventually they seemed to reach some kind of agreement with the detective.

When the conversation was over, Ethel Dalton came back to speak to Noelie. She was upset – the exhumation was being suspended until the following morning. Experts from a unit with experience with limed remains were in transit but wouldn't arrive until around 8 p.m.; work would begin early the next day. The children were going to get some sleeping gear and return to the site: they didn't want to leave their father alone for even one more night.

Noelie and the others said their goodbyes. It was very difficult. Ethel Dalton held Noelie for a very long time.

49

Nearly a week later, on a sunny Friday afternoon, a crowd gathered at the cemetery to attend the unveiling of Egan's headstone. The entire Dalton family – their father's remains finally recovered though not yet buried – were present along with a range of other people connected to Danesfort Industrial School. Ellen was there along with Hannah's extended family. Detective Byrne was present as was Ajax Dineen with his son.

Noelie, Meabh, Black Gary and Martin were thanked by many of those who came. In particular, Noelie enjoyed meeting the men and women who had attended industrial schools and who had turned up to pay their respects to one of their own. They shared a bond and Noelie witnessed hearty handshakes and hugs. It was a privilege to be there and to be in their company. He knew that Hannah would have felt the same and he was suddenly overwhelmed by her absence.

Before the unveiling Noelie had visited Shane's grave. Most of the wreaths were showing their age although a few new ones had been placed at the head of the plot. One was from Ellen and Arthur, another from Irwin and Garret. Noelie told Shane that he loved him and missed him.

Irwin spoke about coming out of the past and fighting to understand your soul. Everyone, he said, had their own journey to make and he reminded them that not everyone got the opportunity to make it. He called for silence so they could remember those who had fallen due to depression, drink, emigration and loneliness. He asked for a moment of silence for those who had had their childhoods stolen and blighted by sexual abuse. He extended a hand of friendship to a representative of the Magdalene Laundry women, also present, and finished with a few words about getting on with life, and making peace with it by finding companionship and love.

As the ceremony concluded they all gathered in a tight semi-circle around Egan's plot, which was no longer bare. The mound of earth was heaped with flowers and bouquets. Hands around shoulders, they stood together and listened as Garret read Patrick Galvin's poem 'Song For A Poor Boy'.

As he said the final lines, the drape over the new headstone was pulled away to reveal a granite stone with the inscription that Irwin said described the character and spirit of Michael Egan perfectly.

> But in the dark he learned to creep
> When all the guards were fast asleep
> And in his house of spinning pearls
> He hopped about in loops and whirls ...

Acknowledgements

Thank you to Sheila Mannix for essential advice at an early stage; and to Dominic Carroll for his support and for picking over the 'first fifty pages'. I would particularly like to thank my editor Patsy Horton at Blackstaff Press for all her work on this manuscript and for making it a much better book. My gratitude to all at Blackstaff Press for their work and for taking me under their wing. Finally and most of all to Mary Favier for her unstinting encouragement and support – this book could not have been written without you.